Song of
SALZBURG

OTHER BOOKS AND AUDIOBOOKS
BY JEN GEIGLE JOHNSON

THE LIBERTY SEEKERS
The Nobleman's Daughter
"Mistletoe Memories" in *A Christmas Courting*
A Lady's Maid

THE PIMPERNEL
Scarlet

STAND-ALONE NOVELS
His Lady in Hiding

ROYAL REGENCY ROMANCE
A Foreign Crown
A Torn Allegiance

OTHER BOOKS AND AUDIOBOOKS IN THE
ROMANCE ON THE ORIENT EXPRESS SERIES

It Started in Budapest by Julie Daines
Wrong Train to Paris by Jennifer Moore
Until Vienna by Heather B. Moore
Song of Salzburg by Jen Geigle Johnson

Song of
SALZBURG

Romance on the Orient Express

JEN GEIGLE
JOHNSON

Covenant Communications, Inc.

Cover photograph by Melea Nelson.
Visit www.meleanelson.com
Cover design by Michelle Fryer

Special thanks to Mark Nelson and the Heber Valley Railroad who provided the trains for the cover photoshoot.

For more information, visit www.hebervalleyrr.org

Cover design copyright © 2021by Covenant Communications, Inc.

Published by Covenant Communications, Inc.
American Fork, Utah

Printed in the United States of America
First Printing: August 2021

28 27 26 25 24 23 22 21   10 9 8 7 6 5 4 3 2 1

ISBN 978-1-52441-760-4

PRAISE FOR
JEN GEIGLE JOHNSON

"A captivating romance from the first page to the last. Freya's frequent travels to Salzburg put her in the path of one of the most unlikely of men. *Song of Salzburg* brings to life the glories of the Orient Express and the magic of music that touches the soul. This wonderful book is not to be missed."
—Julie Daines, author *It Started in Budapest*

"Filled with music and romance, this is one you don't want to miss."
—Jennifer Moore, author *Wrong Train to Paris*

"In *Song of Salzburg* by Jen Geigle Johnson, prepare yourself for all the romance of traveling on the Orient Express when you meet Freya Winter and Erich Schumann. Freya's frequent journeying on the train begins to coincide with Erich's, and their friendship blooms among conversation, shared meals, and their love for music. Readers will be instantly charmed and left with a smile on their faces long after the last page is finished."
—Heather B. Moore, author *Until Vienna*

FOR ANYONE WHO SPEAKS
THROUGH THEIR MUSIC
Thank you for your talents.
Your work changes hearts and always lifts mine.

ACKNOWLEDGMENTS

I AM GRATEFUL FOR MY violin instructors, for my experience playing in orchestras when young, for my time in England as a young teen, and for my parents for introducing a love of music into my life. Though I stopped long before I could have made something of myself as a musician on any instrument, the beginnings ignited in me a love for music. Thank you to Ashley Gebert for her insightful edits and to the Covenant team for making my stories shine. Thank you to my fellow Romance on the Orient Express authors, Julie Daines, Jennifer Lunt Moore, and Heather B. Moore. I love their stories and am thrilled we could bring this train alive for each other and for you.

CHAPTER ONE

FREYA WINTER RESTED THE BACK of her hand on her mother's forehead. "Are you well enough, Mama?" Leaving her mother while she was in a bout of coughs felt like a betrayal.

"I am well enough. We all know I will not die from this, but I envy your crisp mountain air. If I could just leave London and the filth I breathe here every day . . ."

"You could stay in Paris with Grandmother. Then I will see you when I visit from Salzburg."

She closed her eyes. "I am too tired for the journey."

"Or perhaps you will vacation to Brighton as you have so long desired." Freya hoped her father would grant this one wish. Her mother would benefit from the sea air, and Freya could leave for Salzburg with less guilt.

When her mother fell asleep, Freya joined her father at the breakfast table. He was reading the paper. As usual, he'd set the gossip columns aside, perhaps hoping Freya would take an interest in the social lives of those around them. This morning, she didn't even pick up the pages to appease him. "Mother would do well in Brighton."

"Yes." He read a moment more.

"Do you think you will be able to take her?"

After a moment, he lowered the paper, his thick eyebrows, perhaps intimidating to some, drawn together. "I'm doing my best, Freya. It would help if you were also doing something."

The hurt caused her hands to clench and nearly managed to bring tears, but she swallowed twice and then sat up taller. "I will only be gone a few months."

"Yes, and what good is it doing anyone? If you would stay here, take an interest in a courtship, marry . . . I would like to pass along some of my work, then retire and go to Brighton with your mother."

"But perhaps a vacation only? And then, when I return, you might retire." This old, tired conversation seemed to be the only thing her father ever wished to discuss of late. She was not opposed to marriage, but when she compared it to creating music that carried her away, running a violin bow across strings, joining large orchestras, traveling, and playing for others, marriage just seemed . . . meant for a later time in her life. She was not entirely to blame. No men had yet seemed interested in her, not once she started talking about her music and her violin. Their eyes glazed over, and no amount of dowry could convince them that their future wife would be a musician bluestocking. She'd turned many away by her actions before her father realized what she was doing.

"It's expensive trying to marry you off. And when you wile away your time, we wait, your mother ill with the London air. And I work myself to the bone so that we can have all that we do and to keep you here in London Season after Season."

She knew some of his complaints were just talk; he had given his heart and soul to the railroad. What would her father be if not the great mogul of the Stonebridge Railroad? But she also sensed that things were not as successful as they had always been, that he was stressed much of the time and perhaps really would prefer to retire.

"And what does my violin playing have to do with your retirement?"

"My daughter, we have long given up on you marrying . . . After years of staying here, keeping a house on Grosvenor Square, building up your generous dowry . . ." He stopped talking and rubbed his eyes. "But what to do with you? You need a purpose, a situation, a living to care for you once I'm gone. And music doesn't provide that, does it?"

She didn't even feel offended by her father's dismissal. He had good intentions. Her heart was so far from railroads and gas and running companies or even in marrying that she knew she would be hopeless in most pursuits other than music.

"Perhaps if I can make a name for myself in Europe, I can play professionally. I will perform for some of the greatest names in music."

Her father waved her attempts to be helpful aside. "So you have said. And might I remind you of our stipulations? Go. Try. Play. That would be something, a life for yourself. And if you aren't chosen, if this Maestro person doesn't pick you, then be finished with this nonsense once and for all. We shall find a situation for you, a companionship, perhaps a governess position." He stared at her until she nodded. "Talk no more about it. We have agreed to let you go. You are going. Let us speak of other things."

She said no more, and he returned to his paper. As usual, nothing was understood between them, and her father showed as little interest in her music as he ever had.

She returned to her room with two hours remaining before she would go to the train station. She was all packed. Her mother was sleeping. Her father was uninterested. Her fingers ran along the case of her violin. The soft feel of the worn leather brought comfort and teased her fingers, beckoning her to open it. But instead, she lay back on her bed, the case at her side.

She knew better than to play while both her parents were home. There was no need to draw further attention to the fact that she was going to Salzburg for months. Her father's words sank deeper inside. She knew the ultimatum he'd set. She'd agreed to his terms so she could go. *Salzburg.* Then her lips trembled in a sudden panic-filled insecurity. She had no idea what she was about in the world of orchestras and European professional musicians. She barely knew any other instruments outside her own. But she had to go, didn't she? The truth of it all burned even deeper than her father's words. If she didn't go and try, she would regret it with every breath ever after.

When it was at last time to depart, her father left her at the station with these parting words: "Enjoy your time. Make something of yourself. Perhaps if this Maestro chooses you, all the time you've spent on this nonsense will serve some purpose at last. You need a place in society, a useful one."

She nodded, then turned and entered the station without looking back. She was used to his dismissive comments about her music. Sometimes they hovered above her in the air and didn't quite strike home. But other times, like now, they made her question every stubborn inkling that kept her playing and practicing despite discouragement. What if she fought a losing battle? What if she was as unimportant as he suggested?

She gripped her case tighter and forced one foot in front of the other.

When at last she stood on the London platform in front of her train, clutching her violin to her side, her feet would not take the steps necessary to board. Her skirts swished about her legs as people rushed by. Sometimes trouser legs forced the movement. Sometimes it was just the air that flowed between them. Her nose itched. The air felt thick, and since her train had just recently arrived, steam billowed around her ankles.

But she hesitated to board.

She had been chosen to learn at the hands of expert musicians in Salzburg, Austria, to play before kings and queens. Her violin instructor assured her he would not have picked her above all his other students were she not the best, the one who would succeed in such a venture. But she wasn't certain his knowledge of proficiency extended across Europe.

Almost all the passengers had boarded. The conductor on the platform checked his pocket watch, ready to call for the last boarding. A man rushed by her. "Pardon me." He turned and paused, taking in her face in one swift glance. His eyes lingered on her violin.

Her hand rose to clutch something at her chest, anything, even a bit of lace from her dress. The air around them seemed to catch up to his hurried pace, and she was encompassed by the comforting smells of violin wood and . . . rosin. Was he a musician?

He paused in his rushing and stepped closer, seeming to be most intently interested in her. His hat covered all but two patches of chestnut curls at his temples. The corner of his mouth lifted in a smile, and his gaze lingered. Everywhere he looked tingled with a new sense of warmth.

"Oh." Her hand moved to the side of her face.

His blue eyes danced. "Are you here to say goodbye to someone? Perhaps I might deliver a message?"

"Oh, no. I'm here . . ." She swallowed. "I'm here to board."

His eyes widened in obvious pleasure at the thought. "Well then." He indicated she should walk at his side. "We'd best be moving along."

Her breath escaped as the conductor called, "All aboard! Next stop, Paris and the Orient Express!"

The man waited another moment. "Will you be coming?" He took two steps toward the train, looking back over his shoulder, his eyes challenging, inviting. When the whistle blew, he nodded his head once and then moved quickly toward the nearest door, glancing one more time over his shoulder at Freya.

She grabbed her skirts with one hand, picked up her feet, and raced to the train as the huge black wheels began to rock in place. Then she stepped inside just as they began to move.

"You're a brave one. Almost missed it, you did." The conductor stepped in beside her, and they both watched the platform get farther away as the train picked up speed. She stepped farther inside and stood for a moment at the top of the stairs, catching her breath. Her eyes strained in both directions for the man who had rushed past. But he was gone. Well, no matter. Perhaps she would see him again to thank him. She breathed in the new smells of the train—the grease from the wheels and the mixture of people all around her in the train cars as far as her eyes could see. Her heart filled with a surge of energy as the adventure of her life carried her along with every chug and rhythm of the train that sped on more rapidly down the tracks.

She stepped into the passenger car, holding her violin case against her chest and trying to take up as little space as possible. One car up ahead was mostly full. She looked from seat to seat. Large, plush chairs held every kind of passenger. She imagined the Orient Express train cars would be even more opulent once she boarded it in Paris. Freya smiled. This journey would be far brighter and more comfortable than she had imagined.

The faint smell of peppermint tickled her nose. A man with a pipe joined her at her side. He was cheery but dressed all in black. "You'll be wanting zeh ozher car." He pointed behind her.

She tipped her head. "Thank you." Then she turned and, for some reason, following the advice of a perfect stranger, entered the other car.

The spacious and lovely seats looked to be like those in a formal sitting room, placed together in arrangements with tables. Many passengers were reading. Some were conversing, and there were several free chairs. They seemed large enough for her violin to be placed beside her. And she did hope for a bit of tea. The closest passengers glanced up, smiled, and returned to their activities. She made her way down the wide middle aisle and found a large, overstuffed chair in the farthest back corner to sit in. She placed her violin beside her and just as she'd predicted, she and it fit nicely.

Soon a member of the staff approached, and Freya asked for some tea.

Her wide hat allowed a bit of covert staring on her part. She was mostly hidden beneath it, which she quite enjoyed. And she found the hat lovely. Her mother had instructed extra hat pins be placed here and there as a form of protection. She'd laughed at the idea at the time, especially when her mother had made her practice stabbing an imaginary person. But now that she was on the train, traveling alone for the first time in her life, she was grateful for her mother and her hat pins.

Freya adjusted her skirts and leaned back in her seat. No one here seemed to be the sort of person who would require a stab or two with the pins. And now that she was seated with nothing to do until the ferry and then switching trains in France, she began to relax by degrees. The door opened again. Her gaze flitted to the newcomer, wondering after her tea.

She sat up again immediately. The very man who'd walked by her so quickly and convinced her to follow him onto the train—unbeknownst to him, of course—was now sitting on the opposite side of the car in a chair similar to her own. While he was as yet unaware of an audience, she took the time to peruse his well-made clothing, the jacket that fit perfectly across his shoulders and his lovely hat that hung low over his eyes, eyes that she knew to be perceptive, intelligent, and of the brightest blue.

As he placed a satchel on the floor at his feet and lifted out a book, she looked away, not wishing to be discovered in her perusal of his person. Just the very act of looking where she usually wouldn't filled her with an exhilarating sense of freedom. She was here, alone, traveling to another country. And even though she would have chaperones and matrons and instructors looking out for her from the moment she arrived in Salzburg, right now, these hours on the train were all hers to do with as she pleased.

The corners of her mouth lifted. Even though she might have looked a simpleton sitting there smiling by herself, she could no sooner have stopped her personal celebrations as she could the train, nor did she want to.

England moved past in a great blur of landscape. The farther away from London she traveled, the greater her hope rose within. No matter what happened in Salzburg, she was going to work hard and do her best. She lifted her chin, and her fingers itched to get out her violin and play.

CHAPTER TWO

THE DAY PASSED AS THOUGH in a dream. They travelled across the channel, boarded a new train in France, and at last boarded the actual Orient Express in Paris. Nothing could have prepared Freya for the finery. The details, the etching in the wood, the fine brass, the plush materials in rich colors of red, blue, and cream all welcomed her. She found a car similar to her first on the train out of London and settled herself comfortably, preparing for many hours ahead. A man passed her in the aisle, and for a moment, she caught a familiar whiff of wood, rosin, instrument cases. The smell felt as much like home as anything in her life. She lifted her chin to confirm to her delight that the same man who'd travelled with her earlier was indeed still on the train. Fascinating flutters cascaded through her as she saw him seated in the nearby corner. Who was this man and how did he have such an effect? She watched him for a moment, but then, when he didn't pay her a bit of attention, she looked away again. Perhaps she could read. She'd brought her well-read copy of *Sense and Sensibility* by Jane Austen. She opened the book and tried to become lost in the story.

But after only a moment, she knew his eyes were on her. A pleasant sense of awareness tingled over her skin. When she glanced up, he nodded to her and pulled out his own book. He lifted it for her to see the cover, which she couldn't read from where she sat, and then he dipped his head. When he didn't look up again, she exhaled slowly and tried to calm herself. She'd rarely been so intrigued by another person.

Her tea arrived and, when she'd had her fill, was taken away. They'd travelled for hours. The countryside passed by her window and though it was lovely, she had lost interest in the view. A sigh escaped, and her foot tapped away some energy. She was in the last half of her book, and she needed to stretch her legs. Did she dare? Certainly. It was almost dinner, and so she would make her way to the dining car. The man in the corner had left. Perhaps he slipped out the door nearest his seat? She moved in that direction without planning to, slid open a thick wooden doorway, passed through, and closed it again behind her. As soon as a conductor with an Orient Express brass-buttoned uniform crossed her path, she asked, "Would you mind telling me where the dining car is?"

"Certainly, miss." The young man pointed in the direction she was already heading. "If you walk through two more cars, you will see it. We're serving Bolognese."

"Excellent. Thank you." Freya carried her violin and her satchel with her. She doubted her father had purchased a sleeping compartment or any place that was solely hers, so she didn't dare leave her violin out of her sight.

The finery and beauty of the train made her smile. Everywhere she looked, the seats seemed comfortable, the ceilings were especially decorated and elaborate, and the very walls were made of carved wood paneling that had her wondering more than once how long it took to create such a lovely piece of art.

She entered the next car, which was full of mostly men at cards. She looked straight ahead and tried not to be noticed. But much to her pleasant surprise, no man commented, approached her, or in any way made her uncomfortable. She exhaled in relief and then opened the door to the dining car.

Tables lined each side. Each was set with the whitest linen, napkins, cutlery, and a single red rose in the center of the table. Freya was enchanted.

A man dressed in uniform, probably a waiter, bowed to her. "Would you like a table?"

"Yes, please."

"I can seat you with that lovely lady over there." He pointed to a woman with snow-white hair and creamy skin at a center table. She looked cheery and pleasant enough. But before she could answer, he half turned. "Or that man on the other side." He indicated a farther table sitting in the corner, where her handsome man looked down at a newspaper.

"No." Her abrupt tone surprised her and the waiter, if his raised eyebrows were any indication. "The first will be fine. Thank you." She followed him, kicking herself. Why not sit with the handsome man? What an opportunity! But surely he would think her bold. Brassy. Forward. Would he notice she'd joined the dining car once he looked up from his paper? Or what if he didn't notice her? What if all his shared looks and interest were merely imagined on her part?

By the time she had arrived at her table, she knew her cheeks must be bright red because of the heat she felt emanating off them.

As soon as Freya sat, her new table companion called out, "Good heavens, are you ill?" She leaned back and put a napkin to her face, her eyes wide and concerned.

Several others from tables nearby leaned away from Freya as well.

"No, I'm not ill. I'm in perfect health. Just a little warm."

Those around them seemed to relax, but the woman across from her looked skeptical. She seemed an interesting sort of person. A small hat with a polka-dotted veil covered her face down to her nose. She wore a smart yellow, tight-waisted jacket and long skirt. Her lips were bright pink, and she had crisp white gloves.

Freya set her violin and satchel down beside her near the window, away from the aisle, and smiled while she sat. "I'm Freya Winter. Thank you for letting me join you."

The woman's demeanor relaxed. "Of course. I'm happy to have a companion for the rest of my meal. I'm Victoria Manet. Please call me Victoria." They shook hands briefly across the table. Then Victoria said, "A bit odd, isn't it? Eating at all different times with people you've never seen before?" She sipped her wine without leaving any pink on the glass. How had she managed such a thing?

"I think so too. So far, I'm enjoying it." When the waiter returned, Freya placed her order and sipped her wine. She ran her hand along the crisp white tablecloth. "This is lovely."

"Is it your first time on the Orient Express?"

"Yes. I'm travelling to Salzburg."

"Beautiful city."

"How often do you ride on this train?"

"I'm here every other month. I go to visit my son and his family in Vienna." Her smile grew, and the lines on her face softened at the mention of her family.

"How wonderful for you."

"Yes. I remember the days when this kind of travel was a thing of dreams. I'm grateful to see my son so often." She leaned forward. "And to be able to travel alone." She closed her eyes. "In my younger years, I'd have had to bring a companion and a servant if I were to attempt such a journey, and look at you. Are you alone?"

"I am." Freya swallowed, the idea still a foreign concept to her.

They chatted of pleasant things, and the food was delicious. She was aware of the man in the corner, knew when he'd finished his meal, knew when he'd put down his paper. Partway through dessert, Freya knew the minute her handsome man noticed her. She glanced his way, and just as she'd suspected, he was watching; this time his grin from the platform had returned.

Her mouth tugged into an immediate response. *Too large. You look silly.*

And sure enough, Victoria noticed. She immediately turned to see what Freya was smiling at, then turned back, watching Freya a bit too closely. "He's handsome." She sipped her wine again.

Freya ate another bite of dinner even though it was now cold, and she wasn't hungry any longer.

"Do you know him?" Victoria folded her hands in front of her at the edge of the table.

"No, I don't." She had no notion of how to explain her perhaps imaginary connection with someone she'd never officially met.

"Excuse me," said a pleasantly deep male voice above her. Without looking up, she knew it must be *him*.

Victoria's eyes widened.

His voice sounded like every beautiful composition she'd ever heard, rolling through her in waves. For a moment, Freya froze.

Victoria tapped her leg with her foot, and Freya forced her head to angle upwards towards the voice.

His blue eyes sparkled with good humor. The air filled with the now familiar blend of his scent, as if she'd just opened up her violin case. He held up a napkin. "Did you drop this?"

She searched her lap, and indeed, hers was gone. "Oh yes, thank you."

When he handed it to her, his fingers brushed her palm, sending a thousand paths of light through her, as though the world had illuminated and her soul burned with the realization. Her eyes widened, and his did as well. For a moment, she was captured, staring into a face that searched her own, but aware of an audience, Freya looked away. "Thank you."

"You're welcome." Did he sing his response? Surely that wasn't the case, but to Freya, his voice made music.

She tried to think of something else to say. But he dipped his head and made his way out of the dining car.

Victoria immediately fanned her face. "Now that was something special. And you say you don't know him?"

What was special? She reviewed in her mind their words and found nothing extraordinary about their conversation. She shook her head, still unsure of what just happened. "I had simply noticed him." She bit her tongue, not wanting to share more.

"Of course. He is so handsome, the kind of man any woman would notice and look twice. But my dear, the best news of today is that *he* noticed *you*." She dabbed her mouth, obviously pleased. Freya felt both pleasure and anxiety at Victoria's assertion and didn't know what to do next. Was the man returning to their original car? Would she see him later? Should she run after him?

Freya forced her feet to still. "We don't know anything about him."

"True. But you could." Victoria's eyes lit up with a challenge.

And Freya felt a new dose of reckless courage fill her. "You are exactly right. If you'll excuse me?"

"It was nice to meet you, Miss Winter."

"You too. Thank you for your company. And suggestion." Her voice softened and faded as she tucked her violin under her arm, placed her satchel over her shoulder, and headed out the same door as the man.

CHAPTER THREE

FREYA COULDN'T SEE HIM FARTHER up ahead or anywhere in the next car. She kept walking and making her way through the cars until she was back in her original place and happy that her same seat was still free. But his chair was empty. He was nowhere to be seen. She chided herself for chasing after a man she didn't know anything about.

She settled into the plush of her seat, ready to spend the bulk of her day in it, when a conductor approached. "Miss Winter?"

"Yes."

"You have not been to your compartment yet. Would you like to see it now?"

"I have my own compartment?"

"Indeed. Might I see your ticket?"

"Oh, certainly." She pulled it out of her satchel, studying the letters and numbers for a moment.

"Ah yes, see here? This is your compartment. If you'll follow me?"

She felt so foolish not knowing such a thing and equally pleased her father had thought to purchase such a comfortable situation for her. "Certainly." She really knew nothing about traveling alone or otherwise. What made her think she could manage herself and her situation all alone? As she followed the conductor out of the car, she thought she saw a glimpse of the man from earlier up ahead. The conductor led her to the very next car lined with doors on the right side. He slid open a door partway down the narrow corridor. "You are welcome to continue to sit in the public space if you choose, but this is your personal space while you are on the train with us. I am sorry this was not made clear earlier. Another passenger pointed out your situation and I hope you can forgive that I hadn't noticed it myself before this."

"Of course. Thank you." Two benches faced each other, upholstered in welcoming softness. A large window with the countryside racing past, an upper platform area that looked as though it would convert to a bed, even a sink helped the whole space feel cozy and more homelike. She was quite charmed. But lonely. She placed her satchel and her violin on the bench and then peered back out the doorway.

To her surprise, the handsome man was there. He dipped his head in her direction and then continued to walk down the corridor. Was it he who had sent the conductor?

Just as he was about to leave her car, a young woman came rushing in and bumped into him. The contents of her bag were flung across the corridor.

"Oh my. Oh goodness. I am sorry." Intriguing red curls lined the face of a girl who looked to be about Freya's age.

The man immediately helped to pick up her things.

Some of her unmentionables were lying in plain sight. Mortified for the girl, Freya hurried to gather them herself, pulling an armful of garments and other items to her chest. She shared a momentary gaze with the man and then choked on a laugh. She desperately tried to hold it in.

The young woman shook her head. "Oh, you may as well laugh. This is indeed the most humiliating thing to ever happen to me, but I can see it is also the most humorous." She brushed her curls from her face. "Oh dear." Her cheeks colored, and she reached for Freya's armful of her belongings. "Let me take care of those." She shoved them into her bag and then held it open for the man to add what he'd collected. Then she nodded to Freya and to the man, not looking up beneath her own hat brim. "Thank you." She rushed past them. "Thank you," she called back over her shoulder again, and then she opened up the door to Freya's compartment.

Freya put a hand to her mouth and shared another look with the man. "I do believe she just stepped into my—"

"Oh dear." The young woman stepped back out. "I believe I'm the next." Her cheeks matched her hair now. She then fumbled with the door to the compartment and stepped inside, and the corridor was once again quiet.

"Well, that was certainly something." He grinned such an open and easy smile that she couldn't help but return it.

"It was good of you to help her. What a thing to happen." Freya laughed.

"But of course. It was simple enough. She seems a cheerful sort of person at any rate, and I suspect she will quickly recover from her mortification."

Freya considered the next bit of information she'd just learned about this man. He was kind as well as handsome. A friendly sparkle in his eyes made her want to linger a moment. "I saw you a moment ago. Was it you who helped me become aware of my compartment?"

"I merely brought it to the conductor's attention. You hadn't left that one sitting car in so long, and you were asleep earlier." He dipped his head again. "Forgive me for mentioning such a thing."

"No. Thank you. I am in need of rest. I'll have a hurried schedule when I arrive, I imagine, and want to be as rested as I can." She puffed out a breath of air. "I feel quite foolish for needing to be told the details of my ticket." She rocked back and forth from her toes to her heels, unsure what to say or do around this man. "My father usually cares for such things." She supposed she should return to her own compartment, but was it rude to simply walk away? Did she want to leave his presence? Not really.

But he chuckled. "You must not travel very often."

She lifted her gaze to see his reaction. So far, he seemed curious, interested, and not at all derisive. "Ironically, no. Even though my father is in the railroad business, this is my first time on an overnight train."

"And what a train to be spending your first extended journey! The Orient Express is unmatched in luxury." He ran his hand down the woodwork near her shoulder.

"So I am seeing. Do you travel often?"

"I do. I am on this very train frequently in fact."

"Then you will have to share any other tips you might know."

"I would be happy to. What is your destination?"

"I'm going to Salzburg."

His eyes lit with further interest. "The very place I am going. I find it a wonderful place for a musician. I couldn't help noticing you are carrying an instrument. Is music the purpose of your stay in Salzburg or are you visiting family or friends?"

"I am going to further my musical education for a couple months."

"Salzburg is full of music and art. The air breathes it, and the very mountains inspire your spirit." He leaned against the side panels of the train, seeming at ease.

"You make it sound like a magical place."

"It is, in many ways. I have lived there for a long time, and whenever I leave, I long to return." His smile was genuine, his manners lovely. She would not mind staying in his company for greater lengths of time.

"The way you speak makes me all the more anxious to call it home. I suspect I won't ever want to leave." She knew that to be true. But would she have that luxury? Would she be able to stay in such a place beyond her time with the orchestra? Not likely.

"I'm loathe to leave whenever I do." His expression turned wistful. "But we both head there now, do we not?"

"Yes. Are there . . . sights to see that you recommend?"

"Certainly. The cathedral off the Grande Ill. The trolly that runs up the mountain to the fort—the view on top is unmatched. And of course, always remember to look up. The view of the mountains changes by the minute no matter where you are."

She nodded, enjoying watching his face light with an obvious love of the city she so longed to also fall in love with. "Are there many musicians?"

"Yes, the Salzburg Orchestra is the grandest I have ever heard, and the Student Salzburg Orchestra practices every year at this time." His expression was full of questions.

"Oh yes. I will be playing with them."

He raised his eyebrows and gave her a nod of appreciation. "Most excellent. Their students are some of the finest as well. There are assembly halls and cathedrals and great halls where music concerts are performed. I've heard many of the great musicians who pass through as well as the ones who spend their time year round."

Freya didn't think Salzburg could sound any better. "I find myself most anxious to begin my time there. I don't know how many of the grand masters I will hear, but have you heard of the Salzburg Maestro?"

He dipped his head. "He is mentioned in certain circles." He raised an eyebrow. "I'm surprised you have heard of him."

"Oh, I know him well. That is to say, I know his music. I should very much like to meet him."

"Then perhaps you shall. Can I walk you back to your compartment? Or do you wish to go elsewhere?"

"My compartment is just fine. Thank you." After only a few steps, she turned to him at her door. "It was nice to see you, and thank you for your assistance in helping me find my compartment." She couldn't think of anything else to say to linger a bit more with him.

"My pleasure. Perhaps I shall see you again sometime." His face spoke of untold secrets, and she was filled with a desire to unravel them all.

"I'd like that." She lifted her eyes to his, questions teasing her tongue but left unspoken. "As I said, I'll be playing with the Student Salzburg Orchestra. Perhaps our paths will cross at a concert."

"Yes, I would like that." But instead of properly introducing himself or arranging a meeting, he turned as if to walk away. "Enjoy the rest of your journey."

"Thank you. You as well," she called after his retreating form, wanting to cower in embarrassment at her brazen behavior.

The young woman next door with the red curls peeked her head out. "Is he gone?" She blew an errant curl off her face.

"Yes, quite."

"Do you suppose he's forgotten my unmentionables?" She dissolved into a fit of giggles. "I've never been so embarrassed in my entire life. I daren't look at his face. Please tell me he was not young or handsome."

"I'm afraid he was both."

"Oh dear." She leaned back against the wall between their compartments. "At least I can comfort myself knowing I shall never see him again."

Freya felt a pang of disappointment that she would likely also never see that man again. At least, he'd made no plans to do so.

"Thank you for your assistance. Can you imagine my mortification if he were to have touched a corset?"

Freya joined her in laughter. "It was quite the experience. Have you sorted it all out now?"

"Yes, and the lot of it *would* be in my trunk, but there were some last-minute items I couldn't live without, and so I squeezed as much as possible in my carpet bag . . ." She held out her hand. "I'm Gertie Thomas."

"Freya Winter. Good to meet you."

"Yes, you as well. Perhaps we shall meet again after our rest. I didn't mean to eavesdrop, but I believe you said you were tired?"

"I am, yes." Freya liked this new woman and would have liked to get to know her better, but she worried she would not feel rested when she arrived, and her success in Salzburg was more important than anything. A nap would be just the thing, giving her time to refresh. Gertie helped her pull down the cleverly situated bed, then retired to her own compartment.

But after a short rest, sleep never giving her an ounce of respite, Freya decided she much preferred the cars where people congregated. Even if she spoke to no one, she felt comfort that they were near . . . and dare she admit she hoped to see more of her mysterious man? Certainly. That motivation alone took her feet back to their original car.

She was rewarded for her decision because he had returned to his original seat. So she took hers, pretending at first that she did not see him. But after but a moment, her gaze lifted to his, and she found he was watching.

He stood and approached. "Might I join you?"

"Certainly." She sucked in a breath.

He sat in one of the four chairs that surrounded a short table. "I've taken your example and have quite enjoyed a book of my own." He held it up. This time she was able to make out the title.

"*Dracula*?"

"Yes. It's quite intriguing. I'm enthralled despite its incredibly gothic tones."

"Probably nothing like my Jane Austen novel."

"I would not think so. Though I know many who have enjoyed her books."

She nodded. When they returned to their books, she wondered if she'd have more conversations with him, but he didn't say much else. He seemed rather enthralled by his book as he'd said.

She followed suit. They'd somehow acquired a level of comfort together, and she did in truth read a good portion of *Sense and Sensibility* before she nodded off. When she awoke, he was gone.

The rest of the evening and most of the next day followed in the same pattern. Gertie Thomas was her dinner companion for most meals. They shared a table with Victoria once, and Freya was pleasantly surprised the woman did not bring up Freya's interactions with the handsome man even once. Freya saw him now and again. He was always at the edge of her awareness, and the time passed quickly.

Back in her original seat, after hours of exploring every other possible diversion, Freya opened her eyes; the gentle sway of the train changing rhythm woke her from a soft doze. The sky was dark. The timepiece from her pocket told her she would be arriving any minute. Her thoughts turned to the days coming ahead. How would she measure up against the other students in her program?

She placed the book that had fallen to the floor back into her small satchel and shifted the violin case to her lap. Her fingers ran over it without her giving much thought. Its smell and feel beneath her hands were comforting. She was about to step into many unknowns, but her violin would be there. No matter what happened, she would be playing music. She closed her eyes, soaking in the comfort of an instrument that was almost as close to her as any family member.

The train started to slow. Passengers stood to leave her car, and some shifted in their seats, gathering their things.

The man entered her car with his luggage in hand. She sat up taller in her seat. Was he leaving? Was he coming to say something more? To introduce himself at last? Curse her lack of courage. But when had she ever brazenly introduced herself to a man? Never. She wasn't ready for that. Or was she? Her hands clutched the case. She watched him. Because of his hat, she was unsure where his gaze fell until he was standing right in front of her. He lifted the brim so that the brilliant blue of his eyes was visible. Then his gaze travelled over her face. She tingled with expectation. He smiled, dipped his head.

"It was a pleasure to spend this time with you." His voice warmed her all the way to her toes.

Before she could do more than nod and smile, he had continued down the aisle. On her lap lay a card, beautifully ornate edges surrounding a single drawing of a flower in the middle, *edelweiss*. She turned it over. No signature. Just the flower.

She twisted in her seat and watched his back as he stepped through to another car without looking back. Then she fell back in a defeated heap. Was that to be all that happened between her and the mysterious stranger? She clutched the card to her.

He was a stranger, wasn't he? She considered what she did know about him. He was the kind of man who helped a woman pick up her strewn belongings, who helped Freya know she had a compartment to sleep in without being intrusive. He had a kind face. As a stranger, he kept his distance. He was a gentleman. She knew precious little. But she wanted to know so much more, and now he was gone.

The train at last jerked to a stop. Everyone stood. But she waited.

As others around filed out, the train conductor waved a hand to the car in general. "Last stop. Everyone off."

One small family remained in her car along with her. She could delay her exit no longer. It was time to make her way as a musician. She'd been waiting for this moment. Best she grab hold with both hands and never let go. As she stood, a tall, large woman stepped up in the doorway to the train. The conductor was attempting to shoo her away, but she pushed past. When she saw Freya, her eyes travelling over the violin, she nodded. "There you are. Freya Winter?"

"Yes, ma'am." Freya stepped forward.

"Well, come child. No need to be standing there in an empty passenger car. The others are waiting."

Freya followed her to the doorway and stepped down out of the train. Her fingers reached out to trail along the grillwork as she left the familiar travelling companion, large and metallic though it was. The woman who had called to her stopped suddenly, and it was all Freya could do not to run into her.

She turned. "I'm Olga Uberdiche. I'm to be the matron at Frau Munchen's boarding house, your caregiver while you are here, and your instructor for some of your theory."

Freya curtseyed. "Thank you. Good to meet you, of course."

"Hmm." She turned again and took off at a quick pace across the station. It was fairly empty. The hour was late, nearly nine p.m., and Freya guessed that most trains ran during the day. She hurried after Frau Uberdiche. The woman's stern greeting somehow comforted Freya. She could handle stern. Predictable. Rule following. She nodded to herself in a decisive manner. Stern felt like home.

But Frau Uberdiche seemed to be walking away from the train and off the platform.

"Excuse me?"

She didn't respond but kept walking.

"Excuse me."

The woman turned with an eyebrow in the air so high Freya almost laughed.

"My trunk. We don't have my trunk." She would leave the trunk in her new boarding house during the week and travel lighter for all other trips, but in this instance, she had a large trunk that she could not possibly carry, and she assumed Frau Uberdiche would not manage such a thing either.

"We've hefted it with all the others into the carriage already."

"Others?"

"Of course. You don't think you're the only gifted musician in all of Europe, do you?"

"No, I don't." She hurried after Frau Uberdiche, hoping that her trunk truly had made it. When they'd rounded the corner out of the station, she almost laughed at a very happy sight. Four young people, around her age, stood together in a cluster. And one of them was the woman with the red curly hair, Gertie Thomas. What beautiful luck to have met her previously. As Freya's gaze scanned the group, she saw that her trunk was indeed included and fastened on the top of their carriage. "This is excellent. Thank you."

"You're welcome. Now, let's be on our way." Frau Uberdiche plodded away, her larger frame seeming to fall with more solid footsteps, but even that was reassuring to Freya. She approached the group of musicians. They were chattering in English, some French, some German. Freya had a good handle on English, French, and German but greatly preferred English. "Hello." She smiled. She wasn't used to simply inserting herself into conversations without an introduction. In fact, this was probably her first time ever doing so.

But they turned to her and smiled. When Gertie saw her, she squealed. "Oh, of course it is you. I'm so utterly happy at this moment I can't even speak."

Freya laughed. "We should have discussed specifically what we were doing in Salzburg."

"Yes. And so many other things, but there always seemed to be much to discuss besides. No matter. For now we have broadened our topics to include all of this as well." Gertie's embrace was warm and sincere, and Freya held her a little longer. Then she stepped away, her eyes misty.

Gertie continued introductions. "This is Daphne, Eliza, and Frank."

Freya would need to concentrate extra hard to remember all these names. "I'm happy to meet all of you. This is all so new. It's nice to see a friendly face." She held her violin closer.

Gertie sidled nearer, to her side. "Frau Uberdiche has a harsh tone now and again."

"She does, doesn't she?" Freya nodded.

"I suspect she's kind on the inside though." Frank pointed to her as she talked to the coachman. "Someone has to be firm."

"I suppose so." Gertie pressed her lips together. "I don't know why you couldn't say the same things with a cheerful expression."

Freya agreed with them both. Their instruments appeared to have already been loaded, or so she assumed. "Tell me what instruments you play. I play the violin."

Gertie pointed toward the carriage. "My violin is in the carriage."

Frank stood taller. "Cello."

"Oh, I love the cello." Eliza spoke up for the first time since Freya had arrived. Her attention was solely on Frank. Did she just flutter her eyelashes at him? Eliza had rotated her body slightly so that her back was to Freya. Interesting.

Frank was a handsome-enough person. But Freya still had thoughts only of the mysterious man on the train. And anyway, she was here to play the violin, not find romance. Eliza had nothing to worry about from her.

Eliza looked over her shoulder at Freya and Gertie, with her body still positioned away from them and toward Frank. "I play the violin as well."

"And I the flute." Daphne's voice was quiet, but she had a friendly smile.

Frau Uberdiche clapped her hands, and Gertie jumped.

"Everyone load up in the carriage. Sit close now; there's not going to be any extra room. We haven't long to travel."

"Come. Let's go together." Eliza reached for Frank's arm and indicated the others should join them.

Freya raised her eyebrows, but she and Gertie followed along.

Soon they were all sitting pressed together on the carriage benches. Two other men had joined them. With all six and some of them broad shouldered, Freya had to sit forward to give others room.

"Well, this is cozy, isn't it?" Gertie laughed.

The man at her left chuckled. "I apologize if you have no room."

Gertie blushed all the way down her neck, and Freya decided she was even more charming than ever.

"Miss Uberdiche said the ride wouldn't last long," Gertie said.

"Well, I'm Henry. Nice to see you all."

Everyone went through their names again, including Henry's brother, Tobias.

"I heard her say it won't take long, but she sounded like my mum when she says chores won't last long." Henry shook his head slowly. "She always underestimates."

"Do you still have chores?" Eliza raised an eyebrow.

Tobias eyed her as though she had just asked the most obvious thing in the world. "Of course we do. Some of the work is hard and heavy, and my mum can't do it alone."

Freya studied him for a moment but said nothing more. She wondered if they were tenants or if they couldn't afford having people do some of the labor for them. The school cost money, but if a recommendation came from a well-respected professor, then scholarships were possible. Perhaps he'd come that way.

The carriage began to move. Tobias opened the window. "I heard the boarding house sits on the river, the Grande Ill."

"Oh, that sounds lovely." Gertie's smile grew.

"We'll see how lovely it is." Eliza tried to share a look with Frank, but he looked away.

Then Frank said, "I suspect the whole thing will be amazing. I cannot wait to start playing with all of you. The orchestra will be something to remember. I'm certain of it."

"I agree." Freya surprised herself with a strong vocal opinion. She usually kept such things to herself. "I've been hoping for this for many years."

"Oh, I as well." Gertie linked their arms together. "I pinched myself yesterday when I boarded the train in England."

"We live here in Austria, near Salzburg." Henry nodded to his brother. "And I pinched him when we hopped on a wagon this evening."

"He did." Tobias rubbed his arm. Everyone laughed.

"Frank and I both come from France, though different parts entirely." Eliza seemed to lean into Frank, who stiffened, and Freya was beginning to think their interactions might provide a good bit of amusement.

"And you, Daphne?"

She lifted her lashes. "I'm from England, though not London. We live near Brighton."

"Have you gone sea bathing?" Gertie leaned across Freya to ask it.

Freya laughed.

"Yes. We do it all the time." Daphne's face became animated. "But only when the weather is nice. I cannot account for the tourists who come during the season and bathe in the rain or with a chilly wind." She shivered. "I don't know what good the sea will do if you catch a chill."

They continued chatting with each other, and Freya settled into a comfortable cozy feeling. Friends. Musicians. She could find a place here with these people.

"Has anyone heard when we shall meet the Salzburg Maestro?" Frank asked the question most on her mind.

Eliza nodded. "My instructor knows him personally. He was the one who recommended that I come."

Daphne shook her head. "I don't have any lofty associations, but I've played some of his music. And it's perfect. I could play a Maestro piece for hours."

"And some of them take hours, don't they?" Frank swallowed. "I did hear that he's demanding, exact, but intensely helpful. I heard that this whole program is difficult but worth it. We're going to have to work more than we ever have."

"Unless we already work quite hard." Eliza's hint of superiority might stop being entertaining after many hours of her. "My instructor even knows his real name."

"His real name?" Freya had wondered why his compositions always referred to him only as the Salzburg Maestro.

"Yes. He is a person of some renown and wants to keep his identity as the Maestro a secret. I hear he's somewhat modest about it." She shrugged. "That seems odd."

Freya almost laughed. Perhaps to Eliza it might seem odd. "Do you think a person should go around touting their accomplishments? I, for one, can see many reasons why I might want to keep such notoriety a secret."

Eliza frowned. "Are you embarrassed of your playing?" Her self-satisfied assumptions started to burn beneath Freya's skin.

"Absolutely not."

Freya opened her mouth to say more, but Frank pointed out the window. "Look, the Ill. We must be close to arriving."

Gertie squeezed her arm, and that one gesture settled Freya's irritation. Gertie winked. "Well, I did hear one thing. I heard that once you're his pupil, you play for royalty. There is no stopping your fame." Gertie's face could have lit the whole carriage from the inside out. "I'd love to play for audiences."

"I hear the Maestro is so particular he only chooses one pupil a year, and it's always from this group." Eliza looked at each in turn, and Freya wasn't completely certain what she was trying to say but could guess that Eliza assumed herself to be chosen already.

Freya nodded. "The whole reason I wanted to come at all was to be able to play for him."

"I think it will be equally grand to play with all of you. Have you ever played with other talented musicians? Performed in orchestras?" Frank's gaze lingered on Gertie for a moment, and Freya's intrigue heightened. Could Eliza be interested in Frank and Frank be distracted by Gertie already?

"I have never played my instrument with so many. And I think you are correct. I will love that most of all." Daphne's quiet nature drew Freya to her.

"I've never played with anyone other than my professor or a few others at a musicale." Freya smiled, the tremulous hope that she would not embarrass herself among these new musicians rising inside.

As she looked around at these students with whom, among others, she would be spending the next few months, she realized that they might understand her in ways no one else could. For the first time, she might have true friends.

CHAPTER
FOUR

UPON ENTERING THEIR BOARDING HOUSE, which would be her new home in Salzburg for the coming months, Freya was directed to her room, but she took her time getting there. The house smelled deliciously old and comfortable, and the wood floors creaked, but everything was clean. She made her way slowly, experiencing every corner of her new home, expecting to adore every moment of her new experience. Narrow corridors, adjoining rooms, and a maze of disorganized floors made her smile. But she found her new room. The door was cracked open. She pushed on the wood and peered inside. Gertie jumped up from one of the beds.

Gertie's sweet arms winding around Freya's neck filled her with happiness.

"I'm so pleased!" Freya reached for Gertie's hands.

"We shall make the very most of this."

"We absolutely shall," Freya found herself exclaiming and embracing as she imagined most girls would, those who had dear friends. And a lonely part of her heart she wasn't aware existed felt the soothing of a healing balm.

After a moment of girlish delight, they linked arms and made their way to the great room, where Frau Uberdiche had some announcements. The house was typically used for girls, but for the students invited to participate in the program, they had split the home down the middle, the men and women each taking opposite sides.

"There are rules." Frau Uberdiche held up a paper. "We will post these outside your rooms. And you will obey. Pay particular attention to the designated quiet hours. There is to be no playing of your instruments during these hours. Frau Munchen has been very kind to turn her house over to us for the program but might not feel so kindly if there is never a moment's peace."

"I bet few places in the world boast their only concern about behavior to be too much practice." Frank laughed until Frau Uberdiche leveled one stern stare in his direction. He closed his mouth.

"Your schedules this week are in the packets on your beds. You will notice that we are already scheduling performances. Our orchestra is much requested. We will spend four days a week training. You will learn from all manner of experts. We will prepare for the grand gala in which I am pleased to announce that we have just received the final count. Almost all European royals will be present, including Prince Edward himself, for all you English. Queen Victoria did send her regrets. She has been unwell quite a bit, of late."

An excited murmur rushed through them.

Frau Uberdiche leveled a stern gaze that quieted them all. "And now for the news of the Salzburg Maestro."

The room itself seemed to buzz with anticipation. Every face showed the anticipation Freya felt.

Frau Uberdiche stepped closer. "He will be here every day, during which time he will occasionally pull out a student to hear them play. This is a huge honor. He will make suggestions to help you learn how you might play better. Use the time well. Learn, for not many will ever get the same opportunity."

Freya silently vowed to do just that. And then Frau Uberdiche dismissed them all to get ready for bed. But they lingered, as no one felt like they could sleep yet.

"That would be the most wonderful thing in the world, to learn from the Maestro himself." Gertie's dreamy look made Freya smile as much as it clenched her stomach.

"I'd cherish an opportunity to play with the Maestro." Freya's voice sounded quiet to her own ears. She cleared her throat, aware of the eyes of the other students on her. Freya continued. "It could be life-changing for me. My parents said if I cannot succeed with the orchestra, they will not support me in any further musical efforts."

Gertie gasped. "That's so much pressure."

"I know." What she didn't say was that she would likely have to abandon her music almost entirely as her father sent her to work as a companion or governess. She had agreed to this ultimatum only because if she hadn't, they wouldn't have let her come to Salzburg at all.

When at last she and Gertie returned to their room, she exhaled in relief. The mattress was thin and the coverlet a bit threadbare, but it was hers alone, and her adventure was beginning. *"Not many will ever get the same opportunity."* She tried to push the words of Frau Uberdiche out of her mind. Her words had amplified all Freya's concerns about succeeding in Salzburg.

Yet her fingers itched to play.

Was she good enough? If she could just pluck a few strings, it might help her remember or at least help her feel more at home. But it was nearly ten, perhaps too late to play. Once Gertie left to use the toilet, Freya checked the schedule and saw that ten p.m. was the beginning of quiet hours that day. Perhaps she could fit in one little song. She opened her violin case on the bed, breathing in the sharp wood aroma of the case, the rosin, the fabric. As the lovely smells filled her, some of the worry left. She lifted the bow, tightened it three times, then grabbed her bar of rosin and ran the amber block up and down the taut hair, over and over until a powdery substance covered it. Then she lifted the instrument up to her chin. Plucking each string four times as she tuned, she made a few adjustments, and she was ready.

As soon as she drew the bow across the first string, her shoulders relaxed. She closed her eyes and played whatever came to mind. Slow, peaceful, beautiful music poured from her, moving to chords, the rhythm picking up. She reveled in each note. She swayed with the sound until it became a part of her, until she had played all worry from her mind. She'd cleansed whatever insecurity had plagued her, and she remembered . . . What did she remember? As if finding herself again, she remembered that her violin spoke for her, played what was in her heart. She loved to play. And that's all that mattered. If she could express that through her music, she would be fine. No matter what the orchestra decided, no matter who the Maestro picked. For the moment, Freya was at peace.

She drew the last note out to the end of the bow, and then she opened her eyes.

Her bedroom door was crowded with people. She sucked in a breath. Most were smiling, and then Frank began clapping.

The others joined in.

Freya felt suddenly nervous. Then she choked on a nervous laugh. "Oh, thank you. But please. I wasn't looking for an audience. I just felt a need to play a little."

"What *was* that?" Eliza sniffed.

"What was what? The song I was playing?" Freya shrugged. "It was just something I made up."

"You made that up as you were going?" Gertie's mouth dropped. "That's amazing. Do you do that a lot?"

"I think so, really just when I need to remember . . . things."

Frank nodded. "You should write it down. I compose too. Perhaps we can create something, a piece for an orchestra, while we are here. Everyone can add their own instruments."

Freya nodded. "I'd like to try something like that."

"Well, the music we play for Salzburg Orchestra *auditions* is already set. We can't be making that up as we go." Eliza lifted her chin and turned to the others.

The conversation in the room increased as everyone excitedly discussed the music they had been assigned for their audition five weeks away.

Freya had looked over the music again a moment ago. She would need to practice to do well. But she could do it. And the words of her instructor at home were already speaking to her in her memory about how to treat certain parts.

The room finally emptied again, and she and Gertie were ready to turn out the lights when Gertie said, "That was really beautiful. You'll get to be first-chair violinist for sure."

"I don't know. Eliza is right. When we're in an orchestra, we can't just make up whatever we want."

Gertie waved her hand. "That doesn't matter one bit. You'll do well."

Freya smiled. "I look forward to hearing you play."

"Tomorrow."

"Yes, tomorrow."

They both pulled out their schedules to see what the week would bring. Three days in a row of practicing, getting ready for a performance on Friday. Then they had three days off.

Gertie placed their schedule on the short table next to her bed. "What shall we do on our days off?"

Freya hated to dim the excitement in Gertie's face but felt she should explain her situation now. "I will have to leave."

"Leave?" Her nose wrinkled.

"Yes. To visit my grandmother in Paris. I have to go twice per month to see her whenever I have three days off together."

Gertie's brows drew together. "I guess I'll have to go visit the sights with the others." Her small pout warmed Freya's heart.

Freya did want to stay with them, quite badly, so it was a balm to know she'd be missed.

They talked in the dark about what it might be like to meet the Maestro.

"I bet he's old and wrinkled. He would have to be to play as well as he does." Gertie laughed.

"What if he's young and handsome? A prodigy?"

"Even better!"

Freya fell into the deep sleep of one exhausted from her journey but looking forward to tomorrow.

CHAPTER FIVE

THE NEXT DAY, THEY GOT right to work in their first class. Drills. Scales. Arpeggios. She might have found it tedious since she did similar exercises on her own, but the director started them working on different keys, transposing on sight, and harmonizing with each other.

The more difficult the assignment, the more her smile grew.

And then right before they were to take a break, Frau Uberdiche entered with a bell. "Attention. I need Eliza to come with me, please." Eliza stood, a flash of worry crossing her face, but then she hid it, lifted her chin, and moved to leave.

"No, miss. You'll need your instrument. You have been summoned by the Maestro."

Everyone in the room seemed to freeze. Eliza's face went white and then flushed with color.

"Excellent," she said, her voice cracking. She cleared her throat and then reached for her violin. With head high, she followed Frau Uberdiche out of the room.

"Where is she going?" Freya couldn't believe that somewhere in their very building, the Maestro waited.

"Frank, follow her," Gertie called over to him in the row behind them.

A laugh carried across the room. With a grin, Frank kept his seat as she expected he would. "Anyone know what he looks like?"

They all guessed like she and Gertie had done last night. Freya plucked at her strings absentmindedly. "How does he pick someone to listen to?"

Someone a few seats down, who Freya hadn't met yet, answered. "I don't know. But Eliza said earlier that she knew she was going to meet with him. Perhaps she knows him or something? Or perhaps her instructor set it up?"

"I thought he was from Germany." Daphne's voice was just loud enough for Freya to hear from across the room.

"Oh no. The man is either French or English. I'm almost positive."

Everyone seemed to know something or think something about the Maestro.

Freya was beginning to see that rumors abounded of who and what the Salzburg Maestro was.

The conductor had been tolerant of the delay, but now he held up his baton. Everyone immediately sat at attention, and Freya smiled. She loved the professionality. So rarely had she played with a group at all and certainly never one this large or this qualified. She lifted her instrument, and at the conductor's lift of the baton, they played.

To Freya it was exquisite. How wonderful to be able to hear the wind instruments and the percussion as well as strings! She knew the conductor would have comments and replays per section and perhaps some work on dynamics, but Freya had never heard anything so fantastic as the sounds that this group made together.

When Eliza walked back into the room, her face was beaming. She tapped another student on the shoulder, and that person grabbed his cello and hefted that larger instrument out of the room, presumably to talk to the Maestro.

Freya wished Eliza were sitting closer to her. Had Eliza just chosen a student at random? Or did the Maestro request certain musicians? Her thoughts would be consumed by expectation and hope until she met him herself.

But time passed, and she wasn't called back to meet him. Mercifully, her thoughts were frequently distracted as the students prepared three new pieces together. After three full days of lessons, drills, orchestra practice, and private lessons, they were ready for their first concert.

Freya eyed herself in the mirror, satisfied. They had been required to bring concert attire, formal wear, and many specific pieces. Part of the reason her parents had complained about the program was because of the expense, which, again, Freya found unfair. No one would ever accuse the Winters of being on the brink of poverty and ruin. Nevertheless, she humored their ridiculous concerns over cost, and again, Freya had reminded them that it was no more than they'd pay for a new Season's gowns, and if she were to achieve a spot in the orchestra, if she were able to then train with the Maestro, she could pay for future gowns herself.

The shimmering length of her dress fell to the floor. Her gloves rose to her elbows. Black was not usually her color, but something about the night of a concert brought out extra pink in her cheeks, so she was pleased with the result.

Gertie, too, wore black. Her dress was less sleek and more puffy, but it suited Gertie. As the two stood together, Freya turned to hug her friend. "Are we really about to play a concert for an audience in Salzburg?"

"Yes, I think we are!"

They met the others out in the hall. Frank held his elbows out, and Freya and Gertie each took one arm. "Who has your instrument?"

Frank tipped his head behind him. "Henry agreed to carry it for me."

Freya looked back. Henry did not look pleased.

"Well, he lost our bet." Frank's smile was mysterious.

Gertie laughed. "Do I want to know what bet this was?"

"Probably not."

Eliza marched past, her nose in the air.

"Goodness, we're all unhappy about something this evening, aren't we?" Gertie clucked.

Freya suspected Eliza's problems had more to do with Frank's arms being taken than with anything else.

They made their way to the carriages, instruments in hand. Everything about their evening was favorably etched in Freya's mind, or at least, she hoped it would be.

Nothing could have prepared her for the moment when she stood to face her first audience. The exhilaration that flowed through her, then the wonder and surprise at the grand applause for their playing . . . she would never forget it. They played better than they ever had in rehearsals. And at one point, the conductor had pointed to her to stand. She'd played the next part of the piece as a solo.

The audience had erupted in applause as soon as she'd finished.

Freya had nothing else to compare their evening to, but as far as she could tell, everything went as beautifully as it possibly could have.

In the carriage on their return to the boarding house, her friends were much quieter than they'd been on the ride to the event. When no one would meet her eyes, Freya suspected she was the cause. "What?"

No one answered.

"What? Why won't anyone look at me?"

Finally, Frank nudged her with his shoulder. "Why didn't you tell us you had the solo?"

"I didn't know! That was as much a surprise to me as anyone."

"You played that with no notice?" Gertie's face paled. "You know what that means?" Gertie looked at everyone else in the carriage.

"That Freya is excellent?" Frank shrugged.

"No. Well, yes, she is excellent. But this means that the conductor could call on any one of us at any time to play like Freya did tonight."

Daphne nodded. "I'm afraid Gertie is correct. I heard from Eliza that the Maestro requested the solo. He wants to see what kind of musicians we are when surprised like that."

While everyone else seemed to sink into their own fears, Freya sat taller. The Maestro at least knew who she was; he had singled her out with the honor. Surely, he'd call her back, and she would meet him next.

No one said much after that until Freya said, "Does this mean we're friends again?"

Gertie reached for her hand. "Yes. We always were."

Freya nodded. But she wasn't certain how friendly anyone would be with the musician who rose to the top. Was the loss of friendship worth it? It had to be, for she was determined to play nothing less than her best.

The next morning, Freya found herself on the train once more, carrying much less with her. She needed only her violin and clothing for two days, and then she would be back with her new friends, ready to continue her training. Already she felt that weeks and weeks had gone by in just those few short days. Her letters home remained unanswered as of yet, but since it took some time to receive a letter, hopefully she would receive news of Mama soon.

As difficult as it had been to leave Salzburg, Freya did look forward to time with her grandmother. The woman was delightfully eccentric and always had delectable food.

This time, there was no trepidation about boarding the train. This time, she knew she had her own compartment, but she had no use for it. Paris would be only one day away and not even a full day at that. And this time, she knew what she needed to do. As soon as she boarded the train, she asked for the conductor in the dining car. She'd worked it all out in her mind, and so she pushed forward, even though the real-life version seemed petrifying. But was this moment not part of her test? Did she not wish to be a professional musician? At the first test of her determination, would she waver? No, she would not.

The cars were different and in a different order this trip. Some were even more fine, with gold-gilded edges on the carvings. And some were less opulent. The seats were worn in places, and the rug beneath her feet showed wear. As she approached the dining car, she stood taller, attempting some courage. The man who greeted her seemed kind enough. "May I help you, miss?"

"Miss Winter." She held out her hand. "Thank you, yes. I am a student of the Student Salzburg Orchestra."

"That is very impressive." He dipped his head to her.

"Thank you. I must travel from my school to visit my grandmother twice monthly, and I wonder if during my travels, you would be looking to pay for a musician to entertain your dining car?" She held her breath. She'd never attempted such a thing, made such an offer to anyone. What would her parents say about selling her talent like this as a common performer? She had no way of knowing. Perhaps they would be pleased. At any rate, she forced herself to pretend to be professional.

He considered her a moment. And she thought he was bound to deny her the opportunity. His eyebrows lowered, and he pressed his lips together.

Freya's shoulders drooped, preparing herself to step away and hide in her compartment when out of the corner of her eye, the handsome man from her last train ride approached.

Her mouth fell open, and she forgot to close it for so many breaths that her tongue went dry. She desperately tried to wet her lips so that she could speak when needed.

He surprised her further by saying, "I can vouch for her. Your guests will be enchanted."

"Oh, well, if you say so, sir, we shall give her a go, no?" The conductor turned to her. "Show me your music tonight during the dinner hours, and we shall see."

"Thank you!" She smiled. And then she turned her smiles to the handsome man. But he simply bowed to her and made his way out of the car.

Where was he going? He'd moved so quickly that he was soon no longer in sight. She wanted to groan in frustration for now she must talk to him, to thank him, to find out why he would vouch for her when he had certainly never heard her play.

But the conductor was peppering her with questions, and together they chose music to play. He was interested in the tone and type of music and in how she presented herself. When at last he seemed satisfied that her performance would not embarrass the fine quality of the Orient Express, she was left to herself. Her feet rushed after the intriguing man of their own accord. But he was nowhere to be seen. She passed two cars with nothing but a line of doors to individual compartments and suspected he was merely inside his own space, enjoying privacy. She kept going until she stepped into a car with a glass ceiling. She lifted her chin, her head back, watching the sky float by above her.

All the seats were taken in the car. So she stood at the entrance, watching the mountains above, especially their snow caps and deep purple hues with a smattering of green on the lower edges. She stood for a few minutes more and then made her way back down the train. She'd walked the entire length of the Orient Express, stopping only at the door to a private car. She felt silly for her almost desperate chase after a man who obviously did not wish to be found at the moment.

She wanted to be close to the dining car for when she would play her violin. Earning some money would help her situation in every way. And the very idea that she could perhaps earn her own living someday seemed at once preposterous and freeing all at the same time.

She entered the dining car; it too was filling up. She asked for a chair at a table near the front where the conductor had decided she would play and ordered her own smaller meal. Suddenly, her nerves took over. With shaking hands, she brought wine up to her lips. After three sips, she commanded herself to be calm.

No command to calm herself ever worked as well as she hoped.

As soon as she finished dinner and the conductor stood up to introduce her, she closed her eyes in a desperate attempt to control her breathing. Why could she stand and play with a grand orchestra in a great hall without a problem, but here, with this small car full of people, she felt her nerves fraying?

"We will now hear from someone with a relatively new face in the world of musicians. She comes to us every two weeks here on the Orient Express as a premier violinist from the Student Salzburg Orchestra. Miss Freya Winter."

They clapped politely, and Freya stood with her violin and bow already in hand.

CHAPTER SIX

By the time she was into her third number, she relaxed into her playing. The bow moved across the strings, sending perfect vibrations up through the instrument to her fingers. She drew out the last note of the current piece with a touch of vibrato and almost forgot where she was.

The clapping startled her, and then a wave of pleased surprise rose inside. The audience was enjoying her numbers. The conductor seemed pleased. Time to have a little fun. She picked up the pace, started tapping her foot, and moved into a fast number. It was not actually very difficult to play, but it sounded complicated, so it was usually impressive to people who didn't know anything about the violin.

Freya started dancing while she played, and the people in the dining car cheered. Some stood up. Many clapped their hands to her rhythms. She grinned and moved among them playing faster and more intricate notes.

Then the back door opened, and *he* walked in. She grinned wider, her eyes sparkling as she danced and played closer to him.

His gaze flitted up to everyone watching, and then he grinned at her. He stood at her front and started dancing as if they were together, but obviously with her violin and bow in hand, he could not hold her in his arms, though it felt almost as though he were.

She laughed and sped up her playing even more.

Most of the people in the dining car stood, and soon everyone had hands in the air, clapping and moving to the music.

When at last she ended the number, the dining car passengers cheered loudly. She bowed to them and then curtseyed low to the handsome man who had made it all possible.

He bowed in return and then sat at her table near the front of the car.

Everyone else moved to sit again, and all eyes were on her. But she saw only him. She stepped as close to him as she dared, her skirts barely brushing against his legs now and again, then she turned to face the room. "I have one more number." She considered what it could be. And she decided to just play from her heart. She dipped her head to the man at her side and began. The music was cheerful, happy, and light. She thought of her opportunities, of her new program in Salzburg. She thought of the Maestro, and she closed her eyes. One day she would play for him. Her melody dripped with longing, echoing the desires of her heart. She would return to Salzburg in two days and audition for chair placement in the student orchestra. Her notes turned short and full of energy as she thought of all that awaited her.

The man shifted, and she eyed him. His return gaze was intense, searching. Her tune became solid, sure, important. She thought of this man sitting in front of her, his blue eyes seeing her. She wished she knew his name. A great tingling awareness spread through her, and her melody returned to longing, pleading, reaching out with both hands to scoop up every dream, every happiness, and . . . him. In her mind, his hand reached for hers, and she ran to him. Her notes picked up into a great rising crescendo, moving faster and louder until . . . silence. She dipped her head. Then she played two more notes and bowed.

Everyone erupted in cheers. Their laughing, smiling faces, the nod from the conductor. Everything should have been something to celebrate, and they were. But her heart was still pounding, and she hadn't dared look at the man at her side. Her piece had been so . . . intimate. Her face burned.

He hadn't moved. Had he clapped?

She bowed again, and then, before she turned to put away her violin, she forced herself to look at him. For a moment, he said nothing. Then he reached his hand out to her. She placed her fingers in his, and he brought her bare knuckles to his lips. His lips on the back of her skin were soft.

"That was entertaining." His eyes sparkled. Did he linger there, or did she imagine it? He released her hand. "Entertaining is perhaps what's appropriate here."

Was entertaining not sufficient? She found her voice. "Were you pleased?" She wanted to bite back her desperate-sounding tone, but she was as lost to it as she was becoming to this new stranger in her life. She held her breath, waiting for his response.

"Does it matter?"

She sat across from him, almost falling into her chair. "Yes." The word came out in a breathless whisper. But after a moment of no response, she sat up straighter and clarified, purposefully shifting the moment to something more practical. "You were the one who recommended me to the conductor. I was honored and grateful. I wouldn't want you to think your recommendation had been misplaced."

He dipped his head, nodding slowly. "Then yes, I was pleased for the conductor. You performed adequately for this group, for your purpose here. I am certain the dining car will be a highly sought car whenever you are riding this train."

She tried to bask in his approval but could not find much true praise in his words. The word *adequately* squelched some of her happiness. "Would you have me play from the masters? Here?"

He studied her and then tilted his head. "Walk with me?"

She stood and nodded, placing her violin carefully back in its case, loosening the taut stretch of her bow and returning it to the case as well. She shut the case, then picked it up, holding it close to her body.

He lifted his hand toward the door, and she followed him out.

Guests nodded at her or smiled as she passed. Then in the corner, she saw Victoria Manet from her first train ride. The woman had the audacity to clap again as she walked by. The woman's brazen wink emboldened Freya somewhat.

A well-dressed, portly man approached, the soft smell of rosin lingering in the air near him. He bowed to them both, then stepped back, giving them space to pass. "Zeh observation car is largely empty."

"Oh, thank you." Freya turned as they passed him, but he had slipped through the door to another car.

"Odd." The man at her side turned back to her. "But shall we follow his advice?"

"Yes." Now that she was walking with and talking to this mysterious handsome man, she found herself tongue-tied. She clutched her violin case tighter as she worried over what he would say to her. Was he not pleased?

They walked through several cars before arriving at the observation car. The air was a bit colder.

"I think our winter will linger." The man craned his head to see up into the mountains. "Still plenty of snow on the lower hills."

"Traveling by train is nice for colder weather. Better than a carriage."

He indicated they should sit. One other couple sat in the car, deep in their own conversation. He held out a chair for her, and she placed the violin at her side while she sat.

"We have not met officially." His smile was warm and almost delicious. "I am Erich."

Odd, were they to only use first names? Something about that seemed fitting, equally mysterious as their interactions had been. "Freya. And I wanted to thank you. Your recommendation got me that spot in the dining car." She wondered how that had happened. Was he some sort of renowned person? Or did he simply know the conductor well?

"I was happy to do so."

"But how could you know I wouldn't embarrass myself and you?" She hoped she hadn't done either, because again, his own painfully mild reaction to her playing unsettled her insides.

"I had a hunch." He grinned. "Those in the Student Salzburg Orchestra rarely disappoint. I hear their concerts year to year. I admit I was surprised to see you on the train again."

"Yes, and I you." She waited, but when he didn't offer any explanation, she added, "I am going to visit my grandmother in Paris."

His eyebrows shot up. "I go to Paris as well. The exposition is about to start."

"Oh yes. I hope she will take me to see some of it."

"I would venture some of the sights will be difficult to miss. The Eiffel Tower . . ."

"True." She shifted in her seat, impatient to discuss what plagued her unease. "I'm sorry to change the topic, but I can't help but feel . . . that you were dissatisfied with my playing." There, she said what most pestered her comfort.

"Not at all. I am sorry if I gave that impression. You are very skilled. You also have a gift for emotion, for reading your audience, and for entertaining them. Is that not what was needed?"

"Are you someone who appreciates music?"

"I am most passionate about music." His eyes had turned serious, intense.

"Would you like to hear me play again? I can play other things, more complex selections—" Her desire to impress this man, this Erich, blocked out all other thought at the moment. She wanted to play for him something that would make him cry with emotion or stand and applaud in pleasure.

She wanted her notes to reach him, to crowd out all else. And she'd never felt quite this way before. Her breathing increased, but she said nothing more.

He studied her and then leaned forward. "Tell me about your playing."

"Tell you?" She fidgeted. Her hands reached for her instrument and then lowered.

"Why do you play? How do you feel?"

"Well, I love to play. I feel alive. I feel . . . heard. No, it's more than that. I feel like myself when I play."

"I can understand that. I think one way to get to know another person is to hear him or her play." When his eyes met hers, the depth of his searching into her own felt more intimate than intrusive. For the briefest of moments, she wanted to share everything with him, her sorrows of a life filled with no one to listen to her play, her frustrations of trying to force her parents to understand, the loneliness of never finding someone who appreciated this part of her, the part that felt most real.

He spoke again. "Tell me about that last number."

She laughed, the self-conscious sound making her want to wince. "That was a piece of my own making."

"When did you compose it?"

"I created it while I played." She dipped her head. "Do you . . . do you feel that was too bold?"

The pause between them left her almost breathless.

"Not at all." His smile was warm. "In all truth, I was enchanted. And that piece alone said more about you than any other."

Would he ever guess that her thoughts had focused on him during her playing? She willed her face not to heat. How could he know? She exhaled, and some of the tension left her shoulders. Again, she didn't have a true sense of whether or not she had reached him, had touched him. She didn't dare offer again to play for him even though her fingers ached to do so. What would it take to reach his heart? To change him?

"What did you learn of me while I played?"

"You are full of passion." He rested his hand on the table, near hers. "Your notes are exact, and you obviously play well, but there is a hunger, a desire to communicate with your music and I . . . I have never encountered such a thing . . . in others." The words hung in the air around them, and Freya found that she shivered down to her very toes.

"And in yourself?"

He shifted, then he took her hand in his. Her arm erupted in a tingling pleasure, and she bit back a soft gasp.

He ran his fingers along her calluses. "You play often."

She nodded. "I communicate best through music."

"Then we are of one mind in this."

His thumb moved along her knuckles, and she tried to breathe normally, trying not to close her eyes in appreciation of that one simple, slow motion.

"Yes. What instrument do you play?"

"Many, but the violin is my passion." He turned her hand over, running a finger along her calluses again. "These are familiar." He lifted his fingers to show her. "See."

She reached out a finger to brush lightly against his skin. The intimacy of doing so trembled inside her.

The train's momentum changed, but after hours moving in the same direction, even the subtle differences were obvious. The sun had gone down. They would be arriving in Paris soon. Freya didn't know what else to say or do, but she didn't want their meeting to end.

Before he could stand or say anything about the journey being at an end, she asked, "You said once you often ride the train?"

"I do. I'll be coming back to Salzburg in three days." His gaze caught hers.

"As will I." She swallowed. She hated to leave, not knowing if this was perhaps her last moment with him.

The train started to slow. And he stood. "Perhaps we shall see one another again."

"I-I would like that."

"And I as well." He looked out the window toward the approaching station. "Must we go?"

The corner of his mouth lifted, and then he bowed. "Goodbye, Freya."

"Goodbye."

Only her many years of discipline kept her from running after him, clinging to his arm. What had happened to her heart? For years it had beat in a normal fashion, one beat after the other, so much so she hardly paid it any mind. But now, it pounded for a moment, slowed, and then raced. Her face flushed. His tall form exited their car, and she knew she would be counting the moments until she returned to Salzburg, using all of them to hope that he would be on the train.

CHAPTER SEVEN

GRANDMOTHER MADE FREYA LAUGH ON good days and wish to duck and hide on others. Today seemed like something in the middle.

"Oh, my Freya, my dear," she clucked as they left the train station in her new car. "The sights you will see. Paris is a changed city."

Freya was quite amazed at the whole experience. They travelled through the busier streets of Paris at first, and she tried to catch sight of everything. People seemed to be everywhere she looked, even during this evening hour. And many of them were building structures. "Is all this construction because of the World Exposition this month?"

"Yes. They are working on it night and day. You can see the Eiffel Tower from my windows. Much will happen right below. We could promenade and see it next time you come."

"Thank you. I'd like that."

"I'm happy to hear it." Grandmother studied Freya for a moment. "I have a rather full schedule for us while you are here. Tonight, as soon as we arrive, you must change your clothes. You'll find new ones in your closet. I've invited guests, a friend of our family, a dear woman I've known since we were young . . . and her son."

Freya nearly choked, but she knew better than to say anything to cross her grandmother. "Thank you."

"You're welcome. I know you might be fatigued from all the travel, but we will have supper, and I think it will be just the thing."

"Yes, I look forward to meeting your friend."

"And her son." Grandmother's eyes sparkled. "He's very intelligent and appreciates music, so that should be something you can talk about."

They arrived in front of Grandmother's beautiful townhome. Their driver opened the door and offered to carry Freya's bag and violin, but she shook her head. "Thank you, but I can manage."

Grandmother clucked again. "You and that instrument of yours. There are other things in life, you know." Grandmother smiled at her, but it was more calculating than friendly. "As you shall see."

They climbed four stairs and entered the lovely upscale townhome. Freya had visited before and saw that much was still the same in her grandmother's home: her plush furniture, the fineness of her artwork, the draperies that hung at her windows, even the smell. An odd mixture of perfume and spices tickled Freya's nose.

"You must hurry. They'll be arriving within the hour."

"Goodness!"

"You can't blame me. I have only tonight and tomorrow with you really, so we had to fill every moment."

Freya could not imagine the cause of the urgency, but she suspected some matchmaking machinations were at work, which would be confirmed the moment their guests arrived. She went to change into her new clothes her grandmother had purchased. Everything in her closet was exquisite, and she felt grateful . . . and beholden. She donned her favorite, a long, white, lacy tea dress. The sleeves puffed at her shoulder, and the waist was snug. She smiled. Grandmother must have gotten her measurements from Freya's dressmaker in London. She heard voices at the door. Her skirts skimmed along the floor as she stepped forward to greet these important guests so soon after her arrival.

An unfamiliar woman blocked the doorway to whomever was behind, at least for the moment. The woman's pink skirts flared; her hat filled the space so that she had to turn sideways in order to enter. The brim was turned up at one side. A large feather rose up and arched over. In many ways, she reminded Freya of a large, pink cloud.

"Oh, Minerva! Oh, we are so happy to come."

Grandmother fluttered about, hugging and air-kissing her friend, who held a hand out to Freya. "And you must be the granddaughter. Miss Winter?" She raised both eyebrows and took her in with one glance.

"Yes, how do you do?" Freya curtseyed.

"I am Lady Bouchet."

A lady.

"And this is my son, the newly titled Lord Bouchet."

Still unable to see the woman's son, Freya dropped in another curtsey. "Lord and Lady Bouchet. I am honored to meet you."

Lady Bouchet smiled and then patted her shoulder. "Your grandmother and I are old friends. And it has been our dearest wish to get together more often and most especially when you two are both in town."

Lord Bouchet stepped to the side so that he was at last more visible from behind his mother. Striking. His blond hair waved across his head. His eyes were a deep brown, and in every way, he was almost the most handsome man she'd ever met. Almost.

She offered her hand. He bowed over it, pressing his lips to her knuckles. "Enchanted."

Was he enchanted? She searched his face. He seemed bored, but there was a spark of something in his eyes, something that said he wasn't entirely regretting the dinner engagement. And that made the prospect of time in their company at least endurable, if not enjoyable. Who was this lord and why would his mother and her grandmother think that the two of them might be a good match?

At dinner, her grandmother's servants brought in the first course. Lord Bouchet's voice at her side sounded bland compared to Erich's. "I hear you play with the Student Salzburg Orchestra?" His voice was quiet, but every ear tuned in to listen. Lady Bouchet's gaze flitted in their direction, and Freya's grandmother paused her spoon on the way to her mouth.

Freya cleared her throat. "Yes, I do. I feel lucky to have this opportunity."

The ladies leaned closer, watching Lord Bouchet for his response.

He cleared his throat. "And you enjoy the violin?"

The hungry expressions on both their relations grew rather ridiculous in Freya's mind.

"I do play the violin, and I enjoy every moment, whether playing for pleasure, performing, or even practicing. Do you play an instrument?"

"Sadly I do not. But I enjoy listening to music very much. Paris has many opportunities for music lovers."

"Are you often in Paris?"

Grandmother smiled. "Oh, he will be here the whole of the time you are traveling from Salzburg, dear. We are going to have the coziest time of it." She nodded and exchanged a meaningful glance with Lady Bouchet.

"As Mrs. Winter has said, I will be here for many weeks, yes."

"I wonder what Miss Winter would enjoy seeing while you are here."
Lady Bouchet's pointed expression almost made Freya laugh. She turned to
Lord Bouchet, her eyebrow in the air.

"Whatever she most wishes to see. The fair will be a highlight, obviously."
His open expression was somewhat tinged with a waxing discomfort. "Are
you enjoying the sights in Salzburg?"

"Yes, they are lovely from afar. I find much of my time is used in rehearsal."
And then Freya, tired of the situation herself, took pity on him and decided to
liven things up a bit. "Furthermore, I have not met a single eligible man of
interest in the whole of the orchestra."

He coughed, his eyes widening. "Is that so?"

"Yes, quite. We are all so consumed with our music. We don't have much
time to pursue marriage." She clucked her tongue.

Lord Bouchet seemed to have no response, but a great amused twinkle lit
his eyes and perhaps a growing comprehension. "With no marriage potential,
perhaps it is a wasted experience."

"Ah yes, you see my concern." Her eyebrow rose in a daring lilt.

The silence from their audience felt thick, but Lord Bouchet's smile grew.
"Undoubtedly a waste, unless the purpose is to enjoy music?" Could this
man have a delightful wit and humor?

"Ah, but a purpose simply to enjoy music, is that not a waste of time
for those of us of a certain age?"

"Only you could say so."

"Don't you find the process of finding and capturing a good marriage partner to be either the most important of your life . . . or immeasurably tiresome
depending on the company?" She turned her most daring expression to Lord
Bouchet. His eyes widened, and his mouth twitched, and she knew he wanted
to laugh. She tipped her head.

But he managed to regain control. "I quite agree."

The women gasped in unison.

"I find that those of our age have other things to be thinking about besides
simply capturing the interest of someone only to be shackled our entire lives."
His voice broke at the end.

"Too true. Or to be wooed and courted for one's dowry and then be
given pin money portions of an income."

"Or to then be told day in and day out where one might go, to be told
that cards were out or that a family dinner was needed," he said. "Seems a
bit of a freedom crusher if you ask me."

"I sympathize with those of our age who are submitted to countless activities with these sole entrapments in mind."

He leaned back in his chair, his eyes appraising her anew while he brought his wine glass to his lips.

Freya didn't dare look at her grandmother. She and Lord Bouchet got on well and comfortably at that point, so perhaps the woman would be satisfied.

Grandmother cleared her throat, eyebrows considerably higher on her forehead than Freya thought possible. "Tell us about Salzburg. It has been an age since I've visited that charming city."

And so Freya told what she knew of the city, though as she'd said, she had spent most of her time indoors. After a delicious dinner and some lingering conversation, Lord Bouchet stood and turned to Freya.

"Miss Winter, I see a fascinating bit of balcony that looks to have a glorious view of the Eiffel Tower," he said. "Might I escort you out to see it?"

She stood and placed her hand in his. "I'd like that. I admit I haven't even seen the view yet."

"Have you just arrived then?"

"Yes, within the hour of our dinner."

"Singular." He bowed to his mother and her grandmother, and she lowered herself in a curtsey.

Freya followed him up the stairs and then to the right to an upper-level sitting room that boasted the balcony.

As soon as the door shut behind them, he turned to her and crossed his arms, his face all smiles. "You, Miss Winter, are the most intriguing woman I have ever met."

She joined him in laughter, resting the fronts of her arms upon the railing. "I hope I did not come across as overly impertinent, but I could not abide how that dinner was going to go."

"You mean with our conversation under strict scrutiny, every word analyzed?"

"You know they're down there discussing us right now."

"Absolutely." He snorted. "Only now, you have delightfully altered the conversation." He stood closer, his shoulder bumping hers. "And for that, I thank you. I haven't had this much enjoyment at a dinner . . . ever." He looked out over the city. "Would you look at that."

The Eiffel Tower rose up against the sunset-painted sky. "Such a beautiful city."

"Will you be here long enough to enjoy it?" Lord Bouchet seemed almost hopeful that she would.

"I have tomorrow. Then I must hurry back to Salzburg."

"But you return every two weeks?" Was his interest friendly? Or was he intrigued by her in more ways than simple friendship?

"Generally, yes, though I will have some weekends swallowed up by practices. Are you living in Paris?"

"My mother and I are here on a tour of sorts. She wished to come. I am here to show her the things she has never seen."

"How kind of you."

His face seemed strained at the thought of sightseeing with his mother, and she wished to alleviate his discomfort. She added, "I believe we mean to see some of the preparations for the exposition tomorrow. If you and your mother are free . . ." She found she wouldn't mind an afternoon in his company, not one bit.

He turned to her, resting his side against the railing. "Tell me, Miss Winter, has your heart ever been turned by a man?"

Her mouth dropped. *How bold.* But she lifted her chin. "I'm not certain." Images of Erich passed through her mind. "Perhaps?"

His grin grew. "Tell me all about it."

She laughed. "Well, there was this man on the train."

"On the train?" His eyebrow rose. "Who is this man?"

"I don't really know."

"So, a mystery man?" He nodded. "Excellent. How did you meet?"

How to explain Erich to this man? They'd certainly seen each other, conversed even, before they'd met. She determined to stick with the simplest explanations. "I was playing my violin in the dining car."

"And he was smitten by your beautiful music? Couldn't stay away?"

"Well, actually I think he was rather underwhelmed." She frowned. "But he has this manner, this intensity. Sometimes I couldn't look away. I don't really know what drew me in."

"I can certainly guess what might draw him in." His eyes turned appraising as his gaze moved over her face. She felt her face heat. "Is he handsome, then?"

How unusual to be discussing such things with another man, someone she hardly knew, but they had found such quick rapport with one another; it was like they had grown up together. "He . . . is. Very handsome, in fact. Tall. Where your hair is light, his is a deep brown. His eyes are blue. And his smile is warm and sincere."

"And this is what has turned your heart?"

"No, it's something else. I don't know what exactly." The connection she felt with Erich felt deeper, more important, but as Lord Bouchet's questions pointed out, she didn't know him very well at all.

"Now, don't be concerned. You aren't as shallow as this sounds. Everyone is attracted to another at first, correct? Take you and I for instance."

"You and I?"

"Yes, if the well-meaning relatives downstairs hadn't so pointedly thrown us together, we might have met on a train. I might have boarded and met your gaze across the car and then approached with a smile, and there you go. Connection." He tucked a hair behind her ear. "You are a very attractive woman, you know." He said it in such a matter-of-fact tone that she didn't think she would even blush.

"Wha—thank you." She dipped her head. "So are you." She laughed. "I mean, you are handsome." She placed a hand at her forehead. "Goodness. I'm not accustomed to these kinds of conversations."

"That's why they're so delicious. Take our conversation over dinner. Delightful, unique. How often have you heard the ladies of our class being as frank as you?"

She shook her head. "Never. I fear that Grandmother will have words to say to me once you go."

"No, not at all, for we've come up here and conversed, and I am going to ask to come by tomorrow, and they will think their machinations have worked and that your brash comments were just the thing to reel me in."

"You are almost frightfully frank." She crossed her arms. "Tell me, has your heart been turned?"

He studied her long enough she thought he would refuse to answer, but then he said, "Yes." He didn't add more for a moment, and his face turned away. "My heart belongs to another, but I'm afraid she is lost to me."

Freya felt relieved to hear his flirtatious ways were meaningless. What an odd reaction for her to have, for who wouldn't want a member of the peerage flirting with her the way he had?

"So we are each hopelessly distracted by another?" She bumped her shoulder against his this time. "Sounds like the perfect opportunity for some frivolity to keep us elevated from our melancholy separated ways."

"Precisely. We are of one mind." He stood to his full height. "And now I must escort you down and clear you of any nonsense from your grandmother since I promise to call."

"Thank you, Lord Bouchet. I believe I will enjoy our friendship very much."

"And I as well."

They walked down together, and everyone bid farewell. By the time her grandmother's front door was shut and the house quiet, her pleased expression stretched from ear to ear.

"Tell me what you think of that!" Grandmother led Freya into the front drawing room.

"Grandmother, what is he a lord of? How do you know them?"

"His mother and I are dear friends, as we've said. He has a large estate in England as well as in France. He's quite the catch and has not had his head turned by any of the nobility that his mother is aware of. And he wants to come calling tomorrow." Her triumphant face made Freya laugh. "Tell me that isn't more exciting than practicing that instrument of yours."

"I do admit to finding myself much diverted." She patted her grandmother's hand. "Thank you for your willingness to host me, to support my school in Salzburg, and for arranging the meeting of such a nice man."

"You're welcome, my dear. Now. The exhaustion is all over your face. Let's get you to rest so that you are fresh and lovely tomorrow. I have your clothing picked for our day in Paris as well."

Freya kissed her grandmother's cheek and then made her way to bed. Before she had too many thoughts, all of them centered on her handsome man on the train and her new friend in Paris, she had drifted off to sleep.

CHAPTER EIGHT

HER AND LORD BOUCHET'S DAY together with chaperones looking on had been pleasant. Paris had engaged Freya's fascination, and now that she'd seen the preparations almost complete for the exposition, she was longing to return to Paris once the grand event had truly begun. But the longing did not match the intensity of her desire to continue in Salzburg. Her fingers itched to play. Out of respect for her grandmother's tightly packed schedule, she hadn't opened her violin case during her stay in Paris. But now that she was well and truly on her way back to the train, she was almost consumed by the wish to run a bow across strings.

As the motorcar made its way to the train station, she studied the tip of the Eiffel Tower, visible to their left, and laughed. "I did not hear your opinion the other day: to which camp do you belong, Grandmother? Those who adore the Eiffel Tower or those who abhor it?"

"Adore, oh certainly. Although, I do not appreciate this yellow color."

They pulled into the station, and their driver opened her door. "In that, we are of one mind." Freya kissed her grandmother on the cheek. "Thank you. I'll see you in two weeks."

"Oui, my darling."

Freya waved as her grandmother drove away, and then she turned to face the station. Everything seemed larger than when she had arrived in the evening hours. The crowds hurried from place to place, to vendors, from ticket booths to trains. As Freya pushed her way through a much larger crowd than she ever remembered in Paris, her thoughts turned to Erich. His name rolled around in her thoughts. *Erich.*

She picked up her pace, her eyes searching for his hat and tufts of hair. With a grin, she stepped aboard the train, her violin tight at her side. But she saw no sign of him, even after searching through three cars. She told herself she was merely looking for the perfect location to relax for the many hours it would take to arrive back in Salzburg.

The cars were different again, no hint of an observation car. But this time, she was also cold.

A man dressed from head to foot in black dipped his head as she passed. "It is warmer zeh closer you move to zeh steam and coal car."

She shivered, not realizing until that moment just how cold she had become. "Thank you." A faint aroma of rosin filled the air, passing as soon as she moved away from the kind gentleman.

As she pushed on, she discovered the next car was a sleeping car. The narrow corridor felt confining as she clutched her violin case to her front. Then she found a salon, filled with tables and comfortable chairs, cards out, and finally, a warm-looking fireplace.

It was difficult to tell how close she'd come to the engine and coal car. But that fire seemed the most likely chance to warm herself, and so she chose one of two large overstuffed chairs seated at its front. Her violin fit next to her and her bag at her feet.

A conductor approached. "Would you like me to store your belongings for you?" He reached for her violin.

"I'll keep the violin with me. I believe I will be playing during the dinner hour. But you may take the other. Where will you place it?"

"Might I see your ticket?"

She nodded and handed it to him to peruse. "In your compartment, here." He pointed to the number. "I will place it in this room. You will find it in the sleeper car in this direction, closer to the engine." He then took her bag in hand.

She smiled. "Thank you."

Warmth from the fire had started to seep inside her body. How odd. She'd not been so cold on the platform or on the streets of Paris, but the chill had come on quickly once the train had begun to move.

They'd been having unseasonably cold weather of late. She was grateful blizzards hadn't slowed her train's progress. At least she spent most of her time indoors in Salzburg. She closed her eyes, thinking of the magnificent views of her new home. Her mouth curled up in a smile without her thinking much about it. Her new home. Salzburg was magical. The mountains towered up above them in might and power. And the colors. Purples, white tips, deep browns, blacks, the green of the trees. So much depth. She felt cradled at its base. Thoughts of her program, the classes, the practices, even chords of the music she played lulled her into a comfortable sleep.

When she awoke, voices rumbled near her.

"I believe she is to play during the dinner hours," a familiar voice said.

"Excellent. I will inform the dining car conductor." The voices stopped, and the train car went quiet.

"You smile when you sleep." Erich's voice sounded deep and warm.

Her smile grew. Then she opened her eyes, slowly. "Do I?"

"Yes. And now that you've fully awoken, might I know of your dreams?"

She closed her eyes again, the lids feeling suddenly heavy. "I was thinking of Salzburg, the mountains, and eventually, my music. I think I dreamt an entire concerto." She laughed. When he joined her in laughter, she thrilled at the sound, his deep bass and lovely smile warming the last remaining chill right out of her. She sat up. "Forgive me. I think the warmth of the fire put me to sleep."

"They came asking if you were going to play in the dining car."

"I caught some of that. Thank you for responding." She wondered if the conductor would again pay her for her efforts. How wonderfully freeing to have money of her own.

After time spent with her new friend, Lord Bouchet, she was feeling bolder around Erich. "And how did you enjoy Paris?" she asked.

"Very much. I was intrigued by the finishing touches they are placing on the exhibits for the exposition. It is a time for artists."

Her interest perked further. "Are you an artist?"

"Of a sort, yes. As are you. Were you able to play your violin this weekend?"

Her shoulders fell. "No. I'm afraid my playing for the dining car will be my only practice this weekend."

The concern in his expression surprised her. "But are you not trying for a competitive spot in the orchestra?"

"I am, yes. But I am only in Salzburg at all because of the kindness of my grandmother, who wishes more than anything that I would marry instead." *Before her parents sent her off to be a companion.* It was too difficult to say the words aloud, but she thought them often enough that the concern grew by the day.

His eyebrows rose. "And so she discourages practicing?"

"In her own way. She encourages my meeting others and touring Paris and behaving as a debutante might."

"I see." His concern seemed to grow.

"Perhaps I shall try some of my classical orchestra pieces for the dining car. Do you think they will appreciate the numbers as much as my others?"

"I know some will." His eyes sparkled.

"You clearly love music very much. Was there someone who influenced you to pursue music when you were young?"

"My grandfather in particular." He shrugged. "It seems your and my families are at odds with one another. Mine loves and supports music while yours does not." He reached for his book, opening up the pages, turning them as if looking for something. "I would thank him every day if I could."

"Does he live far?"

"Unfortunately, he no longer lives."

"Oh, I'm sorry."

"Thank you. But I visit his old home to take care of things when I can in his honor and to pay my respects."

"That is very noble of you."

"Not so noble as simply grateful." He had stopped leafing through the pages and held a small card in his hand. "I . . . thought of you."

His normally austere face turned hesitant, and she found herself fascinated by the transformation. She wanted more than anything to place her palm at the side of his face, but she could never. Instead, she tried desperately to think of something to say.

But he continued before her brain could function. "I drew this." He reached out his hand with the card.

A card like before but more detailed—a drawing of a small bunch of flowers tied with a string.

"Edelweiss. That's lovely." Her second such gift from him. She wanted to press it to her heart as she had the first.

"We are lucky to have them growing where my grandfather used to live. It is rare. Usually they grow high in the mountains above Salzburg."

She studied his work, the precise detail on the flowers. "You are an artist, certainly. I feel as though you have gifted me with a real flower."

His smile softened. "One day I might." The hint of a promise, of something deeper, tickled her curiosity, but for now she basked in her gift.

"Thank you. I'll use it to mark my pages as I would press a real flower in a book." As she closed the pages of her book, the card sticking out on the page she had stopped reading, she lifted her lashes. "I thought of you too."

"Did you? Even amidst your grandmother's attempts to marry you off?"

"Even so. And I can't help but notice that we have remarkably timed journeys on this very same train."

"That we do." He shifted in his seat. "I travel so often on these lines that I imagine we are bound to cross paths again."

Would they? Oh, she wished it to be so. "I admit that when we parted on that platform, I didn't know when we would next meet, if we would, and I had no way of reaching you." As soon as she said them, she knew her words sounded odd given their short time in knowing one another, but in the spirit of being open, in his acknowledging that he thought of her, the words had just tumbled out without thought. She held her breath.

"I suspect we can count on further meetings." He seemed unfazed by such a bold declaration and responded as though he'd thought the same things. And he seemed surer than she about them meeting again. He had said that he travelled often, weekly even, on this train.

At any rate, she wished to know all she could about him before their time came to an end. "Tell me more of your grandfather's home."

As his words described rolling fields and the hills of the land, as he spoke of the caretakers, she could almost see it in her mind. When the hour grew later and she knew she must stand and make her way to the dining car, it was with mixed feelings.

CHAPTER NINE

IN THE DINING CAR, READY to play, Freya held her instrument up to her chin. Her violin required some tuning, but as soon as the notes sounded true to her ears and her bow was tightened and rosined up, she played one long note. She smiled, lost to the sound.

After an initial slow, moving piece more for her own enjoyment than anything, she opened her eyes and smiled at her audience. For the most part, they weren't paying her any attention. She was a background to their experience. Even Erich, who sat as close as last time, was conversing with a man who had joined his table.

Time to change things up. She pondered the most complex piece she knew. Written by the Maestro, and one her instructor in London had purchased for her, she'd worked at it for months and had played it at a recital for some of London's elite. Could she still manage all the fast-paced fingering? Even if she missed a few of the notes, this audience would not notice.

So she began the first notes of the piece.

Even though Erich did not stop his conversation, he half turned so that his ear was toward her.

Apparently the piece was a good choice if she wanted his attention. She smiled.

The music moved to a rising complexity that soon required all her thought and concentration. As her fingers flew through the notes, she stopped even playing for Erich. Mastering this music had been for her instructor, playing it well had been for the recital and two other gatherings, but now, now she played it for herself. And with every note, joy trilled in her heart. She and the music became one. As she reached the end, moving into the last movement, she altered the music. The original ending was passive, restful, but she was feeling active and urgent. So instead of a slowing resolution, she sought a rising climax, higher and higher, more and more energetic, until her heart might burst with waiting, and then she pounded out the end, one descending combination after another until she herself felt drained of energy. When the last note left her strings, she bowed, trying to catch her breath before she met anyone's eyes, especially Erich's.

After such a performance, she felt bare. But she could only bow for so long. She lifted her head again. The passengers were clapping politely. She felt Erich's gaze, but she didn't dare return it. Instead, she played a common European folk tune that many liked to sing. And with this song, she caught the diners' true attention. Passengers lifted their glasses and sang along, all six verses, cheering at the end.

They called out requests for other common tunes, which she obliged until the dinner car hours were long past for the regular meal, and finally, she sat at Erich's table.

The waiter brought her a drink and her own plate of dinner.

"Thank you."

As she put her violin back in its case and loosened the hair on her bow, she watched Erich. Then she said, "Mr. . . ."

His eyebrows lifted, and he watched her closely. Then she shook her head. "Erich." She pursed her lips. "What am I to call you really? Surely first names are too bold."

His strangely intense expression turned to a smile. "Most everyone in the world calls me Mister if they use my name. Very few call me Erich. It is those few who know me well enough that my first name would be acceptable."

She studied him.

Then he said, "What shall I call you?"

Oh, that wasn't fair to put things in her lap to decide. What were they but passing acquaintances on the train? It felt so much more intimate in her mind. Once she'd learned his name, he was only Erich in her thoughts. She daren't express such a thing, naturally. How could she admit that he wasn't far from any waking thought? She shook her head. "I can think of nothing but Freya for you to call me, though I suspect it to be highly inappropriate."

He toyed with his napkin. "No. How could the familiarity of first names be inappropriate between us? We are of one mind in so many things, are we not?"

She felt as if they were. Her music had united him to her in many respects, but that closeness was surely just a figment she had created. "Then Erich it shall be." She made quick work of her dinner, partly because she was famished and partly because Erich seemed to be waiting for her to finish, making only passing pleasantries.

When she placed her fork precisely on her plate and dabbed her mouth with the white linen napkin, he nodded. "Now tell me. Tell me about that piece you played, the incredibly complex, intricate piece in the middle." His eyes danced with energy. He seemed to wait on her next word with greater intensity than their other conversation.

"That is a brilliant piece by the Maestro. I received a copy before many even knew it was written. If you haven't heard it yet, that is why."

"To which maestro do you refer?"

"They call him the Salzburg Maestro. I believe we discussed him before, so I know you have heard of him. He is a composer, and though I haven't heard him play, he is reputed to be an excellent musician. I've long known of him and followed some of his successes. He has created some of the best compositions and the few of my skill level that really stretch my ability." She felt perhaps bold in declaring something so presumptuous, but she believed Erich would understand.

"And he," she sighed, "he is brilliant. Genius. To be able to train with him would be every violinist's dream."

He watched her even more intently. Then he cleared his throat. Did she imagine it or was there a slight pink to his cheeks? Perhaps she had been too effusive and embarrassed him with her lack of self-restraint. But he said, "It was incredibly complex, the fingering, the energy, and the tempo. I found myself amazed watching you play it so well. I was expecting something entirely different particularly toward the end, but the climax kept building."

She was delighted that her worries about his thought processes were unfounded. And even more delighted he had noticed the song's ending in particular. "Ah, well, the ending was not the original piece, but since I knew that crowd had never heard the original and I was of a mind to play something more dramatic, I improvised."

His eyes widened. "You improvised on a piece you claim is written by the best musical mind of our day?"

She felt her face heat. "I didn't think it would do any harm . . . I was carried away. Perhaps he would not have appreciated the alterations, but he is not present." She tried for a carefree smile.

He studied her a moment more. "Were he to ever hear it, he might be amazed at not only your audacity to attempt such a thing, but also your own genius. You played without a noticeable change in tone or style or feel. The piece sounded seamless."

"And yet you felt it should go in a different direction. What was that direction?"

"Oh, well." He stretched against the collar of his shirt for a moment. "It seemed to me that it might be wrapping up, slowing down, and resolving the conflict."

"See. You have hit upon it exactly, which proves my weak attempts were just that, weak attempts. The true Maestro did exactly as you say. He set us up to crave in that moment some resolution. I could play the ending as it was designed if you'd like."

"I would like that." He glanced around. The car was nearly empty. "Perhaps right now?"

The meal had revived her energy, and the interest in his expression urged her on. Within a few breaths, her instrument was out, bow tightened, and tuning checked. "How about I just play a couple measures before the change and then lead in to the piece as written by the Maestro."

"Excellent. Tell me, does this Maestro have a name?"

She paused and frowned. "I'm certain he does, obviously. But I admit to never knowing it. He is known even on his music as the Salzburg Maestro." She shrugged. "I've always assumed him to be Austrian or German."

"A most logical deduction." He sat back. "Now let's hear the piece how I expected it to be played." He held up his hand. "But if you don't mind, you could begin on the previous page, oh I don't know, perhaps some eight measures before?"

His knowledge of music must be much greater than she realized if he was visualizing measures and pages in his mind. She tapped her toe four times and then started in again. This time, the music swelled and flowed and filled the area around them with a sense of peace. She imagined a stream flowing through a grassy meadow, wildflowers all around. The melody trilled and jumped in happy leaps and flowed in a slow embrace until the last note, which she played very quietly. With a soft sigh, she smiled. "I feel much better."

"Do you?" He tipped his head. "Because I feel like I might go to sleep."

"Well, that's the point, isn't it? To close up and bring peace." She raised her eyebrow. "It is the end, after all."

"And what if the song should be about new beginnings?" The adventurous glint that lit his eyes intrigued her.

"But didn't you just say you felt the piece should have ended in just this way?"

"Yes, but having heard both, I change my mind entirely."

Her smile grew. "I'm happy to have provided an alternative then."

"Just so." He stood and held out his arm. "Would you like to walk with me?"

"Yes. Might we walk to the boiler room? I'm curious about such things."

"Certainly." He led her to the other end of the dining car, and they made their way toward the area where her compartment was located. "Do you think if I left my violin in my berth it would be safe?"

He considered her. "You have the ability to lock your door. I imagine your instrument would be secure, though I understand your trepidation."

"My violin is by far my greatest possession."

He nodded. "Is your berth close?"

"Yes, that is why I ask. We are approaching it right now." She paused outside her door. "That's my number."

"I think you will be safe to leave it here. We won't be gone long at any rate and will pass by here again so you can check on it."

She nodded, then opened the door. Her bag sat on the bench with her key right beside.

"These compartments are rather ingenious, aren't they?" Erich said. "Water to that sink there. Heat from the steam. Have you slept in one of these before?" He reached up and pulled at something near the ceiling. A bed lowered from the wall.

"I had to ask someone to help me sort it out on my first journey. If you recall, you helped me discover my first compartment." She felt silly the minute she'd said anything. Perhaps he would hardly remember when they'd met.

"Of course. Your smile had etched itself on my eyelids. I could scarcely forget such a thing." He was standing close, his arm reaching back above her head to fasten the bed up inside the wall. "I don't imagine you'll be sleeping between here and Salzburg."

She shook her head. "No. Well, no more than you've already seen." She couldn't believe he'd come upon her sleeping by the fire. What if her mouth had been open, or what if she had snored? She looked away and was immediately distracted by the majesty of the scenes outside her window. "The mountains!"

He stepped up beside her in the small quarters. "They are magnificent." His shoulder brushed hers somewhat like Lord Bouchet's had, but with Erich, the feeling was completely different. He shifted away, and her skin felt cool, like a chill that begged for a bit of hot sun. Every part of her hummed with awareness and longing for a connection with him.

He pointed up to the highest peak on a string of mountains. "It is often night when we are travelling right next to those peaks, but that highest one, that is the one my father most often spoke of to me when I was yet a lad."

"Oh?"

He turned. "Shall we sit a moment? Or will this tale bore you above all others?"

"Not at all." She tried to pretend they were two old friends having a bit of a catch up, but she soon realized the futility of such an attempt. For though they sat on what might as well have been a sofa, they were quite alone. Just the briefest touch of his arm had sent her heart into wild flutterings. She'd never been so aware of the beating in her chest.

"My father would come to Salzburg as a boy. He trained with the great musicians of the city and with one very prominent person."

Her interest was caught. "Your father was a musician?" So it wasn't only Erich's grandfather that influenced him in this. No wonder Erich seemed to have an affinity for and understanding of music.

"He was proficient, but even more than his ability to play was his ability to craft an instrument."

"Craft? He made instruments?"

"Yes, violins." He nodded toward Freya's instrument. "Yours is very finely made."

Her eyes widened. "Mine? You can tell its quality by seeing it?"

"More by hearing it played."

"We purchased this because my instructor highly recommended it. I believe it too comes from Salzburg."

"It's made all the more excellent by the person who plays it." The sincerity of his words was validated by his expression and would surely strengthen her in future moments of insecurity.

"But I have completely diverted the purpose of my story." His face was at rest while he talked. He looked up to watch the mountain range draw closer. "My father would talk of that peak when I was a young lad, and he would point it out every time we came to Salzburg. 'That peak,' he would say, 'that is the highest reach in the range. All the other peaks, they are magnificent, but that one was made to reach the highest.'" Erich pointed again. "I think of him every time I see the mountains, and I ask myself, 'Am I made to reach the highest? Is that my destiny?'"

She nodded, and a thought came. She wasn't sure what motivated such a notion, particularly since she had thus far focused all their conversations on music. But the idea grabbed hold and wouldn't let go. "I wonder . . ." She looked away. Perhaps she was being too bold.

"Yes?"

"I wonder if that peak ever gets lonely." She felt her face heat. "That's silly. Forgive me."

When his fingers reached for her hand, she dared to lift her lashes. He shook his head. "Not silly at all. I've wondered the same thing."

He held her hand in his. And she didn't dare move, enjoying the feel of his closeness, his touch.

"And now you must tell me all the things I most wish to know about you." He squeezed her fingers in his own.

"And what are they?"

"Let's begin with your home. Where do you live?"

She fidgeted a moment; mention of home stole the sense that she lived a dream. Suddenly she was reminded rather abruptly that her parents expected results from this venture. But she tried to put that worry aside. "We live most of the time in a townhome on Grosvenor Square."

"Do you? I've perhaps seen the very one."

She nodded. "If you walk along that area or visit the park across the way, you have undoubtedly seen my home." Could they have passed one another on the street one morning and she not even known it?

"And the fountain, in the center of the park, next to a copse of trees?"

"I know the very one."

He nodded. "Excellent. I know your home now. Do you also spend time in a country house?"

She shook her head. "Though my parents wish to move to Brighton, we spend all of our time in London, even in winter, because my father is very busy with his work." And he'd not stopped reminding her that they stayed so that she would marry, but she wasn't married.

He leaned forward, turning toward her as though these minor details mattered more to him than anything else. "And tell me of your governess, your time growing up, your first Season."

She laughed. "That's a lot of ground to cover. I hope that you will do the same for me."

"Certainly." He waved his hand.

"My governess insisted I learn multiple languages. For that, I am very grateful. Especially now at the school, it has been most useful. And one day, I hope to live in Salzburg."

His body went still. "You do?"

"Yes." She tried to make her voice sound normal, nonchalant, but she was afraid every squeak was obvious. "Is that where you live?"

"Most of the time. As you see, I travel, but Salzburg is the home of my heart and where I hope to one day settle with a family."

When their eyes met, his had changed from intent curiosity to a focused intensity.

"That's . . . lovely."

"Yes." He shifted. "What else did your governess teach you?"

"We studied art, history, literature, and music."

"Ah, yes."

"At a very young age, she insisted I attend a musicale. There was a violinist." She smiled, remembering. "A beautiful woman. She swayed while she played. Her face was so serene, so intent. One tear fell down her face while she performed for us." Freya could still see the woman in her mind. "I began pestering my parents for a violin from that moment."

"Did they give in to your petitions?"

"They did, but they were perhaps unaware that I did not wish to merely have a violin for a few paltry attempts, but that I wanted to become that woman, proficient, playing for musicales, respected for her ability, and beautiful." She sighed and then laughed.

"You have probably surpassed her in all regards if I were to guess."

Freya paused in her remembering. "Do you know, I've never thought of it before now, but I suppose my playing might be more advanced than hers was at that time." She was struck by the thought that her first goal as a musician, to become and to play as that woman, had likely been met.

"I'm happy, though, that you did not let your ambitions stop you there." His smile, so encouraging, comforted her in her dreams that had far exceeded the original hopes of a young girl.

"And you, tell me of your parents, your home. I'd love every detail of what it might have been like in Salzburg."

"I was raised in England, France, and in Salzburg. My father was much like I am now, I suppose. He travelled. He had patrons. He worked in his profession."

"And your mother?"

His face softened, all the lines disappeared, and his smile turned tender. "She was an angel and left us all too soon."

"I'm sorry."

He nodded. "Thank you. She loved to hear me play. From what I could tell, my music was what made her the happiest of all things in the world." He laughed, quietly, as if only in remembrance. "Now of course, I realize she probably received joy from many things, her own pursuits, my father, her life. But at the time, her interest, her love, was the greatest gift whenever I wanted to skimp on practicing."

Freya ached with a yearning for that kind of parenting. Though it was too late, she yearned for it all the same. "I played when I knew no one was home, or I was certain they wouldn't be bothered by it." She looked away. "I found a tiny room in our attic that the servants weren't using and converted it to my practice room. I would steal away there whenever I could." She knew so often her parents created other things for her to do the minute they heard sounds coming from the room. The best, most lengthy rehearsals happened when she could cry off a ball because of a headache and then play until the wee hours of the morning.

"Remarkable."

His voice almost jerked her out of her own memories. "What?"

"Remarkable how proficient you have become with those kinds of obstacles."

"Hmm." She didn't know how remarkable it was. "Perhaps just necessary?"

"I went to English schools. Eton felt like prison with so much focus on economics, mathematics, business. I loved the literature, the poetry, the art, and of course, the music."

"Did you attend Oxford?"

"Cambridge. I studied music, but my father only wished me home. At this point, I think he felt my education sufficient for what it was."

"But not you."

He shook his head. "No. To this day, I do not feel it yet sufficient. I wish to know music, everything there is to know. If a new idea has been discovered, I care to know it. Will it ever be sufficient? No. I may be tortured with this insatiable urge all my days."

She nodded. "Sounds reasonable."

They laughed together, and the new feeling of at last finding those who understood the most passionate side of herself comforted her with a warmth that extended to her toes.

They sat together for the remainder of the journey, all thoughts of a walk to the boiler room forgotten. She dozed in and out while he read, and the closeness felt so companionable that she grew quite accustomed to him. When the train began to slow, a wave of disappointment hit her strongly. She wasn't prepared for it.

"Oh dear." The words slipped out before Freya could stop them.

"Not very anxious to arrive?"

"I am. Of course. I love the program I'm in. I am learning, and this week I audition for chair placement in the student orchestra. And I might finally get to play for the Maestro himself." She sighed.

He laughed. "But?"

"But this has been nice. We haven't discussed nearly all the subjects that we must." *And I never know if I shall see you again*, she added to herself.

"We haven't even made it to the boiler room yet, have we?"

"A most important endeavor."

"I agree." He seemed to choose his words carefully, which concerned her. "I travel often on this very line. Perhaps we shall rely on fate to give us another opportunity. So far she's been our loyal friend."

Fate? She wanted to complain about relying on fate. Could they not meet? Could he not come calling? Happy she hadn't verbalized any of those thoughts, lest she be seen as begging for his time, she simply nodded. If he did not wish their friendship to carry past the train, then what could she do? She tried to swallow the hurt.

They said no more about it. The gradual slowing of the train brought their trip to an end much too quickly. He pointed out the window. "Edelweiss grows on those highest peaks. It might seem a lonely existence, but for years, the most dedicated and interested suitors would climb up near the tops to find the flowers to show their commitment to the woman they loved." He tucked a hair behind her ear and then pressed his lips to her cheek. "Perhaps this is why I am so drawn to the flower." He stood and bowed. "A pleasure." Then he slipped out her door, leaving her with only questions and a raging flow of emotion.

CHAPTER TEN

WITH HER VIOLIN AND BAG in hand, Freya stepped out of the hack carriage she'd hired and hurried into her boarding house. Its tall structure standing above the street was a most welcome sight to Freya's music-hungry soul.

Gertie was standing just off the front door talking to a group of girls Freya didn't know well. They giggled and squealed like Freya had always imagined girlfriends did, and Freya immediately felt torn. She'd missed so much bonding, so much time with true musicians. Did she regret her time away? Certainly.

But it wasn't a total loss. In addition to seeing her grandmother, she had made a new friend in Lord Bouchet, and of course Erich . . . She swallowed . . . *Erich.* The power of his words, his edelweiss. She wished she could read his mind. And would she ever see him again really?

As soon as Gertie saw her, she squealed. "You're back!" Her hug was sweet and tight, and Freya felt much better. Gertie sighed in an overly dramatic way. "We were just talking about my love situation."

"No. We were talking about why not Frank." Candace, one of the few women in percussion, leaned closer. "He's in love. We all know it. But then Gertie carries on about this mysterious lord. And honestly, we're saying, Frank is right here. Where is your lordly lord?" With her hands on her hips and her comical expression, everyone within hearing broke down in another fit of giggles.

"Oh, stop already! Can I help it if my heart is still engaged elsewhere? I wish the rest of me was engaged along with it." She grinned, then linked arms with Freya. "Come. I must hear all about your trip." She waved her fingers to the other group, and they laughed her away.

Candace called after her. "We aren't finished with you."

"Yes, yes." As soon as they were out of earshot, Gertie moaned. "Frank is going to hear them. They are dreadfully careless."

"Is it true what they say? Has he made his intentions known?"

"Not really." She shook her head. "But standing by me at every possible moment, opening every door, picking up a lost handkerchief, and most notably, trying and succeeding to hold my hand for several steps before I was able to fenagle it away." She put a hand on her forehead. "And all the while, I'm in love with someone else."

"In love?"

"Yes, don't you remember?"

"I do, but I want to remember all the details." The first night they'd talked of many things, and some of it undoubtedly happened while Freya was asleep. She smiled. Apparently, she'd missed Gertie's most important story to tell.

"So, I was at a house party outside of London, in Buckinghamshire. I had been invited because I have an uncle who is friends with the hosts. We are not as elevated as many of those in attendance." She sighed. "I had little hope of a match or even a flirtation, but I was happy for a diversion. The months outside the Season are so dull."

Freya could not imagine a time when she was merely seeking a diversion. For as long as she could remember, she'd used all her extra moments practicing her violin. "And?"

"I was as surprised as anyone when one particular lord began showing an interest, and I, of course, became quite smitten with him. He's the handsomest man I've ever seen and delightful to talk with. No one would blame me for falling completely in love with him."

"This sounds like a wonderful happy ending."

"Oh, but it's not." Her mouth lowered.

"Oh dear. What happened?"

"His mother." Gertie frowned. "The woman recently made other plans for him, a dear friend's granddaughter. And she has no intention of allowing her son to form any attachments without first exploring that other avenue."

"This other woman. Is she of rank? Wealthy? What is the interest there?"

"I don't know anything else. He hadn't ever met her and knew nothing about her either." She looked away.

"So, the concern is not your social standing or anything?"

"No. And I do have a dowry." Gertie slumped next to Freya while they walked. "But I shall never love another. He is everything a gentleman should be."

Freya thought of Erich and wondered if she would ever be interested in another. Would she be held captive by her own fancies for a man who she knew so little about?

"At least you know him to be of a good family. A title, my goodness. Would you be a lady, then?"

She giggled. "Yes. Can you imagine? All the servants, my friends, calling me your ladyship." She curtseyed. "But I don't care about any of that. I think I'd marry him if he were a tenant farmer."

Freya decided that Gertie was delightfully romantic. She rested her head on her friend's shoulder. "And now we are both to be forever pining for men who are out of our reach."

"What is this? Who is your man?" Gertie turned and put hands on Freya's shoulders. "You must tell all."

Freya laughed. "I'm afraid there is not much to tell." The more she thought about it, the more she realized how silly she would sound to anyone else. She didn't know his last name. He wouldn't commit to anything more than fate to bring them together again. Had she built up and created a relationship with a man that was only one-sided? Her face heated, but she pushed on anyway. "Perhaps there is nothing to this at all."

"Oh, now you must tell me. I am more and more intrigued." Gertie pulled her into a corner of chairs and a table, scooted as close to Freya as she could, and leaned forward.

"We meet on the train."

"Meet?" Her eyes grew wider. "More than once?"

"Well, yes, but we didn't really converse until the second or third time . . ."

She explained to Gertie the sum of her experiences with Erich, leaving out his name and the fact that he was the very man who helped Gertie with her things when they fell all over the train car.

Gertie's bottom lip stuck out as she thought, her eyebrows lowered. "He must think of you. He said he thought of you. And he said he wants to see you again on the train . . . and he sat with you the whole of the day, sat at your feet while you played . . . twice. He must care for you."

"Do you think?" Freya's hope blossomed again into a roaring flame. Then she fell back against her chair. "But I won't be on the train for almost two weeks. We have concerts the whole of this coming weekend."

"What if he rides the train and you aren't there?"

Freya closed her eyes. "This is the most complicated situation I could have ever imagined."

"And he loves music?" Gertie's smile turned dreamy. "He sounds perfect for you."

"So does your lord. Oh, if only it could all work out for both of us."

"What would that look like? You get your love and I mine, and we both train with the Salzburg Maestro?" Gertie shrugged. "Anything is possible." She looked down, her toe kicking at the floor beneath her. "Though, I admit to feeling quite without hope as far as my love."

They found their way to their room, readied for bed, and fell asleep catching up on all their secrets and dreams. Freya smiled as she drifted off. How nice to have a friend like Gertie.

The next morning, she arose early. Full weekends without much practice were going to hurt her playing—she just knew it. Unfortunately, the auditions for student orchestra chair were that day. She rubbed sleep from her eyes on the way to one of the practice rooms. But as she approached, closed doors and various mismatched sounds let her know that all of them were full. She turned, making her way to another hallway. There had to be somewhere she could practice. She stumbled in the low light of morning, clutching her case. Ready to beg the cook to let her practice in the kitchen, Freya turned the corner toward that part of the house when a door opened behind her. She raced back to the practice rooms.

Eliza stepped out into the hallway and nodded. "Oh, I see you've decided to get some practicing in." She raised her nose higher in the air. "Just yesterday Frau Uberdiche said that we would have no hope of getting in the orchestra without practice." She walked by and sniffed. "You will see me in the first chair." She turned the corner without another word.

"Well, good for you," Freya mumbled under her breath. Then she stepped inside and closed the door.

The room smelled musty with hints of rosin. She turned up a gas lamp. Some parts of the home did have electricity, but most held only lamps or candles. She rubbed her hands together. The air was chilly, but she would warm up soon enough.

Her bow hit the strings as though she had been living in a drought. Every note filled her as cracked, dry earth would welcome a drop of water. Every note quenching an insatiable thirst to play. Her fingers flew over the notes. She cradled her old friend under her chin, apologizing for the neglect. But she was rusty on the pieces she tried, and slipped up more than usual. Her audition piece, the portion of a concerto they had been asked to memorize and play, did not sound as polished as she would have liked.

Frustrated, she began breaking the piece down into measures. They had only been asked to play ten. Each measure had to be perfect.

She had no idea how much time had passed when a movement out of the corner of her eye distracted her. Then Frank stuck his head in. "Hey, welcome back." His warm smile eased some of the tightness that had started to build in her chest.

"Thank you. I'm just trying to get ready for auditions."

"You do know they're starting in about five minutes?"

"What!" She jumped, then packed away her instrument. "Oh dear. I had no idea what time it was. Have I been missed?"

"All we've done so far is tune and talk about the schedule. Oh, and they called for a volunteer to meet the Maestro."

"Oh! That's the worst thing to miss."

"But you'll get your turn, won't you?"

"Have you had yours?"

"Oh, yes. I guess I didn't tell you."

She followed him out the door as they both hurried to the practice room for their full student orchestra. "How was it? Meeting the Maestro?"

"Good. I think."

"You think?"

"He was . . . intimidating." Frank rubbed his face. "I know I should be grateful for his critique, but it was difficult to play with any kind of confidence for hours after."

"Oh. Hmm." She hadn't thought of that. "I suppose I might be the same."

"I'm feeling better now, and the things he pointed out really are things I can improve. I feel sorry for the people who volunteered to see him this morning right before auditions."

Freya nodded. "Yes. That would be difficult. I'm not playing well myself."

"What? Everyone is saying you'll be first-chair violin for sure."

"Everyone?"

"Well, except Eliza, but you know how she is."

"True. She's good enough to beat me."

"No way. I'm cheering for you. Frau Uberdiche said we have a new chair audition every week from now until performance, so if you do less than your best, you always have next week."

"That's comforting in a way." She thought it equally disconcerting. Every week people would be competing for her spot were she to win first chair.

"But you want to get it first and keep it. That's what I'm going for."

They arrived at the door. Frank would be sitting on the opposite side of the room. "Thank you for coming to find me," Freya said.

"No problem. Gertie sent me." He looked away.

Freya smiled. "Well, thank you both."

She made her way to the violin section. Eliza already sat in the first chair spot, positioning herself. Freya supposed that's what happened when one arrived on time. But Gertie had a spot open next to her, and Freya much preferred a friendly face, especially today.

Frau Uberdiche stood at the front. "Now that we are all present"—Did Freya imagine it or had she glanced directly at her?—"we will begin rehearsal. It will be disrupted somewhat by chair auditions. You will leave when it is your turn and head through those doors. Follow all instructions precisely and then return, tap the next person, and we will attempt to get a good rehearsal in despite all this disruption."

"No hiding how she feels about chair tests." Gertie smirked. "Can't say I disagree. My stomach is in knots."

Frau Uberdiche lifted her baton, and everyone sat forward in their seats. When she counted four beats with her baton, they began to play.

CHAPTER ELEVEN

Freya believed she had done well in her chair-placement audition. Not exceptionally well, to her way of thinking, but precise and hopefully well enough. The panel of three who heard her play were stone-faced until the very end of her etude when one closed his eyes with a small smile. That seemed to be a good sign. She might have felt better about her performance if Eliza's face hadn't looked a little too triumphant when she returned from her audition.

The rehearsal was coming to a close after many hours of playing, replaying, and going over smaller sections again and again. Freya wasn't sure she could perform one more thing. After the last student had returned from their audition and the whole orchestra had had a fifteen-minute break, Frau Uberdiche stood again on the conductor's platform. The room fell silent.

"We will start by announcing our first-chair violinist. This is our most important chair by tradition. He or she will ensure that the beginning notes are played to keep everyone in tune." She unfolded a sheaf of paper. "Our first-chair violinist for this week and all our performances over the weekend will be . . . Freya Winter."

Gertie grinned. "I knew it would be you."

Everyone clapped. Some faces were sad, but most were encouraging. Freya made her way over to the first-violinist seat. When she got there, Eliza was still sitting. She looked surprised more than anything. But she didn't move.

Frau Uberdiche raised an eyebrow. "Eliza. You will hear your chair placement in just a moment. If you could please vacate the first violinist spot, then we can get on with placing all the other orchestra members here who are waiting." She waved a hand to indicate the filled room.

Eliza nodded, and then she stood. Her lip quivered, but she backed away, her music and instrument in hand.

"The second chair goes to Eliza."

She nodded, then sat back down next to Freya. She put her music back on the stand they would both share and kept her eyes straight ahead.

Once Frau Uberdiche had called out all the new seats, she placed her papers on the stand in front of her and took a moment to look at each student. "Next time I will post the results on Monday. Come in Monday and sit in your appropriate places ready to work." She nodded. "Finally, let us continue."

Freya bit back a groan. At the very moment she thought she couldn't play another note, they were to continue? Determined, she bit the inside of her cheek. Wasn't this why she'd come, to be pushed further than she ever had before?

They worked through their music, all the while Eliza refusing to look at her. When they were at last dismissed, she turned to Freya and held out a hand. "Congratulations. Enjoy this week in first chair."

"Thank you."

"Because it's not going to happen again."

Freya's mouth fell open. All thought left her, and she wanted desperately to say something clever, but nothing came to mind, not one thing, until Eliza had walked out and likely was out of hearing.

"Oh, she's terrible." Freya lifted her case. She would just have to practice more and harder, even when she travelled to her grandmother's, even on the train. Perhaps she could play during the dinner hour for the guests and then practice in her own compartment. She would have to figure something out.

She met up with Gertie, and they moved to take lunch with the other students. They sat family style at smaller tables for all their meals, which Freya had been pleased to discover meant that the food came in serving bowls which were passed around at each table, shared between the table mates.

"Your turn to get the meal." Henry grinned at Freya when she arrived.

"Oh, right." Freya went to the serving counter and picked up two large serving bowls. Eliza walked by, bumping her shoulder enough that Freya almost dropped the food.

"Careful now." Eliza smirked and kept walking.

Freya returned for the water pitcher and the bread, trying to shake off Eliza's attitude, but her hands trembled. She'd feel better when she told Gertie. They could laugh or make light of it or something. But when she returned to the table, Gertie wasn't there.

"Where's Gertie?"

"The Maestro sent for her."

"During lunch?"

"Yeah, I guess he's not having enough time to get to everyone, so he's started using mealtimes."

"Does the man not eat meals himself?" Tobias put a forkful of potatoes in his mouth.

"I don't know." Frank shook his head. "Well of course he eats, just not with us. Maybe he eats later."

"Have any of the rest of you met with him?" A drop of worry festered in Freya's chest.

She knew Frank had, but when Henry and Tobias both raised their hands and Daphne as well, Freya started to feel a bit betrayed. By what, she had no idea, but how was it that she was overlooked? Every time? "All of you?"

She attempted to question them about their experience, but when it became clear no one wanted to talk about it, she didn't press them for details. Well, at least Gertie would tell her everything. But Gertie did not return during lunch or for their classes after.

By the time Freya saw Gertie again, it was nearly time for bed. Freya had spent an hour in the practice rooms, and she was putting her violin away when Gertie plodded into the room.

"You're back! Finally. What kept you?" Freya stepped forward.

But Gertie looked away and then shrugged. "I don't know really. We played together, and he asked to hear me, and then we just . . . talked." She avoided looking at Freya and left to wash up.

Every second she was gone felt like a year of expectation. They had talked? What about? Had she learned any helpful tips? Freya had been nearly boiling over with curiosity, and now Gertie seemed reluctant to share.

Freya crossed her arms. When Gertie came back into the room, Freya couldn't be held responsible any longer for her expression.

"What?" Gertie moved to the other side of the room, preparing for bed.

"We have been looking forward to working with the Maestro since before we even came here. You finally get to meet him. You spend all of lunch and the afternoon with him, and you're not saying anything."

"I . . . um . . . I'm not sure what you want to know."

"What I want to know? Everything! I want to know every little thing. What does he look like? What did he tell you? Does he like how you play? What were his pointers? Even what he smells like. I've been fascinated with the Maestro since I started playing his music over a year ago."

And then, instead of sitting on her bed and spilling all the details, Gertie shrugged. "There's not much to tell."

"So that's how it's going to be? You're going to keep all the details to yourself?"

"I'm not sure what you're talking about, but no, I don't have much else to say about the Maestro." Her face pinched, and she looked away.

And then Freya's heart went out to her. She rushed to her side. "Oh no, are you unhappy? Was it a difficult meeting?"

Gertie turned farther away.

"We don't have to talk about the Maestro, but we can talk about you. Are you well?"

"I'm—I'm well. It's difficult to meet with the Maestro. Ask anyone. I thought I was good at trills . . . before." She turned from Freya and fell onto her bed. "Just ignore me. I'll feel better in the morning." She looked like she might fall asleep right there, but then she lifted her head. "I wasn't with him this whole time. I went to a practice room. I had to work on everything he mentioned."

"Did he . . . did he *like* anything?"

Gertie sniffed. "Yes. He did." She put her head back down on her pillow. "Maybe I'll want to talk more tomorrow."

Freya had to respect that. She lifted her own covers and slipped in, put her head on her pillow, and tried to find the exhaustion she knew was hovering near her consciousness. But her eyes were wide open. The room felt awkward and unpleasant, and her very blood seemed to pound with curiosity.

Frank had said similar things. Was the Maestro an unpleasant sort of person? Could she trust his guidance when it was her turn?

She nodded her head in the dark to herself. Yes. She could trust him. His compositions were brilliant. At the very least, he was more proficient than she. She rolled over onto her side. Tomorrow, she'd play duets with Gertie. She'd hear the trills herself. And perhaps in a week's time, her friend would feel more comfortable sharing what weighed her down the most. Frank had said it took a few days for the critiques to sink in, and then they actually helped his playing.

Gertie was currently fifth-chair violin. She seemed to be well respected, and if Freya were to guess, she had a decent chance at working her way up to a spot in the Salzburg Orchestra.

Hours seemed to go by before Freya was able to drift off to sleep. She dreamed of Erich. And when she awoke, the cloud of melancholy still hovered in her room. No train this weekend meant days full of performances, which she loved, but no Erich.

Gertie seemed only marginally improved after a night's sleep. Freya did not mention the Maestro. They moved about their morning in a veiled silence, which only added to Freya's own dampened mood.

The week continued with more of the same from Gertie. She'd also taken to talking about her lost love. Every second of every day that used to be filled with laughter and fun conversation was now limited to pining over her lord. Her friend needed a confidence nudge.

Once class was over on Wednesday, they had no more rehearsals, just a weekend full of performances. As soon as they returned to their room, Freya pulled out her violin. "Let's play."

"What? We have been playing. All day we play."

"Right, so now let's just play something fun."

Frank's appearance in the doorway made them both jump. "Yes. I've brought mine." Before they could invite him in, he pulled a chair over, sat with his cello in front of him, and lifted his bow.

Freya played a long chord. "Come on, Gertie. Let's play all the silly folk-dance tunes we know."

Gertie watched them for a moment, and then her face softened. "That sounds like fun."

They began a fast-paced number. Gertie played melody. Frank took much of the bassline and became a sort of percussion, and Freya had fun with the harmonies, playing in and out of the melody, rising and lowering on the scale, jumping with her notes to add a little fun, teasing and dancing on her bow through the song.

Soon, they had a crowd in their doorway. Freya waved them in. To her surprise, they started dancing. A couple paired up and jumped around the corridor in a sort of country waltz. Others formed a square, spreading out into the hall. She inched over to see more out the doorway. Two lines of dancers had formed in the corridor in some kind of reel. Freya laughed. "We've created our own ball."

Gertie smiled. "Excellent." She kept playing, her own body swaying to the music, and Freya winked at Frank.

They kept going until past the quiet hour, but no one complained. Finally, Freya shook her head, and Gertie moved to sit. Everyone cheered. Frank stood and bowed.

With a laugh, Gertie and Freya joined him. Then Frau Uberdiche stepped in their doorway. "That was lovely, but it's far past curfew. Off to bed with you."

Everyone hurried out of their room and cleared the hall until only Frank stood in the doorway. "That was excellent." He nodded to Freya. "I'm interested in our first talk of orchestra and sharing compositions. Perhaps in London when we all return?"

"Perhaps. Or even here in Salzburg or Paris?" Freya was loathe to return to London. The only thing London held for her was a domineering father and a life devoid of music.

He grinned. "That was the most fun I've had playing in ages." He looked to Gertie. Her returning smile seemed full and without a care. *At last.* Perhaps their jovial friend had once again found her humor.

"Would both of you enjoy a tour of Salzburg tomorrow? We have most of the morning and early afternoon free."

Freya looked at Gertie, who smiled. "Oh yes. And Freya hasn't seen it yet."

"Excellent. We'll be ready. The group is leaving right after breakfast."

With that happy news, Frank bid them good night and then bid the same to the uncharacteristically patient Frau Uberdiche, who was undoubtedly waiting to shoo him back to the men's side of the boarding house. They could mingle at will until curfew, and as she had reminded them, curfew had come and gone.

This night's rest would be much better than the last. Even though Freya would be missing Erich this weekend, she was looking forward to seeing Salzburg, a place she'd always dreamed of calling home.

CHAPTER TWELVE

They were able to find a larger motorized vehicle made by Benz to take them for a drive around Salzburg. Freya wasn't certain how they'd managed such a thing, but she wasn't going to complain one bit. The vehicle stopped and dropped them off right in front of the Salzburg Cathedral.

Henry, Tobias, Frank, Gertie, Freya, and Daphne all stepped out together. The original group she'd met when first joining the program were still some of her most preferred friends.

Henry nodded at the large white cathedral. "We're playing here tonight."

"Let's step inside anyway, shall we?" Gertie's eyes shone. "The sun won't hit the stained glass at night."

They creaked open a large wooden door, and Freya's breath came out in a soft woosh. The room was stunningly white, the sanctuary brilliantly lit with stained glass windows filling two balconies on either side and a dome up at the ceiling that seemed miles away. She craned her neck.

In hushed voices, they walked along the perimeter, taking in everything around them. By the time they'd spent just the short amount of their morning walking through the hushed and peaceful environment, Freya's smile was larger, and she felt ready to face her situation with more courage.

As soon as they exited into the sunlight, they had joined another group of students, and the whole mass of them walked down the path to the river.

Quaint buildings lined the sides of the water. The river stretched out in a moving calm. She wondered how fast the current flowed. A breeze picked up, and she wrinkled her nose. She had no desire to experience the rush of the river.

"I'd like to take the Festungsbahn." Daphne pointed up toward the trolley that transported people up the mountain. "People say that Hohensalzburg Fortress boasts a view of Salzburg that is unmatched."

Freya squinted up into the sun. White walls and white turrets at the top of a hill reflected a brilliant light. The hill itself was covered with trees that would one day boast a blanket of green. The mountains towered above them all. "I am of the same mind as Daphne. Imagine what we could see from the top of one of those turrets." They walked away from the river. The cobblestone was uneven beneath her feet, but the smooth rocks made her smile. How many boots, horses' hooves, wagon wheels, carts, and cars had travelled those very stones to wear them to such a smooth texture? They arrived just as a funicular was about to leave. Hurrying to buy tickets and crowd aboard the train car, they made it just in time.

The cart started to move uphill, pulled by cables. Freya craned her neck to watch Salzburg fall away behind her, growing smaller as they made their way up the hill. When they arrived, they toured the grounds. The fortress was interesting, but what she enjoyed most was, as expected, the view. Gertie moved to stand beside her, wind whipping around them, shaking their hats. Laughing, they each placed a hand on the tops of their heads. Gertie swept her other arm out to their front. "This gives me a whole new perspective."

"I agree. It's beautiful. And so far away. Look at the rooftops. They look like toys. Have you ever seen such tiny cars?"

"And just think, there's the school, over by the boarding house." She pointed.

"Oh yes, I see it."

"It, too, is very small. Imagine how small that moment when I played for the Maestro was. That tiny moment in time, in a small room, in a small building far away." She spun in a circle. "And yet, it mattered so much."

"Perhaps it is not the size of the moment that makes it matter." Freya considered her own words as a batch of clouds blew by above her head. "But no matter how big or small, this glorious view helps me remember there's a whole world of people out there doing many small but important things all at the same time. And succeed or fail, the world keeps moving. They continue to go about their lives."

Gertie stood closer. "But are you ready to possibly fail?"

"No, I'm not." Freya's determination grew. "And I don't think you are either." She spun in a circle herself. "And when I'm up here, I feel like anything is possible. Just look. The very world is at our feet." She laughed and ran to the edge of the stone wall. "Salzburg Maestro!" she shouted out to the wind. "You seem very small down there. We are going to play so big and so bold that even you will be blown away by us, just like this wind!" Her words flew away, gone as she shouted them. But she felt a rising strength inside.

Gertie shouted. "Yes!"

They stood together until the rest of their group was preparing to take the funicular back down the mountain.

They had by now toured many of the sights of Salzburg but not the birthplace of Mozart. The group had seen it earlier, and even though Freya wanted to pass by it, no one else, not even Gertie, wished to push off lunch any further that day. She stood with Gertie, surrounded by many of the other students, everyone chattering. Freya smiled. The sun shone warm on their chilled skin from the early April air. The mountains soared above them. And suddenly her eyes were drawn to the top peak, white tipped, and she remembered Erich. Her smile grew, and her heart ached a little for him. How odd to crave the company of someone who only a month past had no part in her life at all.

She felt eyes on her. Almost without realizing, she turned her head but saw only the back of a tall man in a hat like Erich had been wearing the first day she met him. He moved away in a hurry, and soon he was lost to view. Erich did travel to Salzburg. Perhaps that was him? She took two steps in that direction, thinking she might follow him, but then someone called out, "The Maestro! I saw him in the café."

She whipped her head in the opposite direction. "Where?"

A woman, one of the flutists, pointed. "Just a moment ago."

The mass of students moved in that direction, and Freya had no hope of getting any closer than the person in front of her. But she did so long for a look at him.

She studied Gertie's face, hoping this sighting would not bring on another bout of melancholy, but she only smiled. Then she turned to Freya. "He was right, you know."

"The Maestro?"

She nodded. "Yes, about the things he suggested. I worked on my trills. I'm actually improving."

"Already?"

"Yes. I can see if I keep at it, I'll be even better than I thought." She shrugged. "I think I just needed to look at things differently."

"I'm happy to hear it." Freya stood as tall as she could. "Do you think I'll ever get to see him?"

"He's supposed to pull everyone out. I'm sure you'll get your turn." Gertie threw up her hands and stopped trying to push through the crowds. "But I don't know what he could find wrong with your playing."

Freya thought of Erich. "I don't know. I wonder if the professional standard is much higher than we ever experience. I'm interested to hear what I can learn from him."

By the time the crowd had dispersed and Freya could see into the shop, she doubted very much the few remaining people were the Maestro, else he be swarmed with students.

She sighed. "I hope I get my turn soon, in enough time to actually improve before my Salzburg Orchestra audition."

They finished out their afternoon, and Freya was even more in love with the city than she had been in her dreams.

Gertie walked at her side. "Are you ready to be first-chair violinist tonight?"

Freya smiled. "I am." She paused. "As long as Eliza doesn't frown at me the whole of the night, I might have a lovely time of it."

"If she keeps her lips pinched like that, my grandmother says one day they might stay. She points out all the women of a certain age, telling me it's much better to have smile lines."

Freya laughed. "In that case, you will have no trouble." They linked arms and climbed aboard their car.

When they re-boarded the same cars that evening, their instruments either safely in hand or loaded separately in their larger cases, they were dressed in full formal concert attire. Freya had taken extra care with her appearance. Her hair was pulled away from her face, a clip with just a few sparkles held her hair up, and her black dress allowed arm movement but hugged her waist. She sat tall, grateful for the countless hours her instructor had spent enforcing posture and correct positioning of the violin.

They pulled up in front of the gorgeous cathedral again. This time the stained glass shone brilliantly to them outside on the street as the lights on the inside tried to penetrate the dark world around her. She paused, appreciating the sight, but then the jostling of orchestra members around her brought her back to the urgency of the moment, and she followed them into the cathedral. In the doorway, she turned, feeling eyes on her again. But she saw no one. For a moment, a hint of sadness tugged at her heart. No one she cared about would be present to see her performance. Her mother would not feel well enough to come, and her father would never think of coming. Her grandmother might, at the very end, but in spite of helping convince Freya's father to let her participate in the orchestra this summer, she was still clearly hoping for a marriage for Freya rather than a musical career. Still, the woman loved her. Freya wished she was there to see her orchestra perform. And she wished her parents appreciated music like she did. She wished they could see what an honor it was for her to be there, for her to be the first-chair violinist, for her to have this opportunity. She looked around, the cathedral starting to fill up. These people appreciated music. But she didn't know a single one.

She lifted her chin and forced her shoulders not to drop, but she had to blink four times to clear the moisture. The loneliness was a sharp pang that crept in at times she was least expecting it.

A growing audience already filled the front three rows. One young girl drew Freya's attention; her gaze followed the entering musicians almost hungrily. Her hands rested in her lap, and her posture was perfectly upright. Freya wondered if she herself was a musician. Freya paused at their row, smiled, and waved at her. The response was immediate—her returning smile large and engaging. Freya almost laughed along with her exuberance, but instead, she nodded and winked before following her fellow orchestra members up to the front. Chairs were in place in the area directly in front of the sanctuary. A brilliant gold altar with stained glass windows behind rose to the top of the ceiling. The raised stand for their conductor was draped with a black cloth. The vaulted ceilings rose high to the stars. Rows of chairs and pews filled the space in front of where she would play.

Freya made her way to her chair. She sat facing the center, her side not five feet from the nearest pews. The young girl who'd smiled so intently sat a few rows back. Freya double-checked the tune of her violin.

The sounds of the other instruments doing the same made her smile. As time drew near for the concert to begin, she stood. All orchestra members quieted, eyes on her. Then she played her A string. The other instruments tuned theirs to her, and then everyone played their A together. She nodded and then sat.

Exhilaration filled her. Clapping filled the cathedral. Her gaze travelled out. The room had filled quickly, and Freya found a new happiness that she could share this music with these people, even if she knew none of them personally. Her eyes travelled to the young girl, who seemed at the moment to be the only friend listening. Then another set of eyes caught hers. Erich. She gasped.

His grin grew, then he nodded.

Freya's heart pounded in her chest. She closed her eyes, trying to keep her smile small and demure, but the thrill of Erich watching her performance filled her with joy. The conductor paused in front of her. She stood and shook his hand, a gesture symbolic of him greeting the whole orchestra, then he made his way to the platform. Freya couldn't spare another glance at Erich, but her whole body tingled with awareness. The happy flush to her skin gave her a rush of energy and a surge of confidence. She had one solo in this piece, and Erich would hear it. She smiled.

The conductor raised his hands. She lifted her instrument. With the first drop of his baton, they began to play.

The power of their notes flowed through her. The acoustics in the cathedral were incredible from where she sat; the sound echoed all around her as if resonating off the very walls themselves. Soon she forgot the audience and became one with her fellow musicians, the rhythm of their piece flowing through her, the beauty of the music the only priority. Only Erich remained on the edge of her consciousness. His quiet presence in the building made everything even more beautiful.

When their concert was over, she stood and bowed when directed. She searched the crowds, but Erich was nowhere to be seen. Surely he would wait for her. But the longer she looked the greater her disappointment that he could not be found.

The young girl and what looked like her parents approached. Her cheeks colored prettily, and she curtsied. "*Vielen Dank.*"

"*Bitte.* Thank you for coming. It meant a lot to me to see someone appreciate the music like you do."

Her eyes lowered. "Thank you. I loved to hear you play."

The man at her side held out his hand. "I'm her father, Herr Bach, no relation to Johann, unfortunately." He chuckled and then straightened. "Our daughter would like to train one day in the same program."

"Pleased to meet you. I'm Freya Winter." She met the young girl's mother and found that the budding musician lived in London for part of the year. Her name was Emilia, and Freya agreed to see her when she was next in town, though secretly Freya hoped to never live there again. She hoped to continue in Salzburg playing with the orchestra.

All the while she talked to the Bachs, she sought some view of Erich. But she never saw him.

The others met her outside the cathedral, their chatter filling the street with sound. Gertie gushed. "I've never heard such a beautiful sound. Have you?"

"No. It was quite overpowering when it filled the cathedral." Freya couldn't help but join in their excitement. And she had seen Erich. Even if he hadn't waited or stayed to talk, at least she'd seen him.

"And your solo." Gertie's grin was contagious. "It was sublime. I saw even the Maestro close his eyes in enjoyment."

"The Maestro? He was there?" The pang of missed opportunity stung, but to hear that he may have enjoyed her playing took away some of the disappointment that she'd once again missed meeting the man.

"Yes! I forget you haven't met him yet. He stood and clapped with great enthusiasm when we took our bows."

"And you say he liked my solo?" Freya was hungry for any reaction from her hero.

"Yes. He smiled, which I've never seen, and closed his eyes like he was eating a delicious ice." Gertie laughed. "Or at least that's what it looked like to me."

Energy coursed through Freya. Well, that was something. He seemed to like her playing. It was he who had requested her first solo. She had hoped that she was not forgotten. "Tonight was an excellent night, was it not?" Her smile stretched so long and so far, her cheeks began to ache. "And now, on to the Salzburg Orchestra!" Freya knew playing with professional musicians could only be that much more sublime.

The faces around hers dimmed their happiness.

"What? Are you not excited?"

"We're excited," Frank muttered. "About as excited as you can be when someone else wins a medal."

She laughed, but no one else smiled. "Do you not think we all have a chance at making a place in that orchestra?"

Frank shrugged. "Some of us might. But it's competitive, isn't it? And we'd be unseating a current member. I don't know how many plan to leave their spot willingly each year."

"Oh, you're right." Somehow in Freya's mind, she knew she'd be competing against professionals for their spots. But the way Frank said it made her realize just how much of a challenge that would be. "Well, we can try, can't we?"

"Of course. We are all required to audition at any rate. It's part of our experience." He shrugged. "I'll give it my best go."

Gertie scooted closer to her in the car. "And you just might make it," she whispered.

"And you." Freya nudged her.

"I don't know, not from my fifth-chair spot."

"You'll do better this go-round. I am certain of it."

Gertie lifted her chin. "I think you're right. Chair tests are tomorrow again, aren't they?"

Freya groaned. "Every week we have to compete for our spot."

"And everyone trying to steal the one we already have." Frank raised one corner of his mouth.

"At least I'm not travelling this weekend. We have a concert every night as well."

"I like it better when you're here." Gertie's grateful expression reminded Freya again how nice it was to have a friend.

"I do too." But of course, a part of her disagreed. A part of her would always prefer any chance to get to see Erich, and this week particularly, since more than anything she wanted to know what he thought of their performance. Had he smiled like the Maestro?

CHAPTER THIRTEEN

THE WEEK PASSED QUICKLY. SHE had auditioned for her chair spot again, and on Monday, the posted paper told her she still had first chair. Eliza was still second chair. She wasn't any more friendly than she had been the week before, but Freya had just taken to ignoring her. Gertie now sat in the third chair, and that made Eliza's frowns more endurable.

In addition to their orchestral work, they were now working more intensely on individual pieces for their Salzburg Orchestra auditions, but still the Maestro hadn't called her back. Freya was beginning to think it wouldn't happen. She approached Frau Uberdiche after rehearsal just hours before she would be taking the train again to see her grandmother. "Why hasn't the Maestro called me back yet?"

She frowned in response. "He will get to you. Don't be pestering him."

As if Freya *could* pester him. She had no way of reaching him. Perhaps next time someone left rehearsal to go see him, she would follow. No matter what the orchestra was working on, she could excuse herself and run after. A week ago, she might have been horrified at her thoughts. Now she was beginning to think it sounded like a great idea. At least then she'd see the man and perhaps talk to him, if not play for him.

As she packed her small bag and hugged Gertie farewell for another weekend in Paris, Freya admitted she was looking forward to the time away. Her grandmother and, of course, the Paris Exposition sounded exciting, but most of all, she hoped that Erich would be on the train. She hadn't seen him at any more of their performances. Had her music reached him? Did he enjoy it?

She'd practiced her Salzburg Orchestra audition pieces every night until late in the evenings in the practice rooms, working with precision, drilling, running her scales, playing measure after measure over and over again. The calluses on her fingers must have grown calluses. If she needed help from the Maestro, it was now. But still she hadn't been summoned. And part of her need for a break was to end the anxious unmet anticipation.

As soon as she boarded the train, she found the dining car conductor, and his smile was overly exuberant as he bowed. "We will expect you at the dinner hour."

"Thank you. Is there a place I might practice?"

He thought for a moment. "We have a storage room off the galley; perhaps you might entertain the staff in there?" He pointed at the other end, and Freya remembered walking past the galley.

"Thank you."

She stopped by her berth and dropped off her bag and her violin case and then carried her instrument toward the galley. So far, Erich was nowhere to be seen. She couldn't feel at ease until she'd worked through the audition piece a few more times.

The storage room was tight and smelled musty, but she had just enough room to hold out her violin and move her arm at the elbow to wield her bow, plus some space above the sacks of flour.

Freya started on the measures that troubled her, but each time, she tripped over the same note. She didn't miss it; she just didn't catch it in precisely the rhythm required. And no matter what she did, her fingers couldn't manage.

At a moment when she thought she might throw her violin from the moving car, the door opened. Erich stood with light behind him, his expression hidden.

Her heart felt lighter. "Erich!"

He stepped inside and closed the door. "Hello, Freya." His face was serious, but his eyes held their same sparkle of energy. She stopped herself from a full embrace, but she was happier to see him than she even expected to be.

They stood close, the small quarters not giving much space. Her violin and bow were between them. The train jostled and sent him forward against her, but he reached for the low ceiling to stop himself from running into her violin and pressing it between them.

"Erich, I'm so happy to see you." She smiled. She stumbled against him, turning slightly to shield her instrument. "I was hoping you would be here." The awkward jostling made her laugh.

"And I you." He placed a hand on the wall behind her, holding himself steady. Then he cleared his throat. "I couldn't help but overhear your practicing."

"You heard it?"

"Yes. I was walking past the galley, so I paused."

"You did?" She was pleased her playing had attracted his attention. "I'm working on a particular piece for an audition." She puffed out her breath. "I'm actually quite worried about it. The others are equally talented, and I assume there are few spots available—if any—in the Salzburg Orchestra."

He nodded. "Might I offer a perspective?" The dim light didn't give her much insight into his thoughts or his expression, but he seemed sincere.

"I would welcome *any* thoughts. I'm obviously making little headway on my own." Saying it out loud only increased her worry about the audition. "I won't have time to practice at my grandmother's . . ."

"If you could, play that last measure you keep repeating."

She lifted her instrument, but he was very clearly in her way, so she shifted her body. "This isn't going to work." Though every inch of her was aware of the slightest brush of his fingers on her skin, the need for some helpful input dominated her sudden irrational desire to stand as close to him as possible.

He moved past her. For a moment, his strong arms circled her to steady her balance, and she tingled with energy at his closeness. Then, to her great amusement, he sat down on the bags of flour.

She smiled and nodded. "Very good." Then she lifted her bow, put her violin under her chin, and began to play. This time, the notes came easier, the flow was smoother, and for the first time ever, her fingers caught all the quick changes and trills for the piece.

He nodded. "Better. What was the difference?"

Her face flushed. "I don't know . . ." Dare she tell him that his very presence sent a confidence through her that helped her play? That she felt stronger when he was near? She didn't dare.

He sat forward. "I do have a few suggestions."

As he explained his perception of her playing, some of her happy confidence fizzled away. Everything he pointed out she then recognized as a fault she had nurtured for years. A part of her knew his comments were meant to help and were in fact very helpful. But staring at faults in her talents, something she worked so hard at every day, was not easy, and she suddenly wished to escape before her lips turned down or wavered or a single tear escaped.

"Try again."

She swallowed. When she lifted the bow, her hands shook. Then she stopped. "I need a minute."

"Granted."

When she turned to him in surprise, he cleared his throat. "I apologize. I help instruct musicians sometimes, and I forgot for a moment that we are on a train and that you are not here to be my student. Let me try again. I should have said, 'If you'd like, we can work through the passages together. But if you need a minute, feel free to take one. I am at my leisure.'"

He hadn't seemed at his leisure. He had seemed quite intent. But then he kept talking. "I see so much potential in you, so much ability. You certainly could earn a place in the professional Salzburg Orchestra. I believe you could play anywhere you want. For that reason, I am trying to help."

"Thank you." His words of encouragement were comforting, and that perspective helped her regain the courage to push through her new doubts and try the things he had suggested.

"Better. That was excellent. You see, you are so quick to learn, to adapt. You have so few habits holding you back . . ." He cleared his throat. "I have rarely heard a musician as powerfully gifted as you."

His words flowed through her. He, of course, was talking of her music, but to her, they sounded intimate, as if he'd come to court her. Her reaction to him tingled through her. Every shift of his body in their enclosed space echoed in her mind.

Desperately clinging to some semblance of rational thought, she cleared her throat. "Thank you." She lifted her bow. "Might I try again?"

"Yes, please do, but first . . ." He rose to stand beside her, his nearness almost overwhelming. She lifted her chin to see into his face. His eyes were unreadable but seemed to see inside her.

"If I may?" He turned her gently so that her back was against his chest. He lifted his arms to adjust the hold of her violin. "I know the instructors teach us to hold the violin thus, but I find more freedom with this tiny adaptation."

Freya concentrated on her breathing. She hardly knew how to think with him standing so close. So rarely was she in anyone's embrace, and certainly no one had enlivened such a response in her, not ever.

Then he rested his hand over her bow. "Allow some movement in the shoulder. The elbow is, of course, important, but here, the shoulder gives a greater diversity of tone . . ." He continued saying something, but it became lost to her ears as his hands and fingers held her close, as he adjusted her stance. When she finally ran the bow over her strings, he stayed next to her, just far enough to give her freedom of movement. She swayed to her piece out of habit, feeling the melody. His body swayed with hers, and it felt almost as if he were playing along with her. Their unity of motion, their appreciation of the music, made her forget all about the precision of her fingers, the mechanics of what she was trying to do. Instead, the feelings washed over her in a wave of pleasure, of delicious anticipation, and the notes flowed. So lost in their unity, she scarcely heard the music that hummed between them until she had played the last note.

He paused, close enough that it almost felt like an embrace. A soft puff of air at her neck sent a lovely thrill across her skin. She swallowed and closed her eyes. And then he stepped away. "Excellent." The emotion in his voice tugged more from her.

"Thank you." The pause in the air felt thick. She turned to face him. His eyes shone with appreciation. She was lost in their closeness. She lifted her chin, their faces so near, the very air drawing them together. For a moment, his gaze flickered to her lips, and she sucked in a breath. She rose up on her toes. His mouth hovered near her own. She closed her eyes.

But then he stepped back, his face unreadable. "And now I think I shall be about my business. Will I see you in the dining car?"

"Oh . . . yes." She stammered through her words, her mind struggling to think clearly. The air between them cooled. "I will play the entire dinner hour again." She looked away.

He moved past her, seeming to make a great effort to touch her as little as possible, opened the door, and closed it after he left.

The bags of flour caught her sinking form as she sat back and closed her eyes. The tingling awareness from his closeness still lingered about her. Memory of the feel of his face so near her own felt so real, even now that he'd left. She almost believed she could look up from her hands and see him still. But he'd run from her. At least, that's what it seemed.

She knew she'd never played better. The magic of his closeness, of his touch, the idea of two playing as one. Everything had been . . . moving. Could she ever recreate such a feeling again? She didn't know. She held her head up with one hand, closed her eyes, and tried to make sense of it all.

He'd almost kissed her. He'd wanted to. But he'd stopped. Why? Was he merely being a gentleman, or was there a reason he couldn't make an attachment at this time? Too many thoughts swirled around in her mind in dizzying circles until she forced them to calm. But nothing can be forced to calm. And she needed to get ready for the dinner hour. She started humming.

She went through every note of her audition piece in her head. At first, her music competed with the intense confusion. But soon the notes drowned out even the most demanding emotion. By the time she was finished humming the piece for the third time, the world was still, and she felt more ready to be a part of it.

She stood and crept to the door, opening it. No one was in the passageway outside her closet, so she crept out and hurried toward the dining car. She didn't know what time it was, but she suspected dinner was already being served.

When she entered the car, the conductor's face lit up with a grin. "And here she is, ladies and gentlemen. Our very own Orient Express Maestro!"

She gasped at the new title, then smiled.

He clapped his hands, and the other members of the car joined in. Every eye turned to look at her.

Freya stood taller and held her breath a moment before she made her way to her usual spot. Erich was not sitting at the next table as he had before. Perhaps he had gone? Where would he go? She lifted her violin to her chin. She knew her instrument was in tune, and she began to play.

She chose easy songs, pleasant background music tunes, and relaxed into her performance. The feeling of playing by muscle memory and enjoying her own music was such a delight she let her thoughts drift.

Dinner came and went, another success with more money to her name, leaving the conductor as pleased as ever. She packed up her violin again in its case and returned her instrument to her berth, all the while trying to pretend she wasn't disappointed that Erich had not joined her in the dining car.

She spent the rest of her journey in public cars, wondering if she would run into Erich. After the remainder of her time passed without seeing him, she exited their stop in Paris with slow, heavy steps. He'd left without another word. Had he felt their interactions to be too much? Was he hiding from her?

She made her way across the platform and out on the street, unsure who was coming for her. For a moment, she saw no one familiar. Then she laughed at a cheery group sitting in a car with their hands in the air.

"Hello, Miss Winter!" Lord Bouchet waved, half standing in his seat. Her grandmother's pleased expression and Lord Bouchet's jovial welcome lightened some of her confusion caused by Erich's disappearance.

Lord Bouchet hopped out of the car. "Your grandmother and I are happy to see you." He reached for her bag but not her violin case. "How was your train ride?"

Her grandmother's face lit with happiness and a smile that was far too pleased with herself. She looked from Lord Bouchet to Freya and back with such a calculating expression that Freya felt almost guilty for allowing her false hope to continue.

Freya grinned, some of her angst slipping away, then leaned closer to Lord Bouchet. "It was . . . eventful."

His eyebrows rose. "Indeed?"

"Yes." She'd found such a unique friendship with Lord Bouchet that now she wished to tell him everything. Would they have a moment to converse alone?

He winked. "Tomorrow I would love to accompany you, your grandmother, and my mother to the exposition. Perhaps you could share the news then?"

"Of course. I will look forward to it."

They climbed into Grandmother's car, and her driver pulled out of the train station area and through the crowds.

Lord Bouchet, Freya, and her grandmother sat very close together. With her legs pressed against her grandmother's, she said, "How was this past weekend?"

"I enjoyed it very much. Although, we would have enjoyed it far more if you had been here." Grandmother nudged Lord Bouchet. "We missed her, didn't we, my lord?"

"Yes, very much. All of Paris has been as dull as the moors."

Freya covered her mouth with one hand, trying not to laugh. "And the Paris Exposition?"

"Boring." He snorted.

"The dinner parties? Soirees? Balls?"

"Dreadfully slow."

She laughed.

"There is but one solution."

"Oh? And what is that?" Freya said.

"We must attend the exposition again, now that it is open."

"I would be delighted."

"Excellent. I shall return on the morrow with my car."

They pulled in front of her grandmother's house.

"And I will hear all about your adventurous and *eventful* travels."

"Oh yes." Freya smiled. He kissed her hand, and she bid him farewell.

On her way to bed, her grandmother chuckled to herself. "You and Lord Bouchet have quite a rapport." Her pleased smile almost made Freya laugh again. Should she tell her theirs was only a joke, that they had no more interest in each other than anyone else?

Not yet.

"Good night, Grandmother."

CHAPTER FOURTEEN

THE NEXT DAY, FREYA WAS happy to forget about her violin audition. She never predicted she'd ever think such a thing, but she was in great need of diversion and amusement, and the Paris Exposition was just the thing.

Lord Bouchet arrived full of smiles, which she readily returned. His mother sat in the front seat near him and Freya and her grandmother in the back.

"I feel thrice blessed today." Lord Bouchet grinned. "For I am going to the exposition with three of the loveliest ladies in all of Paris."

Her grandmother giggled, and Freya shook her head.

He adjusted his hat. "Where shall we go first? The Camp de Mars, the Trocadero, the Esplanade des Invalides, or along the banks of the Seine?"

"Could we see the Palace of Electricity?" Freya would be pleased to see any of the exhibition, all of it, really.

Lord Bouchet raised a finger into the air. "Yes! She's done it. She's picked the best first spot. And then how about we see as many of the different countries' pavilions as we can."

Freya couldn't agree more. "I should very much like to see the Rue des Nations. Perhaps China, Sweden, Hungary."

"And England, naturally."

"Certainly."

As soon as they were out on the street, walking in the crowds, Freya felt even more free from her cares. Young families, people in love, the elderly all walked past them. The exposition was for *all* people. Everything around them had been built up, created—even full structures—to celebrate the exposition. The Eiffel Tower rose above them, still as yellow as she'd ever seen a monument but impressive all the same.

"And now I've found a spectacle we shall all enjoy." Lord Bouchet led them across the square to something Freya had never seen before.

"Is that . . . ?" She furrowed her brow, trying to make sense of what she was seeing.

"A moving walkway." He rubbed his hands together. "Come. Let us try it out."

His mother reached for Grandmother's hand. "Certainly not. I don't want anything to do with that nonsense."

Grandmother shook her head. "That won't sit well with me, not at all. You two go on."

"Yes, you two go on, certainly." His mother waved them on after they made plans to meet again in two hours.

As soon as Freya and Lord Bouchet were out of earshot, he breathed out. "And now we can really get somewhere with our conversation. Come. Let's try this ridiculous moving walkway."

"It does look rather interesting, don't you think?"

"I've never seen one before at any rate." They stepped onto a platform and then onto the moving path.

After a moment, Freya began to think she could walk faster than their current pace. "It moves rather slowly, doesn't it?"

"I suppose." The path moved forward, taking them across the plaza. Freya found she could not look at the sights around her long enough. Everything held such beautiful details that she would need a week to capture it all.

Lord Bouchet pointed up ahead. "Oh, here we go. Now it gets faster." He led her to the next level. They stepped up and grabbed hold of tall posts that clipped along with them. Freya squealed in happy surprise as she moved even faster along the edge of the exposition.

Once they'd been moving for a moment, she turned to Lord Bouchet. "Tell me how you met the woman you love."

"Now? I was hoping first we might discuss your travels. I assume that your mystery man made an appearance."

"Yes, he did." She smiled. "And we had a rather close encounter in a closet." She grinned.

His eyes widened. "Well that *is* something."

Freya shook her head. "It was nothing improper, just an unusual circumstance. But he's behaving oddly now. In fact, he left without saying goodbye."

Lord Bouchet nodded. "Hmm. That doesn't bode well, does it?" His tone sounded forlorn, but his eyes sparkled with humor.

"I don't know. Stop toying with me. This is hard enough as it is."

"Yes, I too know what it feels like to pine for something that can never be." All teasing had gone from his expression.

"Tell me. Tell me about her." A suspicion had begun to build, one she didn't dare express until she learned more.

"She has delightful red hair with a smattering of freckles."

Freya's heart sped up.

"She has the best sense of adventure, fun, humor."

"Yes, and?"

He searched her face. "What is going on?"

"Just tell me."

"We fell in love. She with me as much as I with her. How often does such a thing happen?"

"I . . . I don't know. Where were you? Was it at a house party?"

His mouth dropped open. "How could you know that?"

"What is her name?"

He studied her for many moments, looked away, and then turned to her again. "I am not certain why you ask these questions. Can I dare to hope that you know something, that you have some glimmer of something?"

"Tell me her name." She pressed her fingers into his arm.

"I'm afraid to say it."

"Come now."

"Oh, all right. What can it matter? Gertie. Her name is Gertie Thomas."

She gasped. "I knew it. Gertie Thomas. You fell in love with each other at the house party, but your mother forbade it, saying she had someone else in mind, someone whose grandmother was her dearest friend." She clutched his arm tighter. "Me?" She shook her head. "This is all so . . . How can this be?"

"I don't know." He stood very still, his expression hesitant, almost fearful.

"I know her. She is a student with me. We share a room." She reached for the lapel of his jacket. "How can this be?" she repeated and shook her head. "But . . . but I know what we can do."

"You do?"

"You must come to our final performance, a ball. Come as my guest. And we shall see what we can make of this."

His mouth opened and closed, and he swallowed multiple times before he seemed to find words to speak. "What do you intend?"

"I believe we can straighten this out. Come. We will tell everyone you are coming at my personal invitation. They will jump over each other to make it happen. I can't wait to see Gertie's face when she sees you. She's my best friend, you know."

He eyed her appraisingly. "Yes, I can see that. She would be, wouldn't she?"

"She's lovely. I can see why you love her and she you."

"Does she? Does she still?" The hope in his face, his eyes, so dear. She wanted to rest her hand on his cheek, to smile and tell him they would make it work for him. He asked again, "Can it be true?"

"Oh yes. That's how I knew your story. She loves you still. She can't love another." She shook her head. "In fact, there was a time I heard only of you from her mouth for days on end. Can you believe that I know how you prefer to take your tea?"

He looked away and put a fist to his mouth.

"Are you all right?"

When he turned back, she was stunned to see his eyes welling with tears. "Yes, I'm fantastic. For the first time, I have real hope again." To her great surprise, he pulled her into a hug, right there in front of everyone.

She choked. "You're welcome."

He nodded. They laughed together for a moment, and then his attention was diverted. He studied something behind her, over her head. When he looked down into her face again, his expression was earnest, serious. "Turn around."

"What?" She turned. "What am I looking— *Erich*. His tall frame, broad shoulders, curly hair at his temples etched in her mind. She turned back to Lord Bouchet. "Oh." She clutched the lace at her heart.

"Is it him?"

Erich stood across the way from them in the middle of the street. "Yes." Her voice came out as a whisper. "How did you know?"

"He was staring daggers at me." He shook his head and waved.

Erich picked up his pace, attempting to walk at the speed of their moving walkway.

"So, him?" Lord Bouchet pretended to size him up. "Really?"

"Yes, really." She put her hands on her hips. "Why is that so difficult to believe?"

"It's not, but I don't know. Well, take his breeches."

"His . . . breeches?"

"Certainly. You can tell everything about a man by the fit of his breeches."

She turned to look and then felt her face flush. "I'm not interested in the fit of his breeches."

Lord Bouchet tipped his head back and laughed. "But I made you look, now didn't I?" His grin was too much and she wanted to swat him. He diverted his gaze back to her. "But really. He's the one, is he?"

She stood at his side as they both watched Erich attempt to keep pace with their moving walkway. He was falling behind.

They approached one of the stops for the walkway.

Lord Bouchet turned to her. "This is what we're going to do. We get off here. You go spend time with your man. I'll get myself a beer at the German pavilion, and I'll meet you in front of the Palace of Electricity."

Her heart skipped in happy swirls. "Are you certain?"

"Yes, I'm certain. Now hurry. You only have two hours before our venerable chaperones become suspicious."

"Right. Thank you." She linked her arms with Lord Bouchet's. Then they both stepped off the moving walkway and onto a platform.

Lord Bouchet lifted his hat and bowed in Erich's direction, then nodded to her and hurried off toward the German pavilion.

CHAPTER FIFTEEN

ERICH. AT THE PARIS EXPOSITION. Freya picked up her pace, feet hurrying to him. It was all she could do to keep from breaking into a run.

His steps were slow, but he approached with a growing smile. She was pleased Grandmother had made her wear such a lovely dress. The hat she had picked out was exquisite, a bit larger and more elaborate than Freya would have purchased, but the peach color brought a rosiness to her cheeks. Never had she considered her clothing when meeting with Erich on the train. But here, worlds collided. Here, where clothes and presentation had always mattered, she suddenly cared very much that she appeared lovely for him.

Here with Erich. Lord Bouchet. Her grandmother. Did they belong on the same page of her life together? Her breath came in shorter, shallow gasps the closer she moved to Erich. For years, she'd wondered what else mattered other than her music. And now that something might, Erich might, she could only wish to celebrate just a bit. Her feet skipped a moment, which tickled a smile out of Erich.

Her heart called to him in great thunderous poundings that rushed behind her ears. She wanted to run to him and hide all at the same time. But her feet kept moving, one at a time, in his direction.

Until at last he stood at her front and held out his hand. She placed her fingers in his palm, and he tucked her hand in the crook of his arm. "Freya."

"Erich." The last time she saw him, he'd left without a backward glance.

His other hand covered hers on his arm, and he led her toward the river. "Shall we walk?"

"Yes, but Erich, how are you here?"

"In Paris?" One eyebrow rose in a mocking fun that made her laugh. "I came by train."

She shook her head. "I know, but how are you here at the exposition right when I am?"

"I came to find you. Since it is your only day in Paris, I assumed you would come. I came early to the front gate and waited."

Her mouth tugged at the corners in a smile. "You did? But you left the train before I could talk to you. I thought . . . I worried something was wrong between us."

He nodded. "When you were practicing . . ." He paused in their walk. "I'm sorry I did not stay in the dining car. It was rude of me to rush off without explanation, but I admit I've never felt that way. I needed time to think."

So he had run. She had never felt that way either. She'd never felt any of the things she felt for Erich before. "Is that . . . a good thing?"

He lifted her fingers to his lips and then smiled. "I think so now."

A trickle of relief healed her previous concern. "I don't think I'll ever play that well again."

"You will. Didn't I hear the conductor call you the Orient Express Maestro?"

She laughed. "Oh stop." Then she frowned. "You heard that? Where were you?"

"I was outside the car."

"Why didn't you come in? Was I . . . ?" She wanted to say, "too forward," but she couldn't dare admit she had thought he might kiss her. She frowned deeper.

"What is this frown?"

"You were there, but you didn't come in to hear me, and then I didn't see you after that at all." She studied him.

He looked apologetic, but suddenly, *thinking* wasn't a sufficient answer. She wanted an explanation.

"What did you need time to think about?"

"How a man can only handle so much from a beautiful woman."

She must have looked as confused as she felt because he grinned and said simply, "I will tell you all. I will. For now, I don't feel free to say everything that my heart feels, just this one part." He tapped the end of her nose.

"And what is that? What one part?" She held her breath.

"I cannot go a single day without thinking about you. I might not be ready to say everything that is in my heart, but I'm here. I waited for you today. I look for every chance I can to be on your train again." He paused and then laughed to himself. "I've said too much already. But there, you see. You, my dear, have captured me in ways I never expected."

She caught a laugh before it bubbled up, then tamped it down in a respectable place. Then she blinked back the mist that started to blur her eyes and grinned. "That's—" She leaned so that her shoulder pressed into his. "That makes me very happy."

"I hope so because I haven't been this happy ever in my life. I have even found myself sitting in a room by myself smiling for no reason." He placed his hand over hers on his arm again. "I have nothing I can offer you except my time and only that in limited quantities." He reached over to place a finger below her chin so that she looked back up into his face. "Yet I hope very much that our situation might change."

Her eyes met his, and she saw unexpressed promises. And his complete sincerity. They walked a few more steps in silence before he grinned. "Now. Tell me more about your playing, oh Orient Express Maestro."

Her frown returned.

"What's this? Do you not wish to be called such?"

"It's not that, though I certainly don't deserve to be called a maestro. The Salzburg Maestro—he is the original. When the conductor said the word, I stumbled." She walked at his side, still not believing that Erich was there, at her side in Paris, aside from any association with the train. "But I'm frowning because I still haven't met him, the real Maestro."

"Has everyone else had their turn?" He stared straight ahead.

"No."

When his face turned toward hers, his expression was somewhat guarded. "What will he tell you that you don't already know?"

She thought for a moment. "I don't know. That's the point, really, to learn what I don't know. Just as you told me things I needed to focus on." But perhaps more importantly, the real problem was tied up in actually meeting him. If she didn't meet him, he couldn't possibly choose her.

He hummed a moment. "But everything I said, couldn't you have discovered it if you had really applied yourself?"

"Some of it, I suppose. But it was painfully helpful nonetheless."

"Critique is only painful if you doubt your ability to change."

She walked on for a moment, pondering his words. They had opened a door the tiniest sliver of a crack to a higher way of thinking about her practicing, and she wanted to linger in that place longer, perhaps push the door open further. "That's really quite profound."

"I had a professor once. He was the harshest taskmaster, and for years, I loathed him. Nothing I played was ever good enough. He would make me play measures over and over and then tell me I still hadn't mastered them. I begged to quit. But my father told me he was the greatest teacher in all of Europe, that if I studied with him, I would be even better than he was."

"What happened?"

"That's when I realized my greatest frustrations were all tied up in my thinking I'd never please this man and that I wouldn't be able to perfect the piece in the way he desired. I had given up in a weird sort of way."

"I understand. Even though you practiced until your fingers felt raw, you weren't practicing with any hope that you'd improve."

"Precisely."

She nodded. "On the train, in the storage closet before you arrived . . ." She sighed. "That was me."

"And my critiques?"

"They were of the most painful kind."

"But when we played together?" He stopped again and faced her. They stood close, and by the movement of his chest, she could tell his breaths were coming faster. They were close enough she could almost feel them, could almost feel his heart pounding against hers.

She lifted her lashes. The world around them went still. "That was magic. It was the most powerful musical experience I've ever had."

"I feel the same." He lifted his hands, and for a moment, she thought he would embrace her, but then they dropped. He teetered closer to her, his face only inches away, the lovely lift right above his mouth, his strong jaw, the flecks of yellow she'd never noticed before in his striking blue eyes, eyes that were seeing through her, straight into the vulnerable parts of her soul. Everything that she'd always admired about him filled her sight and her heart, and she was almost overcome. She reached out to rest a hand on his arm again, meaning to steady herself, but it was more of a clutching than a gentle pressure.

"Perhaps we should sit for a moment?"

Freya nodded, her mouth too dry to form words.

He led her to a stone bench situated in the shade of a tree. As soon as she felt the cool of the stone beneath her, she relaxed somewhat. As least she wouldn't swoon.

His face was serious. He reached for her hand and held it in his own. He must have cleared his throat three times before speaking. "I don't know how to proceed."

"Proceed?"

"Yes." He shook his head. "Forgive me. I've never felt this way before. I'm quite unprepared. In the storage closet I felt . . . like I should wait." And then his face warmed, his eyes twinkled at her, and the smile she'd found so stunning the day they met returned.

"And now?"

"Now." He grinned. "Now I feel somewhat liberated. I'm admitting much more to you than I was ready to. But first, tell me more about your parents. They don't approve of your music?"

Sadly, much of the magic of the moment seeped away like wisps on the wind.

"My . . . my parents? Why?"

"I'd like to know more about them, to understand."

"I think they want other things for me, the life that they lead."

"And you don't want those things?"

"I don't have anything against socializing, moving my way among the peerage, even learning more about Father's business if that's what it takes, but only if I can also play the violin." She avoided the word that pounded through her with him sitting so close. *Marriage.* They'd given up on her ever marrying. Did Erich care that most of the people in her life at home thought her a spinster?

"And they won't allow both?" He tipped his head.

"They . . . they have supported me all this time but reluctantly. My instructor teaches me for a paltry sum. He said—he said that if I can become a maestro myself, it will have been worth it." She looked away. "He says that is payment enough."

"Are your parents . . . Do they struggle with money?"

She shook her head. "No. Father is highly respected. We live in a lovely house off Grosvenor Square. Have you heard of Stonebrook Railway?"

His eyes widened. "Certainly."

"That is my father." She shrugged. "I think they hoped I would marry Lord Tolleson. Or Lord Hemming, and then it was Mr. Fenway." She lifted her eyes to his again. "But none of them would suit."

"And what about a craftsman? Would he suit?" A new insecurity flitted across his face as he lifted his chin and turned his face toward the river.

"Which craftsman?" Her voice sounded quiet to her own ears, and she was astounded at her courage.

He responded at first with only silence as he turned again and searched her face. He brought his hand to her cheek and cupped it in his palm. "This most loyal craftsman."

She held her breath for fear that a simple inhale might disrupt their moment. Then he took her hand in both of his own, his face full of smiles again. She didn't answer him, though she was full of hope. Would her father approve of a craftsman? Perhaps marrying a craftsman would be more elevated than being someone's companion. But did she need her father's approval? Not if she could make a name for herself in Salzburg, not if the Maestro would choose her as his pupil. But so many factors affected him ever selecting her. And the familiar stress of him not even deigning to hear her play tightened inside her.

Erich stood, lifting her hand so that she should stand beside him. "I think we must now amend our overly serious ways and ride the *Grande Roue de Paris*." He pointed high into the sky at the chairs that circled slowly, rising well above their heads into the air.

She sucked in a breath. "What? That is so high."

His eyes filled with a glint of adventure. "Do you dare?" He nudged her in the direction of the line of people standing outside the Roue.

"I dare." Her hand found his, and they moved as quickly as they could, at almost a run, toward the *Grande Roue de Paris*.

"I forgot to mention I need to meet with Lord Bouchet. My grandmother will expect that he and I are touring the exposition."

He stopped again. "That man you were laughing with? What is your relationship to him?"

"We are friends and co-conspirators. I am helping him reconnect with his lost love."

Erich's grin grew. "That sounds like quite a story."

"He will be my date at the ball."

"The ball?" Erich frowned.

"The ball for my performance at the great Student Salzburg Orchestra concert. I have an extra ticket."

He turned away while they kept walking, and she realized her mistake. "The woman he loves will also be at this ball."

"Ah. The woman he loves." Erich smiled again. "Who isn't you."

"Not me."

"And you hope for them to meet there?"

"Yes, I'm rather excited about the moment they will once again be together. Lord Bouchet and I just recently figured out that his greatest love is one of my best friends." She stepped closer to his side.

"That's incredible what you are doing for them. I think when someone finds another who makes them truly happy, they should hold on and never let go." He squeezed her fingers in his hand. She felt the power of his grip and his words. Then he grinned. "Look at that!" He pointed to a large earthlike globe surrounded by flowers. "What do you suppose?"

Though taken aback by his abrupt change in conversation, she forgave him because of the singularity of the sights all around them. This globe seemed suspended in the air.

But the Grande Roue de Paris rode even higher.

"And we are to go up in that?"

He grinned. "Yes." They passed by the signs for the globe. "The Globe Celeste. It is a planetarium."

She leaned over his shoulder to read along with him, the happiness of being so close bubbled up inside. "Ah, so we could look at the stars." She shielded her eyes to look up at the globe that hung above them.

He led her to the wheel. "And now we shall see all of Paris."

She tried to calm her rising fear. "That does sound nice."

As soon as their passenger car on the Grande Roue de Paris began to rise in the sky, she relaxed. "Oh, this is wonderful!" She twisted to look over her shoulder.

"Not as bad as you feared?"

"Nothing is ever as bad as you fear. I think the worry beforehand is the worst part of any experience."

"Hmm. Most certainly true." He put his arm around her shoulders. "I'm happy we could fit in this time together today."

She snuggled into him. "I never told you. Thank you for coming to my performance in the Cathedral of Salzburg." She rested her head on his shoulder. "I was in the very act of feeling sorry for myself that no friends or family ever come to hear me play, and I saw you."

"Does no one ever hear you play?"

"Certainly I play at musicales, but usually I play only for myself and my instructor." She shook her head against him.

"What a loss for everyone in your life." He started to say something, then stopped. Freya lifted her head. "They are missing out on one of the most beautiful expressions of who you are." He paused. "I am too bold." He looked away, his cheeks turning a fascinating pink. "But it is the truth. That moment of your solo, I could hardly stay in my seat. I was so carried away in your playing. No, it was more than that. Your emotion. You bore your soul with your music."

Tears rushed to her eyes and fell into her lap, but her smile grew. "Thank you."

"What's this? Tears?"

"The happiest kind."

He reached out a thumb to wipe them away. "By the time you were finished, I felt like I knew you better, like on the train." Paris spread out in front of them as their car rose again into the sky. Their time together couldn't be any more beautiful. "I cannot explain exactly what I mean. I'm afraid I'm much better with music than words."

She reached out a hand tentatively and then placed it on the heat of his cheek, her fingers moving a trail down the side of his face. Could this man, her mysterious handsome man from the train, appreciate her music the most about her? What a singular thought.

"I feel we are alike in this. Do you feel at last whole when your bow runs across the strings?"

She nodded, once, slowly.

"Do you sometimes feel like you are speaking real words while you are playing, but of course no one hears them but you?"

She nodded again, a great warmth growing. "Though some might send us to Bedlam for saying so."

"And do you ache for music with a pain that is palpable whenever you haven't played for the normal amount of hours in a day?"

"Yes, most of all *this*. I need to play every day." She smiled. "Allow me to ask a question of my own. Do you feel lonely, as if everyone around you lives by a certain understanding and you another?"

His nod followed. "Even among some who play instruments, those who play music passively, as a fleeting part of their day."

"I believe you understand me on a level that no one else can." Her words, barely a whisper, were meant more for her own ears, as if spoken in a cathedral before the great sanctuary.

He lifted his hat off his head. To her delight, his curls, usually only visible at his temples, filled his head and seemed to dance in their new freedom up in the wind.

Freya lifted her chin. "There was a time I wondered if you were even real."

He placed a thumb and forefinger at her jawline, lifting her chin farther. His face moved closer, his mouth hovering above her own. "I wonder the same about you all the time." His murmur sent a shiver of warmth from the puffs of breath on her mouth to her very toes. He searched her eyes. "Shall we find out?" His eyes danced with caring, amusement, and desire, then an intense sincerity that stole her breath. For a second, she was filled with only yearning. Then he pressed his lips to hers. And after the first touch, she no longer noticed anything but the rush of emotion. She leaned closer to him, her hands rising to his chest. Everything in her life swirled in a great confusion for a moment and then stopped, centered on this space, and at once seemed to fit perfectly together.

His lips searched hers, pressing in a soft caress that spoke to her with every touch, sending tingles up and down her arms, and then he paused and smiled, his mouth still moving over hers with his words. "You've captured my heart, I do believe."

She was sure her smile mirrored his own. "And I shall never let it go."

CHAPTER SIXTEEN

"Dim your smile." Lord Bouchet nudged her.

"What are you talking about?"

"You are so sickeningly obviously a woman in love, and I don't want my mother to think I've completely won you over."

"Oh, hmm." She tried a frown.

"No, not that. I can't have her thinking I've insulted you."

"Goodness, Lord Bouchet, we are in a bind, for I'm the happiest I have ever been and can't imagine I even lived before now."

He chuckled. "Well then, I'm happy for you. But truly." He stopped. "Could you manage a pleasant, bored expression? Mimic those of all the debutantes during your first Season. You had a Season, didn't you?"

"I did, of sorts. My parents were particular about who I was able to meet. Little did they know, I was even more particular myself." She looked away. They might not be overly thrilled she'd fallen in love with a craftsman. She paused. "I don't even know what Erich does. What is his business? His financial situation? His social position? His father was a violin craftsman . . ." A small worry began to grow. "My parents will certainly have opinions about him."

"And mine as well about Miss Gertie. But we shall conquer this situation together. You will marry your man and I my lady."

She gasped. "Marry." The word came out soft. Neither that word or even the word *love* had been spoken between her and Erich. But at least he had set up a time and place to meet for their return journey to Salzburg.

"Why does he travel so often from Paris to Salzburg?"

"I don't know," Freya said.

"What is his purpose here in Paris?"

"I don't know."

"And you don't know what he does with his time when he is not on the train."

"No."

He frowned. Then tapped his chin. "He did seem a respectable sort of chap though."

"I don't know what you do with your time. Today, it was drink beer in a German pavilion for all of the afternoon." She raised an eyebrow in challenge.

"I did that for you, you traitorous whelp."

She gasped. "What did you just call me?"

He snorted. "Forgive me." But his laugh had already started, and she couldn't help herself. She joined him. By the time they had walked the remaining distance to meet their chaperones, both were wiping tears of laughter from their eyes.

As Freya was preparing for bed, smiling to herself, her grandmother stepped into the room. Her smile was tired. "Might I come in for a moment?"

"Of course, Grandmother." Freya sat at the end of her bed and patted a place beside her. "I had such a wonderful time of it today. The exposition is so much more than I could have ever imagined."

"Isn't it? I feel blessed to live in Paris. Except for the crowds. Lady Bouchet and I had such a time of it when a group of youngsters tried to join us." She clucked and then paused, her face growing tired again. She reached out a hand to Freya, clutching her fingers as though truly concerned.

"What is it? Are you well?"

"Yes, child. I am pleased that you have found such an easy friendship with Lord Bouchet. It is excellent news indeed." Something about her tone warned Freya that more was coming.

"Yes, he is quite amiable. An amusing but also caring person. I enjoy him immensely." She waited. It was not like her grandmother to be reticent.

"I've received a letter from your parents this week and another addressed to you." She reached inside her housedress pockets and held out a sealed note. "I suspect your note contains much of the same missive as mine. You might not find it to be good news."

Freya's hands shook as she took it from her grandmother's hands.

"Your mother's health is worsening. Your father wants you home. He would like to sign over his business to an heir, to see you settled. They've run out of patience. They're talking of an arranged marriage." She cleared her throat. "I think in my overexuberance about you and Lord Bouchet's friendship, I raised marriage hopes they'd long forgotten."

Freya immediately thought of Erich. "But . . . but what if my husband would not want to be the heir of a railroad?"

"I thought the same. What use would a peer have of a business in trade?" She shrugged. "Except to make money. Perhaps Lord Bouchet would be amenable. Others could be employed in the running of it. But someone has to own it, and your father is looking forward to a seaside rest with your mother."

It all sounded so kind and good from her grandmother's lips—caring parents who just wanted to live out their days in retirement. Perhaps that was all they ever wanted, to secure a future for her, to pass on the business to her by way of her husband, but she had refused to court any men. "And my violin? My opportunities in Salzburg?"

Her grandmother put a hand on the side of Freya's face. "You know how they feel about your musical pursuits." She cleared her throat. "They have written that this wonderful experience be a culminating glory of your hobby, that you enjoy it the best you can and then return, ready to move on with your life."

"And what if the Maestro chooses me? What if I am to be trained by the Salzburg Maestro? What if I earn a spot in the professional orchestra?" Had that one caveat been taken as well? Did her success not matter after all?

"But will you, child?"

Freya slumped against her. The Maestro hadn't even heard her play as of yet. "I don't know. I have done very well so far and have been selected as concertmaster each week. But there are other instruments in the orchestra besides violin . . . It would be such an honor, one recognized all through Europe. Prince Edward himself would gift the honor. I would be invited to play at his court." She swallowed, growing unhappy as her grandmother's expression had not changed. "I have been invited to play for the Prince already." She sputtered to a stop because her grandmother's eyes were filling with sympathy, pity almost, and Freya couldn't bear it. "Does Father not care for any of that?"

"I'm afraid not. But perhaps . . . perhaps if you could show him the connections you might make in such company, the benefit you might bring to the business?" Her Grandmother shook her head. "Lord Bouchet surely would not be opposed to adding such a legacy of wealth as the railroad would provide to his estate."

"Surely not." Freya choked out the words. Lord Bouchet's parents might welcome the alliance, but would Erich want such a thing? What did he do with his time? How did he make his living?

She could think of that later. The news of her mother's illness getting worse put much of this in perspective.

"Is Mama . . . Is she . . ."

"She is not dying."

Freya breathed out in relief.

"The London air is harmful. But she will be well. Never fear. If your parents want you to make a decision influenced by her illness, know there is no harm that she will die of this ailment. But your father has worked hard all his life. She is uncomfortable away from the sea air. The two of them would like a rest. Your father could sell the railroad, but he wants to pass it on to you if he can."

Her grandmother stood and kissed her head. "I'm sorry. One day you will see this is for the best. Honestly. Most women would not be so devastated at being the heiress to a great fortune."

Freya pressed her lips together. It wasn't that simple. She was heiress if she did as they wanted, heiress at the cost of her violin, heiress only if she married the right person. *Heiress* had less the ring to it than most people would expect. In reality, *heiress* should be packaged with the bars and the isolation that came with it.

"Good night," Grandmother said.

Freya responded but hardly heard herself. A rushing sound pounded in her ears, and with shaking hands, she broke her mother's seal.

Dear Freya,

By now you have heard that your father is more anxious than ever to pass along his empire. When we heard such happy news as a possible alignment with someone so well respected as Lord Bouchet, he became even more enamored with the idea. He's purchased a smaller estate in Brighton and wishes to move there, to be landowner gentry from now on. As you can imagine, this news is happy news for me and my health. The air will be beneficial and the days of relaxation good for my nerves. I have one worry. You. I do not want you to be sad over the loss of musi-cal dreams. If it is true, that Lord Bouchet is the amiable chap we heard him to be and he has caught your heart, then my own happiness will be complete. Please open your mind and heart to such a union. We hope you enjoy our gift to you of this time in Salzburg. Enjoy every last moment with the excellent musicians, playing for our Prince Edward, goodness. And for all the diver-sions. Enjoy, for it will be your last. We have no more time to delay our lives. Father must have an heir. He always designed his company, the great work of his life, to be yours. Or your hus-band's. It is time to make your way into society as an adult. You will always have your violin and your instructor here. I know you will be able to treat it as the hobby it was meant to be.

With great love,
Mother etc.

The hobby it was meant to be. The word *hobby* felt bland on the tongue. *Hobby* just couldn't possibly have anything to do with the violin. The passion and joy that filled her with every note, the drive to excel, the beauty of the music an entire orchestra created, the notes that rose to the heavens and sank into hearts that inspired emotion and journeys of the mind. No. Playing the violin was not her hobby. It was her life. It was an extension of her soul. Could she give it up other than as a quietly personal pursuit? Certainly. It might break her heart, but she could do it. But why? Why give it up? So that her parents could rest, her mother return to good health, and Freya's new husband continue the legacy her father created.

Her shoulders slumped, and she reread her mother's letter again. What choice did she have? Her grandmother's suggestion to continue her pursuits and wait to see if her parents might be amenable to another solution seemed to be her only tiny window of hope and escape. But would it be enough? She began to fear that it would not.

But if she could be taught by the Maestro, if she could play professionally in the orchestra, play for the King's court, make a name for herself, perhaps they would listen, perhaps they would understand that her dreams could also benefit them. It sounded like that hope was gone for her parents, but Freya clung to it, nonetheless.

She choked on a painful twist in her heart. Obviously, her dreams on their own were not enough for them to matter to anyone else but her.

Except perhaps to Erich.

But even Erich might be lost to her if she chose to submit to her parents' wishes.

CHAPTER SEVENTEEN

Erich peered in at Freya in the storage closet.

But she wasn't playing. She was staring into the musty darkness. She'd played so much she couldn't even think about the notes anymore, but somehow nothing sounded right. Nothing felt satisfying. Every time she lifted her bow, she fought the pressure from her parents, the knowledge that her choices weren't helping the family, that this was her last time to attempt to be a professional violinist, that she had to marry and her husband had to run Stonebrook Railway.

Erich stared at her for a moment. "Why can't you play?"

"You heard?"

"A little."

She sighed, her breath leaving her in one long, slow response.

He took two steps, and she rushed into his arms. Without saying anything, they rocked back and forth to the movement of the train. And then he took her hand and tugged her out of the closet. "I think we've had enough of the violin for today."

"But my dinner performance." She didn't get paid a significant amount for her service, but to her, it was incredible that she'd earned her own income.

"Fine, but that's not for hours yet."

She nodded and followed him.

They dropped her violin off at her compartment, and she pocketed her key again after locking the door, letting him lead her along toward the front of the train. As they walked, passing the many doors along the inside of the train car, he said, "There's a man on the train I see often. He dresses all in black, an older portly gentleman. His name is Nicholas. Have you met him?"

She pressed her lips together in thought. "I don't think I know a Nicholas. But there is a man I notice quite often. He has a pipe."

He held up his hand, a triumphant look on his face. "But it's never lit."

"Exactly. He smells of peppermint. Or sometimes rosin."

"Does he? I think he smells of the wood shop where I used to watch my father working. Or oregano."

"Oregano?" She laughed. "He seems harmless." She wondered why he mentioned him.

"He's the one who always tells me where to find you."

She stopped. "He does? How very odd."

"I thought so too. I wondered if you knew him."

"No."

"He's also the one who told me about this car up ahead where we're going. It's an empty private car. We can sit and talk if you like or play cards or backgammon."

"Backgammon?"

"Yes, they've been playing it in the East, but it is spreading. I find it diverting." His fingers squeezed hers. "And it takes my mind off worrisome things."

They walked through two more sleeper cars and then entered a luxurious private car. She ran her hand along the dark wood, the marble pillars, then the plush seating. She took her spot at a window. Erich sat opposite and opened a game. "This is backgammon."

"Ah yes, I've played it before, though I didn't know it by name." She grinned. "It might be more entertaining than whist for two."

"Whist for two. That seems a perfectly pointless exercise."

After they'd played for a moment, Freya smiled. "Thank you for this."

"You're welcome."

"Tell me more about you. You were raised by your father, who was a world-renowned violin maker. And your mother?"

"She was from England. I was sent to all the schools. I think I told you I started at Eton and finished a Cambridge man. I learned to work in business, but my heart always returned to the shop."

"Did you ever make violins like your father?"

"Regrettably, I do not have his particular gift or patience."

"So, you returned but didn't make violins."

He toyed with his piece before rolling the dice and then moving two of his chips along. "I wanted to play instruments, not make them."

"I can well understand that. Was your father . . . was he disappointed?"

"He was, I think, at first, but he did whatever he could to encourage me along. You can imagine we came in contact with many musicians. And I acquired gifted mentors through those associations."

"And are you pleased with the results? Are you happy you pursued the occupation of your heart?"

He studied her for many moments. "I am. And up until recently, I have had no regrets."

"Recently?"

He gazed out the window. "My occupation does not offer much time for . . ." He turned back to her. "Courting." His smile and the slight pink to his cheeks almost made her laugh in pleasure.

She reached across for his hand.

He shifted in his seat. "Nor does it leave much room for a lifestyle that some might expect." He withdrew his hand and adjusted his jacket.

"Are you saying that you are busy with travels? Or that you don't have much income or that you are distracted by your work?" Freya didn't understand. He had always been such a mystery, and he wasn't being overly clear even now.

"I would like to be more straightforward about both my complications and my intentions, but I'm afraid I cannot at this time."

Her heart leapt. Intentions?

They shared a gaze for many minutes while she tried to read his mind, and he seemed to search her soul. But nothing more was said. This was not a proposal, though she felt he wished to move in that direction. Nor did she have any more information as to what his occupation actually was nor whether or not he would want to be her father's heir.

"Am I speaking in riddles?" he asked.

"Yes, you are." She all but begged for answers with her eyes, unsure what to ask him to receive the responses she sought.

"I am bound in a way. But I will not always be so. If you could be patient a few weeks more, all will become clear."

She nodded slowly.

"But do not suspect me of insincerity. If I am anything when I'm with you, it is sincere."

"I believe you." On the inside, she sighed a very impatient womanly sigh, for she most desperately needed to understand his intentions. But on the outside, she nodded and agreed to wait until he was ready.

Their journey was much more companionable than ever. Her time spent with Erich was comfortable and a pleasant respite from the newfound intensity of her pressures in the orchestra. This time when she said goodbye to Erich, he bowed over her hand and said, "I will see you on our return trip to Paris."

That sentence carried her through the next couple of weeks. As things turned out, she needed something to look forward to. All that week she found her performances lacking and encountered multiple problems in her practice time. It came as no surprise when the following week she saw that she had moved down to second chair.

Sitting next to Eliza with her triumphant smiles was almost too much. Even Gertie couldn't abide the woman's smug attitude. "You'd think she had suddenly become superior to us all."

"Do us all a favor, Freya, and win back your first-chair spot." Henry surprised her and whispered those words as he passed by.

She would. She was determined. Although determination seemed to be only one of many requirements for true proficiency.

Everything felt dark. Even Gertie had once again lost her shine. The rehearsals were getting longer, their instructors and conductors more urgent in their efforts to encourage better playing. The students smiled less. The pressure seemed to be mounting. And right before the end of rehearsal on their last day that week, Eliza was called back to play for the Maestro again. Freya had not been called back to see him even once.

When Freya boarded the train again for Paris, her heart dragged down to her toes. One thing consoled her: she would soon see Erich. But would she have to give him up as well? If she couldn't even make first chair of her student orchestra, how could she establish herself well enough that her father would take her playing seriously?

She went in search of Erich, but he wasn't anywhere she would expect to see him. After a time, she gave up. Instead of practicing further in her closet, she found the original car she'd sat in on her first day, placed her violin beside her, basked in the warm sun filtering in from the window, and read a book.

For the first few minutes, she checked the car entrance often in hopes that Erich had arrived, but once she'd been disappointed enough, she forced her attention to remain focused on her book.

She must have dozed off because the next thing she noticed was a conductor standing above her. "Excuse me, miss?"

Freya blinked a few times and then sat up in her seat. "Yes?"

"I am sorry to disturb you, but a very distinguished guest has asked that you come play for him."

Confused, Freya collected her book and stood, her violin case clutched in her other hand. "I don't understand."

"If you'll come with me?" He gestured. "I was specifically charged to tell you that your friend Erich is there as well and will accompany you on his own instrument."

"What? Oh, that will be excellent!" A rush of relief filled her that Erich was on the train like he'd promised and that he had called for her. She also felt a frisson of anticipation at performing with him. She'd never even heard him play before. "And who are we playing for?"

"Prince Edward himself, miss."

She faltered and reached out a hand to steady herself against the wall of their narrow passageway in a sleeping car.

"Yes. We are trying to keep the information quiet. Your friend has been entertaining his party since we left Salzburg."

She picked up her pace.

"He attaches his own private car to the Orient Express. It is finer than even our cars. You must be an excellent musician, miss, to be recommended in this way."

"Thank you." His words brought on her now familiar self-doubt. Hopefully she would be able to play the simpler entertaining pieces. Though she had no idea what Erich had in mind.

Again she felt grateful that Erich was on this train and that the reason she hadn't seen him yet was that he was detained by the Prince of Wales. She wasn't sure what to do with that information. Surely her parents would have to listen when she played for royalty. And Erich. Who was he that the prince would request him? The conductor seemed to think he was a highly sought-after musician. The dining car conductor certainly thought the same.

At last, they approached a door. It was ornate with gold filigree, engravings, and bars. The conductor knocked. A window opened above her head, someone nodded, and then they let her in.

The car was lined with plush red-velvet walls. The chairs were overstuffed and . . . large. Everything in the room seemed extra-large. Each chair could fit two people certainly. When her eyes found Prince Edward, she immediately understood why. He filled the largest chair to overflowing. He sat at a table with all manner of sweets and fruits.

She sought Erich, but before she found him, the prince waved her forward, his fingers adorned with at least four rings. After guzzling from his cup, he nodded.

She dipped into her lowest curtsey, waiting to be spoken to.

The conductor bowed beside her. "Your majesty, Miss Freya Winter, the violinist."

"Ah yes, welcome, Miss Winter, welcome."

She rose. "Thank you, Your Royal Highness. I'm honored. I hope my playing will be pleasing."

"I'm certain of it. With a recommendation such as the one you have received, how could it be anything but awe-inspiring?" His laugh started in his belly and moved to his chest, followed by a fit of coughing. He waved her away off to the side. She turned in that direction and at last saw Erich. He sat behind a harpsichord in a back corner, his face all smiles.

As soon as she was close enough, she smiled back, albeit a little weakly, and whispered, "What's this?"

But he just winked. "Let's tune you up."

After a moment, she and the harpsichord were in tune.

The Prince called out, "Come now, let's have some music."

Freya swallowed. "What shall we play?" She worried her courage might falter. Everything about this summons was overwhelming.

Erich's eyes sparkled with adventure. "Let's see if you can keep up."

He started on a rapid-paced English country tune, his face challenging. Her insecurity forgotten, she almost laughed at the joy of the sound of it. She began the tune, playing all notes as chords, using two strings at a time, testing one at a time along with his playing.

"Impressive. But can you do this?" Erich ran his fingers up and down the instrument, adding arpeggios where there might just be chords, complicating single notes with many. She was enjoying that a country tune could sound so complex.

She added her own, counterbalancing his, beginning where he would stop, sometimes cutting him off to take over a rising scale, which he would pick up again on the way back down. They played as one. For the first time, she felt almost as if she could read his mind, predict what he would play.

The beat was catchy, the tune fun, and the other members of the prince's car were tapping their feet and clapping along.

When at last they ended the number, the members of the car applauded.

Prince Edward lifted his glass to them.

"I think that means we are to keep playing." Erich laughed. "Well done. You are exceptional. I've never enjoyed myself more." He studied her face. "Why don't you take the lead on this one?"

She thought about it for only half a second and then chose one of the Maestro's pieces, an earlier, simpler one, but it left room for embellishment.

His expression darkened in intensity and appreciation. He nodded, and they played again. This time, Freya improvised, and Erich followed. The same general approval followed from their audience, and then the guests started calling out requests.

After an hour of some of her most creative playing, Freya felt more energized than tired. But the prince called them to him. "Thank you. You have made the journey a pleasant one."

Freya curtseyed, and Erich bowed.

Prince Edward clucked. "When Erich here told me we should summon you, I knew you must have exceptional talent, and he was correct. I am most impressed. Are you in London, my dear?"

"I am, sir. My parents live there."

Prince Edward adjusted his sleeves. "Your father owns the Stonebrook Railroad."

"Yes, Your Highness."

"I enjoyed your playing so much I would like for you to perform for me at St. James for the royal court. I'll send a summons."

"Thank you, sir. I would be honored." She placed a hand at her stomach and tried to breathe normally even though she'd just been offered the most amazing opportunity of her life thus far, though perhaps just barely topping the one she just experienced.

"In two weeks I will be attending the royal concert in Salzburg. I believe Erich will be presenting some of the awards."

Freya nearly jumped. "What? I mean, I'm sorry, sir, I just hadn't heard about that."

The prince looked to Erich, who shrugged sheepishly.

The prince eyed him for a moment and then chuckled. He beckoned Freya closer. "Do you not know who this man is?"

She looked at Prince Edward and back to Erich. The prince seemed to her a rather odd man. "I . . . I thought I did?"

The prince's chuckle turned into a laugh. "The two of you. I'm astounded. And tell me, Miss Freya, what does your father think of your musical ability?"

"He wishes me to focus on other things."

The prince pressed his lips together. "He is unenlightened."

Freya wasn't going to disagree, but she couldn't disparage her father in front of the Prince of Wales. She said nothing.

"A wise woman to treat her father's name with honor." He nodded approvingly. "Off with you now. I look forward to seeing you in a few weeks' time."

She curtseyed again, low, and then she and Erich made their way from the car.

CHAPTER EIGHTEEN

Freya had questions about how Erich had become acquainted with the prince, and what other instruments he was proficient at but was mostly exhilarated at having performed with Erich and for the Prince of Wales, no less.

Freya felt brave. Questions could wait. She wanted to play the important pieces, the ones she'd been avoiding. As they made their way back through the train, her steps bounced with energy. "Would you mind listening to my audition piece, the one for the Salzburg Orchestra?"

Erich's eyebrows shot up, but he smiled and nodded approvingly. "Not at all."

They moved down the train until they found a car with few people in it. She lifted her violin again and played her piece. She'd implemented all his suggestions from the last time, feeling much better about it. She simply enjoyed the piece as she played.

When she was finished, he studied her for a moment.

"What did you think?" she asked.

"You are almost there."

"Almost?"

"Yes, almost. The difference between excellent and the unremarkable is but a fraction of time, the barest change in rhythm. It is more a matter of feeling the piece than the precise mechanics of it."

He reached for her instrument. She widened her eyes. No one had ever played it but her. But she handed it to him. "Thank you." His eyes told her he understood the significance of her trust.

Then he played the first measures of her piece, and it was as if the Maestro himself had touched the measures. She stared in awe at her violin because she almost didn't dare look at Erich.

"You try. First, mimic what I did, then keep going and speak this piece to me through your own ever so slight interpretations."

Freya nodded, trying to grasp and remember precisely what he had done. She played through the measures reasonably like he had, but then, as she pushed on, the magic of what he was trying to portray flowed through her. By the time she finished the last note, she had forgotten he was even there.

She opened her eyes.

His eyes were misty. "You have made the piece your own. You are the Maestro now."

She lowered her violin, relief washing through her, and stepped into his arms.

"I've never heard it played so well. You are beautiful." His thumbs caressed her face. She trembled with happiness at his praise, his closeness. His lips found hers, and that similar unity they'd felt playing, the great confidence and approval he poured into her with his words, filled her with a heady, daring desire. She responded with the strength of her love, the passion she felt playing with him, the hope to be with him. His lips were both firm and tender, and he smelled of wood and sheet music and old violins and a hint of something earthy, something raw. She smiled, and his lips moved to kiss it away, tugging at her response.

After another moment, he paused and rested his forehead on hers. "I wish you were mine forever."

She closed her eyes, allowing the approval to wash over her. "Can such a thing be possible?"

"That is the question." He stepped away and led her to a set of chairs.

Clapping from the other end of the car interrupted them. She turned her face, mortified to be caught.

"Zhat was lovely."

"Ah, Nicholas." Erich nodded. "The man who has come to my rescue so many times."

Freya smiled, not certain if she should be relieved or more mortified that he knew the man who'd seen them kissing. "The man with the peppermint pipe."

"Peppermint? No, surely it is oregano." Erich looked to Nicholas as though to confirm the correct aroma.

But Nicholas looked from one to the other and puffed at his pipe. No smoke left the end. "I am happy to see you togezer. Love vill alvays find a vay."

He stepped out of their car, which Freya was relieved to notice was now empty. She hadn't heard Nicholas enter. Anyone could have seen them. As her face warmed, Erich ran his hand down her skin. "Love."

Her gaze lifted to his, her heart full of questions. The tenderness, the regard, even the love that stared back stole her breath away.

They sat together, and she remembered Prince Edward's question. *Do you not know who this is?*

"How are you and Prince Edward acquainted?"

His eyes shot to hers for a moment, obviously taken off guard, but then he waved his hand. "I am a musician too, of course, and he loves to be entertained. I believe it was one of my father's old clients who recommended me to him." Erich always said so much without saying anything at all. She suspected there was much more to the story than he let on.

"But do you often play for royalty? What is your profession? More instructor or entertainer? Do you work as a musician?"

"I do."

"Then it's possible? To make a living as a musician?" His two simple words filled her with hope and courage.

"Very much. For you? Absolutely. You saw already just on this train what you can do to entertain an audience, how people appreciate that kind of thing."

"Yes, but that was parlor playing. It doesn't pay that well, and there aren't many reputable locations for me to play."

"But was performing in the royal train car truly any different?"

"It was much better because I was playing with you, but no. I see what you mean if I could find upper-class audiences."

He dipped his head. "Precisely." He lifted her fingers one by one, almost absentmindedly, but every touch sent a thrilling path of wonder up her arms. "My playing is not my only source of income."

"It isn't?"

"No. But I must tell you about it more another time. Now, I promised the Prince I would return."

"Oh?"

"Yes. On this trip, I am his personal musician."

His personal musician. She couldn't believe any of this was really happening. "He said he'd ask for me at St. James. I'm so honored by that. It means more than you can possibly know right now."

"To share the time with you was more my pleasure than *you* can possibly know." He bowed. "But regrettably, I must return." After a lingering kiss on the back of her hand, he made his way out of the carriage, and she was alone.

In a rare moment on the Orient Express, she returned to her own compartment, rested her head, and fell asleep to the rocking motions of the train.

She did not see Erich again that day, but she didn't expect to. She was used to his strange behavior by now but this time assumed he had responsibilities to the Prince. Her visit in Paris was short and uneventful, for which Freya was grateful as she longed to return to Salzburg. To her disappointment, she did not see Erich even once on her return journey.

When she arrived back at the Salzburg station, she took a hired hack as she had also become accustomed to doing. Living this independent life was growing on her. One look at the boarding house reminded her that she wasn't entirely independent. Frau Uberdiche treated them like boarding school youngsters, but nevertheless, Freya had a sense of freedom here in this program she'd never enjoyed before—particularly the ability to travel alone by train. Victoria, the woman Freya had met on her first trip, had it precisely right. The added freedom of train passage was as much a blessing to women as anyone. She patted her hat pins and laughed again at her dear mother. Not once had she yet thought to use a single one in self-defense. But she was ready if ever such an occasion did arise.

After little sleep Sunday night because she spent the whole of it in a delicious chat with Gertie, she awoke nevertheless wonderfully invigorated. She was the first one to show up for rehearsal and saw the chair announcement. Her smile didn't leave as she marched right over and took back her seat in the first chair. Then she went through her audition piece for the Salzburg Orchestra, which would be a little later this afternoon.

The morning went by in a blur. Looking back, she couldn't even remember if Eliza frowned or ignored her or sniffed in disapproval as she sat in her second chair seat. All thoughts of Erich brought a smile to Freya's face and a strength to her playing that stuck with her. Even anticipating the audition did not leave her overly nervous. Instead, she felt greater energy. As she left the audition room after playing her piece, she could only feel pleased. If the judges' happy expressions and ready smiles were any indication, she'd done well. They would announce results at the banquet for those who made it. The banquet. The grand ball. The Musical Celebration for European Royalty. She was pleased to be a part of it all. As if to remind her that the heart could overflow with joy, thoughts that Erich might love her leapt around in happy dancing. Love. He'd almost said as much.

She only had one more trip to Paris to see her grandmother and, therefore, Erich. And then what would happen? How would she ever see him again? She didn't know. But hopefully he would come courting, or perhaps she could stay on in Salzburg, or they could work together. Or he'd propose to her and take her away to wherever he lived, wherever he travelled to, and she could keep playing her violin with him. So many hopes and nothing decided.

Her parents' wishes, never far from her mind, came rushing back in. Perhaps they would marry and Erich would want to take over her father's business. And give up his playing? No. Never. She could never ask such a thing of him. But he had said he learned business at university. If he had the right managers, perhaps he could do both.

As much as she'd tried to pretend her parents were not a part of this decision, they most certainly were. Unless she found a way to provide for herself or prove the worth of her musicianship or marry a man who would be able to and want to run her father's company, she was still in the same bind she always had been. Her parents would insist she be a companion or governess, and they would leave London. If they weren't concerned about a house on Grosvenor Square, about all her gowns and the expense of a continued presence in London, her father could retire, and they could enjoy Brighton, one smaller home, and a life of leisure.

Even though her bind was still the same, she found herself much more able to bear it. After all, the memory of Erich's kisses was never far from her mind. Nor was the opportunity to play for His Highness. She allowed the thoughts of her weekend to carry her.

Days passed. One morning in rehearsal, Frau Uberdiche clapped her hands. "Has anyone here not seen the Maestro yet?"

Freya looked around. No hand raised but her own. "I haven't yet." Was she really the very last person to be chosen?

Frau Uberdiche considered her for a moment and then made a note on her paper. "Very well. I will let him know." She addressed the class. "For the rest of you, I hope you will consider with all seriousness the critiques you've been given by the Maestro. He is well known all over the world for his ability to tell you precisely what you lack as a musician. For those who are able to master what they lack, their lives as musicians are changed forever."

Freya thought that useful. But wouldn't it be rather more helpful if one could also show a musician's strengths? She thought of her last visit with Erich when she had moved him to tears with her piece. Nothing had empowered her more. A gentle thought nudged her. She'd felt even more empowered by his praise because earlier he had pointed out some areas she could improve. And she'd worked incredibly hard at them.

No matter. She knew it was only fair, part of the program in fact, to have her own time with the Maestro. And she desperately wished to speak with him, if only to try to aid his decision to possibly choose her as his student.

She waited until all the students had left before she approached Frau Uberdiche. "Excuse me."

"Ah yes, Freya." Her smile was large and genuine.

"I have really enjoyed my experience here in this orchestra."

"I'm happy to hear it. You've grown much. I don't know if you can yet see or measure your progress, but you arrived a talented musician, and you have given every indication you might leave as a maestro yourself."

Freya's eyes widened. "Do you mean that?" She could hardly believe it. High praise. She'd heard Erich say something similar, but for some reason, hearing it from the ever-disgruntled Frau Uberdiche made it sink in even deeper to the place she catalogued all kind thoughts, all praise to remind herself of later when her doubts returned.

"As you know, I don't give out empty praise. Now, I suspect you are here to talk about when you will be called back to see the Maestro."

"Yes. If you don't mind, I am most anxious to be his student, and I feel I would never be able to do such a thing if he doesn't hear me play."

"Understandable. Though I do want you to know that he has heard you. He's heard you quite a bit, as a matter of fact. His notes on you are extensive. That is why I was surprised to see your hand up."

"His notes are extensive? But . . . when would he have heard me play?"

"He does listen to rehearsals at times. He would certainly have heard all your solos. He comes to our concerts. Beyond that, I don't know. But you are correct. You should have a time that is for you alone to play for the Maestro." Her eyes turned kinder and softer than Freya had ever seen them. "His comments about you are positive indeed."

She warmed to her toes. "Are they?" She begged, not with her lips, but with every thought, every bit of energy in her, for Frau Uberdiche to say more. The woman stayed silent.

Freya curtseyed. "Thank you."

"Have a good evening, Freya."

Freya thought she might have had a good sleep before she knew that the Maestro had notes about her playing. But now that she could speculate what might be written about her, every ounce of anything so relaxing as sleep would elude her forever.

Or if not forever, for the whole of this night at the very least.

She passed the common areas in the boarding house on the way to her room. She was too distracted to stop, but a group of students looked to be having a pleasant time of it. She paused, considering joining the friends she'd met on the first day. But then what? She didn't want to talk about the Maestro. Too much of her life's happiness rode on the possibility that he might choose her to train. But truly, how would he ever choose to train her if he wouldn't even hear her? And how did he have extensive notes on her abilities if he'd never really heard her play except at performances? She smiled at her friends and kept walking, too much distracting her from being pleasant company.

CHAPTER NINETEEN

A HALF HOUR LATER, FREYA flopped onto her side. "Are you asleep, Gertie?" Freya's question sounded small and lonely in the dark of their room.

"No."

"I can't sleep. Do you suppose the others are up as well?"

"The others?"

"Yes, Frank, Daphne, Henry, Tobias . . . Do they linger in the common areas for long?"

"Sometimes. It's not very late yet."

Freya sat up. "I'm going to be driven crazy if I stare at the dark any longer. Would you like to join me?"

"Absolutely." Gertie threw off her covers, and the two dressed quickly.

On a whim, Freya reached for her instrument. "Bring yours. What if we play?"

"After hours?"

"We haven't broken a single rule since our first day here."

Gertie giggled, but she reached for her violin as well.

Freya hurried them through the dark hallways to the common area where she'd seen their friends earlier, and she breathed out in relief that they were still sitting in a group, chatting.

Frank smiled at their arrival, and the others turned. "Hello. We were just thinking about turning in."

"No. I can't sleep. Could you all stay a little longer?"

Henry looked at the others and then shrugged. "I've got nothing else to do."

"Nor I." Frank grinned. "Why can't you sleep?"

She shook her head. "So many thoughts flying through my mind."

After she and Gertie settled in with them, everyone was quiet for a moment. Then Frank laughed. "One thing we haven't done yet is share a moment when we embarrassed ourselves with our instruments."

Freya smiled, her ready laugh tumbling out of her mouth. It felt good to laugh. Some of the tightness in her chest lessened. "One time my parents were throwing a party. I was invited to attend though I was too young to be out in society yet. And someone, one of the guests, requested that Miss Winter entertain the group. Thrilled to be able to share with any audience at all, I ran for my instrument, which was just in the other room, came back with it out, my bow ready. I stood at the front of the room and only then noticed one of my aunts sitting at the piano. She began to play. Hardly anyone had even noticed me at all." Freya placed a hand at her forehead. "What if I had begun?" Freya had been much more devastated than she let on. She had been so excited to have her first chance to perform.

The others laughed a little bit and nodded. Then Henry shared how he'd been out on his farm tending to the pigs when one of them ran under his legs just as a woman from the big house walked by, the prettiest one of them all. Henry had ended up in the air and on his backside in the mud.

"What did she do?"

"A real gentle one, that. She placed a hand over her mouth, and she hurried along as though she hadn't seen."

Everyone shared some of their embarrassing moments, and then Daphne raised her hand. "I think my most embarrassing moment with my instrument might have been during my meeting with the Maestro."

Although Freya dreaded a return to that heaviest of topics, she leaned forward so she could hear Daphne's quiet tale.

"I was so nervous that I almost tripped walking in the door. And then I played terribly, my hands trembling, everything. And he was kind. I was so petrified that I think he was afraid to say anything negative. I was so thrilled at his kind words that I waved and said, 'I love you,' as I walked out the door. Like I was talking to my mum!" Her face turned the brightest red, and she looked away. "I can't believe I'm saying this out loud."

Freya laughed with her belly. The others too. Soon they were imitating "I love you. Goodbye!" to each other, and even Daphne thought it was funny.

"Perhaps he will give you extra points." Frank cleared his throat. "I've been thinking about this, about how Freya hasn't heard anything from the Maestro yet. How about we give her some tips he gave to us?"

Everyone nodded, and their smiles warmed Freya. Though she was loathe to think again so soon about her own situation, she eagerly thanked them.

As they went around the circle, each sharing the things the Maestro had said to them, she couldn't help but think that she had been well prepared before now. Many of the suggestions she knew she'd worked through already. But a few she would definitely try to be aware of.

"Thank you. You are all so kind."

Gertie added one more tip. "One of the best things he ever said to me was to pay attention to the tiniest of changes in timing. I think it totally changed the way I will ever play again."

Astounded at the similarity to the conversation she'd had with Erich, she just nodded. "That's remarkable. Thank you for sharing that." Freya lifted her violin. "Frank once suggested we create our own orchestra. How about it?"

The others still had their instruments at their feet. None of them had ventured upstairs since after rehearsal, she guessed. They looked from one to the other and then unloaded their instruments as well.

Gertie nodded. "As Freya said, we haven't broken a single rule yet."

"No time like the present." Henry grinned.

Freya played an A, and they all tuned to her instrument. Then she started in on a country piece she'd played on the train.

"Wait! I don't know this," Gertie complained.

"Improvise!" Freya laughed.

Gertie was timid at first but then jumped in with full enthusiasm.

By the time they'd played the last notes, everyone's smiles were large, and Freya could only appreciate this group all the more. What a rare privilege to be able to associate with each of them. "Tell me. Tell me of your families. What are your plans after the concert?"

Gertie sighed. "I suppose I shall go back home to my family. I don't imagine the Maestro will want to train me. I shall have no other reason to stay here in Salzburg—not in any manner in which to support myself, at least, which I would need to do if I were to stay on."

Frank watched her for a moment. Freya wondered if he was still hoping to catch Gertie's eye. "I shall likely return home also, although if the Salzburg Orchestra would have me, I'd enjoy playing with them for a time."

"Is it . . . Do they pay enough for one to live?" Gertie's hopeful expression reminded Freya just how much she too would like a means to support herself in Salzburg.

Frank shrugged. "To live, yes, but I doubt it would be enough if I weren't single. I don't know about the life of a musician and a family, a wife, a house. Surely some have done quite well, but not all of us can be Mozart, and he was more famous after death, wasn't he?"

"He seemed pretty famous in life as well." Gertie seemed to be interested in the lives musicians could make for themselves, almost as much as Freya herself was interested. Frank had expressed a desire to work as a musician. Freya eased into the happy realization that she was with people who understood her.

"Famous yes, but not overly wealthy."

"True." Freya frowned. "Is there no way to live out our dreams and play and be paid for our skills? Perhaps as teachers?"

"Of course there's a way." Henry snorted. "Just depends on what kind of lifestyle you're hoping to live, doesn't it?"

His brother nodded. "We'll be needed to farm the land, but I imagine we could make a good bit of extra with our instruments in the right crowd."

Henry's broad, strong chest seemed to expand. "If your needs are simple, your life can be too."

No one said much after that. But Freya felt some of her dreams waver, like a candle in a draft. She cleared her throat, suddenly wishing to share her burdens. "I've had some difficult news from home."

They turned to her in concern.

"My parents. I think I've told you they don't love the idea that I play. And they've pretty much given up on me ever making a suitable match. Before I came they told me that if I don't get some kind of accolades here, if the Maestro doesn't choose me, then they are going to arrange a position for me, whether as a governess or a companion. But more recently they have indicated that instead, they may arrange a marriage. Even if I do receive accolades, they still might insist upon my return home."

Gertie's face had gone pale. "You'll never perform again?"

"I suppose I'll play small pieces, but not the complicated numbers, nothing the Maestro would compose, nothing besides the little country numbers we just played."

"I'm sorry." The sincerity in Daphne's face comforted Freya.

"Passing on Stonebrook Railroad is everything to my father right now. He's proud of what he built, but he can no longer run it." *Or let it go.* The idea seared into her brain. *Let it go.* But why would he ever let it go?

"What will you do? Surely a person cannot be forced to stop playing?" Frank, of course, would assume such a thing. He behaved in every way as a man of means. And since he'd probably been denied little and certainly never been a woman, he would never understand how easily a person could be forced to do all manner of things.

"I shall attempt in every way possible, as I always have, to be able to play my violin. But unless I make a significant means for myself, then I will be forced to quit. At any rate, I'm certain I will be married."

"Married? To whom?"

She glanced at Gertie for a moment and then looked away. "To someone of my father's choosing, someone who could take over his business. Insisting I marry is rather ridiculous, if you ask me." Thoughts of Erich countered her statement with hope, hope that somehow they could be together.

"It doesn't sound ridiculous." Daphne spoke louder than usual. Freya was pleased not to have to strain to hear her.

"Why do you say that?"

"Well, as we've just discussed, you cannot just count on making a living with your violin. And do you want to be alone the whole of your life? You must at some point move on to marriage."

Freya thought of Erich. With Erich, she might be able to marry and play music, but with another? She'd be hard pressed to find a man who would want to move with her to Salzburg or who would be able to just leave his work. Perhaps if she married a lord, like Lord Bouchet, they would be at leisure to do what they wished. Her dowry might enable some freedom, but she'd still have to find a different gentleman. And she wanted no gentleman but Erich.

Freya appreciated everything Daphne had just said. "I'm sure there's truth in that, Daphne. It's all just so difficult. All I have ever wanted to do, ever, was to play the violin. It has been my dream since I was a little girl to play for kings and queens and to have a professional life as a violinist. I could play and perhaps compose and even instruct." She started to pack her violin away. "Take that away, and I don't even know who I am."

Gertie reached for her hand. "Perhaps that's what you need to find out."

"What?"

"Who is Freya Winter when she doesn't have a violin under her chin?"

Freya didn't say so, but she couldn't imagine why such a question even mattered. She and the violin were one and the same.

She wasn't anything without her violin.

And that's what scared her the most.

CHAPTER TWENTY

THIS TIME WHEN TRAVELLING BACK to Paris, Erich met her at the station. He bowed over her hand, took her bag, and followed her into the train.

The sound of his feet behind her, climbing the steps made her grin. "To what do I owe this great pleasure?"

"To the fact that I couldn't wait one more moment to see you."

She nearly stumbled, pleased surprise rumbling through her.

"Careful now." The smile in his words made her laugh.

She turned to face him once they'd entered the first car. "Where are we going?"

"How about my compartment?"

She had to swallow twice before she trusted herself to speak. Then she said simply, "Where is it?"

"It's not what you think, though."

"Oh? And what do I think?" A new brazen bravery made her grin and attempt such a little tease.

"Well, I don't know what *you* think, but it's not what *others* might think. I realize that might have sounded untoward . . ." His face colored in a fascinating shade of red. "I will stop talking. You'll see."

"And now I'm curious."

They moved farther down the train cars. Even though the Orient Express traded out different cars on every journey, all felt as familiar as home to her now, and she found she hardly noticed the sway of the cars as the train began to move.

"Is it odd that I wish to ride this train forever?"

"I will miss this time with you."

"Exactly." She sighed and stepped closer to him in the already narrow corridor.

"Then we shall hope for the longest train ride possible."

She smiled. Was this really happening? Did he care as much as she?

"My car is just up ahead."

"Your . . . car?" A beautiful door with engravings, different from many of the others, led her to believe they were entering a private car. "What is this?"

"This is where I stay when it's available."

A conductor stood at the entry and opened the door for them.

As Erich passed the man, he paused and said, "We will require a conductor with us and also some repast this morning."

"Very good, sir."

Freya stepped into a beautiful carriage. It was smaller than Prince Edward's, but it had a staircase. The floors were blue, the walls were deep, rich wood, and the chairs looked comfortable. "This is lovely. I'm surprised you ever leave."

"I've had a pleasant, compelling reason to sit in all manner of public cars."

"And does this car belong to you?" She felt intrusive asking, but the question slipped out. She smiled. If he was a musician and he could earn the means to travel the Orient Express by private car, then all was not lost to her, either for her own prospects as a musician or for her if Erich were to ever pursue her as more than a companion on the train.

Would he? She felt her face heat, and she turned away.

"When it's available, it's mine to use. We will have attendants here. I've asked a conductor to remain with us. Are you comfortable?"

"Oh, yes. Very much so."

"I thought this might be an improvement on your storage practice room." He laughed.

"An improvement. Yes, so much an improvement. But I still don't understand."

He studied her for a moment. "One of my patrons—in fact, the very reason I travel to Paris as often as I do . . . one of the reasons—he asks for this to be linked to the train whenever he's not using it so that I might do so in comfort. In that way, I'm at his call when he needs me, when I don't have responsibilities in Salzburg."

"Our schedules have been remarkably aligned."

"True. They have." He looked about to say something, but then he just smiled.

A conductor entered, the blue of his uniform matching well with the red and blue in the car. He left a tray on the table and moved to stand in the corner.

"Shall we?"

"Yes. I didn't eat before I left."

As soon as they were eating the cakes and drinking tea, Erich asked, "So how were the last two weeks?"

"Oh, I've had the most interesting time of it. First, of course, I must thank you. I regained my first-chair spot in the orchestra. I felt so much more prepared this time. Your assistance has meant so much to me, especially since I've not been able to meet with the Maestro." She looked down, suddenly much more emotional than she planned to be. "Forgive me." She dabbed her mouth to hide its sudden downturn. When she at last felt in control, she lifted her eyes.

His face was full of sympathy.

"But as I said, your help has been all I need."

"I'm pleased to hear it. And your orchestra audition?"

She exhaled slowly. "I did well. We won't hear the results until the actual banquet, but they seemed pleased."

"Excellent."

"They asked me to play a solo for our performance that evening, the Musician Celebration for European Royalty, a long one this time. They plan to feature a violinist for almost the entire movement. Me." She smiled.

"I'm not surprised. A bit of advice?"

"Certainly."

"There are always surprise solos at these types of events. Those who plan them, the royalty in particular, seem to think we always have a repertoire of excellent music we can play at any moment."

"Oh? So I should be thinking what I would play if asked."

"Yes. Have two or three mood pieces, one technical one, and one you know Prince Edward might enjoy." His eyes danced with excitement.

"Since I have already played for him." She grinned. "Thank you. That alone might save my dream of being able to play the violin."

"It was my pleasure to have someone as proficient as you at my side, and as I've said, I look for all ways to keep you at my side or in my sights."

She wished to swallow up his words and keep them inside her forever. "Do you remember the first time we saw each other?"

"Naturally. I saw you when I entered the platform. I didn't think you'd noticed my feeble attempts to gain your attention. But I stood at your side, perhaps slightly outside your vision."

"What? You did?" she asked.

"Yes. I was there. I even remarked on the time."

"You did not."

"It is the truth. But your mouth was puckered in what I have decided is the expression you make when deep in thought. And you were not hearing me. I wondered if you heard the conductor's first call to board."

"I had. I was debating in that moment whether or not to come to Salzburg at all."

His eyebrows rose. "This surprises me."

She shrugged. "My whole life I've been told by my parents that I'm not meant to be a violinist; I have other, more important things to do; the instrument is a waste of my time. Honestly, only my determination has kept me playing at all, that and the kind interest of my instructor."

"Ah, so your last-minute jitters are why I finally had to almost walk into you?"

"Then I noticed you." She laughed, astounded she could have missed seeing such a man at her side. "In fact, I might have let the train leave without me had you not rushed past me the way you did."

He shook his head. "A tragedy that would have been."

"They would be just fine without me. Everyone there plays beautifully. They could have learned what they needed to, and Eliza would be happy to be first chair in my place."

His eyes turned sad. "While I don't know if I agree with any of that, I was referencing not having ever met you. That would have been my own personal tragedy."

His sincerity was obvious, and she was overwhelmed with the truth of his words. He reached for her hand. "This is perhaps our last train ride together." He toyed with her fingers, sending happy thrills up her arm. "And we must make the most of our time. Would you like to play?"

She thought for a moment. "Perhaps. I think you've helped me with my most recent weak spots. Although . . . could I play for you later? Just run through my solo?"

"I would be happy to listen." He nodded. "And now, should we read?" His face seemed overly pleased.

"What are all these smiles?"

"Why shouldn't I smile? I cannot think of a more pleasant manner in which to pass the time with you, doing as we please, reading if we want, playing if we want, with hours ahead of us." He stood and reached for her hand. "Shall we?"

When she stood, he led her over to the side bench along the window. Watching such a picturesque view with him at her side made everything magical again, as though it were her first train ride. "I'll never tire of this view. It changes so completely every time I look outside."

"Which do you prefer, the countryside with the green, rolling hills or the rugged rocks of the mountains?"

She studied the countryside that passed by at the moment. "I don't know. I've noticed your father's peak every time I see the mountains now, so that will definitely influence my decision." She reached into her bag for her copy of *Sense and Sensibility*. She still hadn't finished. "But this view now, with rolling green hills as far as we can see, is so peaceful, isn't it? As if everything will always continue on in so cozy a fashion." Her heart ached with desire that it would be so. Or that if there were any changes, any stark, rocky mountains, that they would be the kind that led her to Erich and the violin.

She read aloud, and he laughed or cringed or exclaimed at all the right places, and she realized she could spend many an hour doing just precisely this and be perfectly happy. When they paused for a break, she reached for his hand.

His eyebrows lifted in pleased surprise.

Freya squeezed his hand in between her own. "I just realized something."

"And what's that?"

"I find enjoyment in other things besides my violin."

"Do you?" His one eyebrow wiggled wickedly, and she felt her face flush, unsure just exactly what he was thinking.

"Yes. This for example, these simple moments watching you pretend to enjoy my novel."

"Pretend? Never. I am on the edge of my seat in distress until I find out how dear Edward can work his way out of this conundrum."

"Edward? As if it's Edward we're concerned with. What about Elinor? She is the most deserving heroine I've ever seen. Can we not worry for her happiness?"

"Of course, but it's all tied to Edward, isn't it? And the chap that I am relates to his dilemma. He's being the dutiful son, and honorable man, first, isn't he? At great personal sacrifice." He placed a hand at his heart. "I feel that."

His words, no doubt, were meant to be charming. But they niggled at her conscience. Was there room for her to be more dutiful to her family? Should she give greater attention to her parents' requests of her?

Not liking the direction of her thoughts, Freya just shook her head. "Of course you would see it solely from his perspective. But have you thought he had no business raising expectations if he knew he was not free to do so?"

"But could he help it? Sometimes people connect. Or in their case, *one* time. And that's all it took. They shared something real. It was immediate, and it was important."

Was he talking about more than the book now?

"I see that. Of course." She thought of that first day on the train, her smile, their connection. Had they connected that first day? Certainly. But more and more as the weeks went by, her love for Erich had grown like dew that drips from the grass in the morning. *Love.* Could she be falling in love with Erich? Certainly. She'd never met a man like him.

She put her book back in her bag. "And now what shall we do? I don't suppose you have a surprise prince here somewhere that is expecting a performance?"

"No. No surprise princes. But I'm guessing my friend Nicholas is here somewhere. Perhaps he and another would enjoy a game of whist?"

"Oh, that would be lovely. Good idea."

"And then of course we can return to this car, and we can go over your solo if you like."

"Did you bring a violin?"

"I did, in fact."

"Then above all else, I should like to play with you."

Something powerful moved between them. Freya couldn't yet define it, but the idea of playing the violin with Erich sent tingles all through her. She rubbed her arms.

"I should like that as well. For now, let's find ourselves some opponents, shall we?"

As they walked out the door, he nodded to the conductor who held the door. "We shall return and would perhaps like some tea."

"Very good, sir."

"Now tell me, Freya. How are you at whist?"

"I've never lost."

"How intriguing." His smile held challenges and promise and adventure, and she suspected he thought of much more than a simple game of whist.

CHAPTER TWENTY-ONE

THEY ENTERED THE MAIN PARLOR car. People were gathered at tables. Games of cards and backgammon, chess, and checkers were being played. Erich seemed to hesitate at the entrance to the car for a moment and then nodded his head toward the far end. "I knew he'd be here. It's uncanny."

She followed his gaze. "Nicholas." She squinted her eyes. "And Victoria." She turned to him. "Do you remember her? I sat with her at dinner one time."

"I certainly do. I think she was in support of me, no?"

"Oh yes. She most certainly was."

"Shall we join them?"

As they approached, Nicholas waved them closer and then held up his cards. "Whist? We are ready for you."

"Victoria, it's so good to see you again." Freya sat beside her.

"And you, my dear. Miss Winter is it?"

"And how are your children?"

"Wonderful. And how are you . . . both?" Her gaze flicked from Freya to Erich and back.

"We are wonderful as well." Erich sat across from Freya. "It's good to see you again."

Nicholas shuffled the cards and dealt them, filling the air with the smell of peppermint.

"You have a most uncanny pipe, sir." Erich nodded in his direction.

"Yes, peppermint, isn't it?" Freya watched him.

Then Victoria shook her head. "Oh no. It is most definitely sandalwood. Reminds me of my dear husband long since passed."

"And I say it is wood shavings. Sometimes oregano." Erich and Freya exchanged glances, and then he organized his cards.

After organizing a card or two in her hands, she was ready. Erich winked at her, and she thought in that moment that this game of whist might be the most enjoyable of her life. He laid down a ten of hearts. Nicholas a six. But she knew she could keep control if she beat him, so she placed her ace.

Erich's mouth dropped open until Victoria played her king. Then Erich nodded approvingly. Freya kept the lead until they won.

Erich tipped back in his chair and laughed. "You know, she told me she never loses."

They played until the dinner hour, then Freya smiled at their cozy group. "I would love to invite you to come hear me play. I will entertain the dining car in a few moments. Perhaps if you take your dinner there?" She stood, and Erich joined her.

"Oh certainly, dear. I will be there. Nicholas, would you like to accompany me?"

"Yes, but a word of advice first?"

They all paused. His eyes had turned deep and ponderous, and Freya stepped closer to hear what he might have to say.

"Zings are not vhat zey seem. You vill find in zeh end zat zey are much better. And zis man here." Nicholas puffed invisible smoke from his pipe. "Zere is still much to be discovered, isn't zere?"

"Yes, I think so." Freya turned to look up into Erich's face. What would he be thinking in response to Nicholas's words?

But Erich said nothing. He held out his arm and led her back to his car, where she picked up her violin, and then he surprised her by collecting his.

Her heart skipped a couple beats in happiness. "Oh, this is fine news indeed. Will you be performing with me?"

"If you'll have me."

She paused in the walkway and turned to him. "What did you say?"

His eyes turned serious, and he brought one of her hands to his lips. "If . . . you'll have me."

"That's what I thought you said." She wondered if she might sink right into the depths of his soul, as though his gaze alone could swallow her whole. Then she slowly nodded once. "Yes." She laughed, the spell somewhat broken. "Yes, I'd love for you to play with me."

"Excellent." He continued walking. "On both counts."

She breathed out slowly, trying to keep her steps measured and her smile within normal bounds.

They entered the dining car, and when the conductor saw Erich's violin case, he looked like he might faint from ecstasy. Freya would have laughed, but she was instead quite amazed at the man's bowing and simpering gratitude. "We will never forget that you have chosen to grace this humble car with your beautiful sounds."

Erich nodded his head. "Thank you. Now, shall we stand in her usual place?"

"Yes, that would be most excellent."

As soon as they were far enough away, Freya turned to him. "Who are you?"

"Excuse me?" He opened up his case and, with great reverence, lifted out a stunning violin.

"Oh. That is beautiful. Is it one of your father's?"

"His best."

She studied it. "The lines, the grain of the wood." She held her violin next to his. "It looks like it could be a twin of mine."

"Yes. Check the date inside and the insignia."

She tipped the violin to see the signature. "1810. Salzburg. S. W. S."

"The very same as mine." He plucked the strings. "I suspected as much when I first saw it."

"So mine was made by your father?"

"Yes." Their eyes met, and she knew she was on the verge of understanding something important about him, but he wasn't about to reveal it.

"Then your father is one of the best violin craftsmen in all of Europe. My instructor told me so."

"That he was."

"And our violins are arguably the very best ever made."

He laughed. "You are a competitive one, aren't you?"

"No." She plucked her own strings. "Yes."

He laughed again. And she loved this side of Erich. If only they could spend many hours together. She was falling in love with the talented and ever mysterious Erich . . . S?

"And your name—"

He whispered in her ear, so close that her neck filled with delicious goose-flesh. "See if you can keep up with me." Then he burst into a melody of sound, full and rich and using every string, quick and bright and full of energy. She was struck in amazement for many moments before she even remembered that she was supposed to play also.

He laughed again and then shifted into another rising and falling melody.

Freya studied him for a moment and then decided to play off of him in a new rhythm. Her notes came out long and slow and poignant as the backdrop of his flight. And though she wasn't certain what he would play next, she tried to feel the piece, to sense the musical journey he was on and, in a way, predict what he might do. After a time, she picked up her pace somewhat, and he joined her. He teased with a tune, practically begging her to join on the end and continue, which she did, then she did the same back to him. They spun harmonies and wove their melodies up and down the scales. And then, without warning, Erich moved into a well-known country song, and it was so perfect that she almost gasped. The audience clapped and cheered and immediately began to sing along.

She gave him the melody, adding chords and harmony to embellish his notes while the whole car sang in such a boisterous manner.

When they finished the number, they bowed together, and the cheers grew. Her eyes were wide. She could feel the wonder all over her face. But she didn't know what else to say.

And then he nudged her. "Now it's your turn. You lead."

She nodded and turned to the crowd. They were still excited. Many were on their feet. They seemed like they were about ready to start a country dance right there in the dining car.

She laughed, then started into another fast-paced well-known number. Erich tapped his foot and then started dancing around her, his bow in the air, as proficient as any of the *ton* at a ball. She wondered yet again at his background. Who was Erich S?

They played until at last the conductor sent everyone out of the car, leaving Freya and Erich to themselves while he helped the staff to clean up the room.

Freya watched Erich while he carefully put away his instrument, loosened his bow, and closed his case. Then she did the same for hers. "You really are the most remarkable musician I have ever heard." She shook her head. "Will I ever know who you are? You ride in the cars of wealthy clients. You play for the Prince of Wales. You dance like a noble."

His eyebrow rose. "You noticed my dancing?"

"Of course. You circled me." She laughed. "How could I not?"

"I know you saw me. But you *noticed* me as well. That is something completely different."

"You're avoiding my question."

"Was there a question in there somewhere?" He tapped his chin. "Ah, yes. Will you ever know who I am?" His tone was light, fun, teasing, and she fully expected him to laugh it off. But he moved his chair closer. She paused all other thought and watched his face. Was he about to tell her something important? Would she learn enough to unravel his mysteries?

He picked up her hand and brought her knuckles to his lips.

Her immediate response to him tugged a ready smile to her mouth. Then he turned her hands over and ran his fingers over the calluses of her left hand as he had the first time he'd held her hand. "Playing with you, hearing your music, watching your heart shine out your eyes, I know all I could ever need to know to convince me I want you always in my life." His eyes held hope and the smallest insecurity. "I know you. And perhaps that is all that is needed."

"But what if our lives aren't compatible? What if there are expectations? My parents . . . my father's business. They don't want me to play anymore. They said if I'm not chosen by the Maestro, I'm finished playing. Father wants to hand the running of his business over to my husband." As the words came pouring out of her, Freya couldn't do a thing to stop them. She'd kept them tight inside for so long. Once she began to open up, everything had to be known. She hoped in telling him he would give her a solution, that something wonderful would present itself and she would be free of her family's expectations. "And you. I don't know what you do exactly, but you don't want to do all that. You and I, we are meant to play. If I can play for Prince Edward, if the Maestro chooses me, if I earn a spot in the Salzburg Orchestra, then perhaps Father will see that my playing is of use." She stopped talking for a moment. "He won't need to support me. He can let me go . . ."

Erich's eyes seemed troubled. His face closed off, and though he still held her hand, he'd stopped running a finger along her calluses. He at once looked to be a hundred miles away. When he noticed that she'd stopped talking, he patted her hand. "Love will find a way."

Was he talking about their love? Did he love her? He hadn't said so precisely. And for some reason, this mention of love only concerned her further.

"A person must always decide how badly they want something and then, if there are sacrifices to be made, make them. Love will find a way." His face had become inexplicably sad. But then he sat up, released her hand, and said, "I think a good exploration of this train is in order. I, for one, am interested in which cars they've attached this time."

She followed him and then placed a hand on his arm, unsure what to think about his change of demeanor. He seemed the same and yet not. But his words had sunk deep inside. Her whole life she'd always thought that what she wanted most was to play the violin. And now the man she wanted most came with her violin in a nice package if he'd have her. But what about her parents? The business? She'd never cared about her father's work. Should her life be tied into keeping and sustaining the business that had kept them all living comfortably? If only she had been born a son. None of this confusion would be part of her life. She'd have been raised to run the railroad. But she couldn't feel completely satisfied in that, could she? For that scenario erased all music from her life. And what was life without her violin? What was life without Erich?

As she followed Erich out of the car, his silence seemed to match her conflicted heart, and she wondered if he even saw the cars as they meandered through them. She knew she wouldn't remember anything about them.

CHAPTER TWENTY-TWO

THE REMAINING TRAIN RIDE TO Paris had been pleasant. But neither Erich nor Freya brought up anything more about their future, her goals, or even his hopes that they could be together. She wasn't sure what had changed, but there was a new distance between them. And she didn't know what to do about it.

Right before she stepped off the train, he pulled her into his arms and clung to her. His kiss was intense, powerful, and quick. Then he stepped away, walking through another car, leaving her clutching her stomach with one hand, the other clinging to the wall of their corridor.

By the time she also exited the train, he was nowhere to be seen. But she wasn't expecting to see him. Passengers rushed to board behind her. Then she thought she glimpsed Erich boarding a train on a different track. Where would he be going? Perhaps she'd imagined it. A part of her panicked that he wouldn't be on her return trip. What if she never saw him again?

Unsettled, as she searched the train platform, she looked for Lord Bouchet or her grandmother and saw neither. She lifted her satchel and her violin and moved farther out into the crowded Paris station. The crowds closed in around her, and she pushed her way through the jostle and the brushing of other passengers all the way out to the street. There was her grandmother's car, or she assumed. She approached the driver. "Excuse me."

He turned and then smiled. "Miss Winter, your grandmother sent me."

"Thank you."

The driver's kind eyes gave her a measure of comfort. He took her bag and then opened the door for her.

Their drive through Paris was the same as it always was, but she knew it to be her last visit. Perhaps she would come again with her parents. Or . . . did she dare even wonder if she could be with Erich? He'd kissed her.

He said he wanted to be together. Was such a thing possible for them? He seemed odd, like he was waiting for something, as if something was holding him back. She couldn't know. They had one more journey together and then everything would end. One more journey if he made it. She couldn't shake the feeling that he had continued on toward London. What if that last kiss was goodbye?

Her breath shuddered through her.

The streets of Paris were as crowded as ever. She trained her eyes to see what she could of the exposition. A group of people ornately dressed in costume, white faces, and long flowing kimonos walked by.

"A group from the Japanese pavilion." The driver pointed them out. Freya studied them, awed at a culture so different from her own.

At last they arrived in front of her grandmother's townhome. Freya thanked the driver, who placed her bag just inside the door.

For a moment, the home was quiet. Then Givens, the butler, arrived and bowed. "Welcome back, Miss Winter. Your grandmother is in the drawing room."

"Thank you." Her feet moved slowly. She appreciated the ornate woodwork of her grandmother's front entryway. How sad to think Freya would not often be back, if at all. The footman opened the door to the drawing room, and Freya hurried in, suddenly anxious to see her grandmother.

She sat at her tea, a lovely spread of food on a table nearby. Freya's stomach rumbled. "Grandmother." She hurried to her and sat at her side. "It is so good to see you."

"And you, child." She reached for her hands. "How was your travel?"

"Most excellent. I think after all this time, I will miss the train."

"I'd imagine so." She patted her hand, her face seeming strained. "Have some refreshment. I hope this will suffice. I didn't feel up to a full meal at this hour."

"This is perfect. I had dinner on the train." She didn't tell her that she mostly ate small bites and that it was cold, but she really didn't want something heavy to eat. The sandwiches and tea looked just right. "Have you seen much of the exposition?"

"I have a bit. Lady Bouchet and I have discovered that if you go in the early morning, most people are not out yet and you can walk without being encumbered about by people everywhere." She fanned her face.

"What has been interesting?"

"Oh, all of it. We've taken to visiting the national pavilions. She and I don't travel as much as some, not even as much as you." She clucked. "And these pavilions make me feel like I've visited their countries."

"If you could, where might you go?"

She waved her hand. "I'm well past dreams. I learned long ago that dreams are but the silly fancy of a young girl's heart. Practicality and reason rule the day when it comes to real life." A certain intensity reflected in her eyes, and Freya wondered what more she was really trying to say.

After they ate their fill, talking pleasantly of their comings and goings, Grandmother placed her teacup on the table with a certain finality. "We've had further news from your parents."

"Have you?" Freya's stomach twisted.

"Yes." And then her grandmother's lip quivered. She lifted a handkerchief to her face.

"What? What is it? Mother?"

"No, they are well. I'll let you read the letter yourself, but this is the gist of it: Your father has come to the realization that if you could still marry someone like Lord Bouchet, then you could marry someone of his choosing just as well. If he is to pass on his business to your future husband, it may as well be someone who knows the business. He's chosen a man from his own team who already works for him and wishes for you to come home immediately to accept his hand."

"Immediately?" Her hands shook. "Before the concert?"

Her grandmother's hand reached for hers. "That is what he says." She shook her head. "I don't even know what I'll tell Lady Bouchet. We had our hearts set on Lord Bouchet as the perfect match for you." She searched Freya's face. "Will your heart break at his loss? No, but you will miss him, won't you? At any rate, we know nothing about this man your father claims to have chosen, not even his age. The letter is so cryptic. How am I to feel settled at all about your life if we don't even know if the man is agreeable?"

"Dear Grandmother, you are so kind to me. I don't deserve such goodness. But I don't understand. What would Father have me do?"

"He's included tickets for passage on the next train to London. I'm afraid he's quite serious."

Her world tilted. She clutched at the arm of their sofa. "And I still have the tickets to return to Salzburg?"

"You do, but surely you can't think of disobeying. He would be furious. Where would you go, child? What would you do?"

"I can't desert my orchestra, Grandmother. I'm the first-chair violinist. I have solos. They are announcing the winners of grand prizes. I could make the professional orchestra, not to mention I have one more week of my program to finish." A determination like she'd never known tightened inside of her. "No."

"No?" Grandmother's eyes seemed to hold a glimmer of hope. "Can one just say no?"

"I don't know, but I'm saying it."

"There's further news."

Freya nodded, swallowing. "Let's have the lot of it then, so that I might consider my situation."

"As I say, you are to come, to marry this man who he does not even name. This new man would receive your dowry and eventually the lot of your father's business and your hand in marriage. He'd better be worthy of you." She dabbed her eyes again. "If you do not do as he says, you are without dowry or means and are cut off from any inheritance."

Her face clenched, and tears fell without her even knowing at first. "But why? Why should he care so much? He doesn't need me."

"I believe he does. Railroads aren't the great investment they once were. He was certain when they'd discovered gas that it would be the wave of the future, but he has no means of funding all the exploration and research it would take to do that. He needed another partner and investor."

Freya waited to understand how this had anything to do with her.

"You and your dowry are part of that bargain."

Freya closed her eyes. "I see." She thought for many minutes, memories whirling around in her mind. Then she shook her head. "I don't care about his timing . . . his demands that I return right now before the concert . . . ridiculous. But I will consider doing as he says *after* I complete my obligations, after the ball, and after I finish my program." She would look for any and all avenues of escape from the life her father had chosen, but if she had no other means, then she had no other means. She would return and do as he said. Though she felt the very jaws of a life of misery opening up to swallow her, she patted her grandmother's hand that was clutching her forearm. "Lord Bouchet is to be my date to the ball, did you know?"

"I didn't know." She studied her face. "Are you certain? Your father is not used to being defied. If you are cut off, darling, you don't have any way to care for yourself. You cannot simply live in Salzburg by yourself. How will you eat? I could send you something from time to time, but you know I cannot defy your father either."

"I'm certain. To you, I might seem like a woman without options, but to me, I am a woman who has a bargaining chip. I just learned how much he needs me. If I cannot live in Salzburg," she sighed, "I will at least finish my experience in Salzburg." She choked on the last word. Then she stood. "Thank you, Grandmother. I think I'll retire."

"Certainly, dear. Whatever you wish."

Freya ran from the room.

CHAPTER
TWENTY-THREE

THOUGH SHE'D TRIED TO SOUND strong to her grandmother, the sobs that stole her breath and choked through her now that she was alone were anything but strong. Despair threatened as each minute passed. Sleep did not come for many hours. She lay in the dark, trying to accept that if something rather miraculous didn't occur, she might soon be marrying a man she'd never even met before. How could that be? She supposed she had known it was coming. But she had held out hope.

Could she still play for Prince Edward? Undoubtedly. Even her father wouldn't dare argue with that. If the royal house summoned her, she would no doubt go.

She had curled into a ball, and yet sleep had still not come hours later while she fought off despair. But even as the early hours of the morning turned from a hazy glow into the bright sun at the horizon, she could see little reason to resist the dark tugs at her heart, the inclination to never leave her bed.

But she must resist, or she might regret missing the concert and ball for the rest of her life, especially if they were to be her last moments with an orchestra. By force of will, she arose early, rang for her maid, and dressed. While watching the maid work on her hair, she decided to get out, to move one foot in front of the other. "Could someone accompany me to the exposition?"

The maid curtseyed. "Certainly. I'll send a footman to the front door."

"Thank you. And ask for the car?"

"Yes, miss."

Freya hadn't spoken with her grandmother of today's plans but left her a note and hoped she would understand Freya's liberties. If Freya were to spend an entire day in Paris, defying her father before boarding the train back to Salzburg, she would need some distraction, without the demands of conversation. Already her heart was pounding at the thought that her father was expecting her to board a train in just a few hours and return home to London. What would he do when she never stepped off the arriving train?

The car stopped in front of a long walk of the different pavilions of nations. "I'd like to get out here."

The footman opened her door and then walked behind her. She was happy to see he was almost not with her at all. She needed time to think. Time to accept her new life. The pain of her father's demands, an unknown future rolling out in front of her, was almost so distracting that she couldn't see the amazing sights around her.

Excited, happy faces surrounded her, and their energy lifted her spirits somewhat. People jostled her right and left. The whole surrounding was much more crowded than last time. Then a woman ran into a man, dumping all the contents of her cup full of lemonade ice. They talked excitedly together for a moment, and Freya enjoyed their energy.

Freya laughed and turned away so as not to add embarrassment to the scene. She walked toward the Grand Palais. Good artwork by talented artists always lifted her spirits. The artwork was impressive, and every piece was well done, she supposed, but she was not as yet touched until she passed by a painting of a woman surrounded by lilies on the edge of water. She paused a moment. Luc Paquet. Her grandmother would love this painting, and Freya wished to lose herself in the peaceful scene. But she moved on. How strange to defy one's parents. Was she alone in the world? Left to fend for herself? Surely not . . . not yet. If things didn't change, she would return, cater to her father's wishes. Her feet dragged slower as she left the Grand Palais.

She stepped up to a smaller pavilion, a white building with a dome. It looked like it might be from Greece, but as she entered, a large flag of the United States of America at the front welcomed her. Mild curiosity about the United States nudged her inside to investigate further. She hardly saw even the railway and oil exhibits as she wandered through. Too distracted to become interested, she was about to leave when her attention was caught by a statuette in the back corner. A plaque read, "The Exhibit of American Negroes." A tall man in the statue looked distinguished, determined. She stepped closer. Frederick Douglas. She knew nothing about him. *Freed slave.*

Goodness.

She ran her fingers along his clothes, his face. The statue didn't show the color of his skin. She imagined his to be of the deepest brown. She kept walking and immediately became lost to the stories being told. The purpose of the exhibit was to honor the lives of the Black Americans and their successes. She studied a glass case that featured four thick volumes of patents owned by Black Americans. Their stories were fascinating. They had been slaves or their parents were slaves or their grandparents. To rise from such a beginning . . . and they were making lives for themselves, leading universities in research.

She entered a section of photographs. Five hundred images stretched before her on the wall. A family in one, standing in front of their homestead, acres of plantation behind, now owners of it all. A man in the next holding a diploma. A church in Philadelphia, the first church to be owned by a Black American. On and on the pictures went. She looked at each one. Their lives were celebrated, some with very public success, some private, some simple and others outstanding, but each one noteworthy. What a transformation in each soul. She tried to imagine if she had been a slave, to imagine if her parents were slaves, if she remembered the life of a slave in her own lifetime, how would that change things? And then to think, to rise from those situations to become successful. Was the climate in America even friendly for them now? How would it be to overcome that kind of societal thinking? She knew her own situation held only the tiniest challenges in comparison to the people featured in the exhibit. A measure of grim determination began to settle inside. Each story seemed to call out to her, "*You can.*" The man who stood, clutching a wife at his side, grinning broadly for the camera whispered, "You can." She turned in a circle hearing two words from every situation. "You. Can."

By the time she'd finished, Freya felt changed. The wise and oldest teacher, perspective, had left its mark on her heart, and she wanted to salute Frederick Douglas on her way out. When she stepped back out onto the walkway, she knew she was finished touring for the day. She'd made the right choice to go to Salzburg instead of to return home. Beyond performing, she hoped the way would light itself because she had no new ideas. Nothing had changed in her situation to merit any hope. Only one very clear idea still sounded in her heart. *There might as yet be a way. You can.*

She said little to her grandmother the rest of the afternoon, and when it came time to once again board the train Sunday morning, she kissed her cheek. "Will you be coming to watch my performances?"

"Yes, of course. But I wouldn't expect your parents."

She shook her head. "I know. Thank you, Grandmother."

"Are you . . . well?"

"I am well." Freya stepped outside the door, climbed back in the car, and waved over her shoulder until she could no longer see her stout yet stately grandmother waving from her front doorway. The next time she would see her, Freya would be wearing concert attire in the great hall filled with all the monarchs of Europe.

Soon the car dropped her off and she walked up the steps and into the train station. Erich was once again on the platform to meet her. He was not carrying a bag, and his eyes looked more tired than she'd seen them before.

"Hello!" She approached with a smile and embraced him. For a moment, she imagined they were together, officially, and he would swing her around and kiss her for all to see.

Then he pulled a hand from behind his back, holding flowers. "For you."

"Edelweiss." She lifted the small bouquet of white from his hands. Her heart tore at the symbolism, at the message that sacrifice was required. "Did you climb the mountain peaks to get these for me?" Would she soon be telling him that she was to be married to another? That she herself had made no climb for edelweiss? In answer to her rising despair, the words *you can* repeated.

He laughed. "In a way, yes." The flash of grim determination in his own eyes matched her feelings from earlier, and she looked twice before it passed. Then he bowed over her hand. "Might I escort you inside?"

"Certainly." Some of the tightness in her chest lessened. His hair fell into his face for a moment. His boyish dishevel brought a growing grin. "Seeing you is just what I need right now."

"And seeing you is always what I need." He led her inside the train and to the nearest car with group seating. He sat next to her. "Now you must tell me all about Paris this weekend."

"Did you not see it yourself?"

"Unfortunately, I did not."

"What do you do on these trips you make so often?"

He dipped his head. "I usually come to play for my patrons."

"And this time?"

"This time." He looked away and seemed reluctant to speak. When she peered closer at him, a slight pink to his cheeks made her smile. He reached for her hand. "When I came from Salzburg this last time, I came only for you."

She widened her eyes. "You did?" She could not even stop the pleased smile that spread across her face. "You left Salzburg and traveled . . . for me? All the way to Paris?"

"Yes, I did. And today I am here because someone had to bring you the edelweiss."

She lifted it again to peer at the soft white flowers. "I have always loved edelweiss." She leaned back in her chair. "Paris was not as enjoyable."

"Not quite the same as riding the Grande Roue de Paris?"

"Nothing like being with you." She opened her mouth to tell him her terrible news, but no words would form. She couldn't think of how she would tell him that her hand had been promised to another. She would force the words to leave her lips before their arrival in Salzburg. Even though she was determined to find another solution, it was only right to tell him of the situation. But until then, she'd live in happiness for a few hours longer.

She ran a hand down her arm. "Do you want to go in one of our compartments? I think it would be warmer."

He turned to peer out the window, and she followed his gaze. "Is that snow?" he asked, incredulous. Flurries fell, barely visible as they sped past.

"I had so hoped that we might be ready for spring."

"Happily, the steam warms the cars as well as cooks our food. If not, we'd have a real danger of freezing in here, like those cold ice-block cars."

She didn't like the sound of any idea that would make her colder, and she stood. "Mine is just down that passageway, so it must be the closest."

As soon as they stepped inside her compartment, she felt much warmer. "Oh, this is just the thing." She sat on a bench next to the window. The compartment had two benches facing opposite one another with a window at their side. The snow was falling much faster now, and the flakes looked large. "I would say that is a magical sight if I didn't know how cold it was outside."

Erich reached for two blankets above them and sat close at her side. "And now we have the entire journey to be together."

As she sat shoulder to shoulder with this wonderful but mysterious man, she wanted nothing more than to be with him forever, but for now, she'd settle to learn more about him. "Tell me something you've never told anyone."

He hummed. "I've already said so many things to you I've never said to anyone else. But let's see."

The snow fell faster and thicker, and the area outside became covered in a white blanket the closer they moved to Salzburg.

"I've always wondered if I might become more than a musician someday." His voice was quiet, determined.

"I don't understand."

"Like your father, for example. I admire what he does. I've always wondered if I might have what it takes to do something like he's done."

Her heart nearly leapt out of her chest. It pounded so quickly for a moment. "Father has built a successful business, but he has no time for anything else." She knew it would physically hurt Erich not to play, not to perform. She knew because it was physically hurting her to even think about being prevented from performing.

He nodded. "He might not have wished to, up to this point. I don't know, but I would presume if he wished to do more, he would have. From what I've seen of business, there are different levels of involvement possible. But what about you? What's something you've never told anyone else?"

"I'm afraid of high places."

He turned to her. "What? But the *Grande Roue*!"

Amazingly, she'd been fine. "Yes. I thought I would be petrified. But the other thing I've never told anyone is that I have a cure for whatever ails me."

"You do?"

"Yes." Then she lost her courage. Shyness overtaking her words for a moment, she stared out at the falling snow.

"What is your cure?" His gentle voice drew her eyes to his.

She swallowed twice before braving her admission. "You. You're my cure. When we are together, nothing else in the world could possibly go wrong."

He reached over and unpinned her hat. Then he placed it on the bench across from them.

She didn't even care that her hair must look a sight, because she forgot everything but him as he ran the back of his hand down the side of her face. His eyes filled her with the love she saw in them. Then slowly, carefully, he placed his lips over hers. "I won't let anything happen to you."

She nodded in the unrealistic hope that he could actually make such a promise. She pushed away all thoughts that attempted to interrupt her happiness and just drank in his confident declaration. Perhaps. Perhaps if she just stayed with him, everything else in her life really would work out.

She laced their fingers together. "Tell me three things that make you unimaginably happy."

His grin grew so large she had to laugh in pure delight. "Do you know you have the best smile?"

She couldn't even feel shy at so bold a statement.

"And that is what I most admired about you that first day on the train." He grinned. "But the very first thing I *noticed* about you was this gentle, focused concentration and the slight pucker to your lips while you stared at the train as though you might not ever board."

"I forgot you notice I pucker my lips." The thought was pleasant, that he was looking, and she didn't try to stop the gentle warmth to her face.

"You mean for things other than kissing?"

She gave his arm a gentle push. "Oh you. Stop. Yes. For other things."

"Another thing that makes me happy is hearing you play the violin. When you play, I quite forget myself."

Her eyes widened.

"You are the most beautiful when you play." His expression turned almost wistful. "You have this exquisite concentration, this look of supreme happiness as though . . ." He paused for a moment. "As though you are about to discover a long-awaited dream." He turned to her. "You are meant to play, as if your very soul longs for your violin."

"It does." A tear dropped from her eyes. She hadn't even known she was welling up. His handkerchief was in her hand before she could reach for one. "Thank you."

"I'm sorry to cause distress."

"You haven't. No. You are the one to make my distress disappear. I dread the moment I must once again leave this train. Oh, that we could be stuck here forever."

"I would never complain of such a thing." He tapped her on the nose.

The compartment filled with the smell of peppermint. She immediately looked around.

He sat up. "Are you looking for Nicholas?"

"Yes. I am smelling his pipe."

"Rosemary and oregano?"

"No, peppermint."

He shook his head. "Uncanny."

A shadow moved past their door, but neither jumped up to see if it really was Nicholas. Freya was too warm and happy. "Now, what else makes you happy?"

"Easy. You. You. You."

She shook her head. "I love hearing that. What else?"

"The perfect vibrations when my bow sits just right on a string."

"Mmm. Yes." How could she have met such a man? "What else?"

"When a student will begin to understand what I'm trying to show them about their playing, and they start to sound like a maestro." He tucked a hair behind her ear. "Like you."

At mention of the word *maestro*, she remembered how badly she had wanted the Maestro to choose her. What did it matter now? "We should play."

"Yes. That's the next thing that makes me . . . how did you say it? Unimaginably happy?"

"Yes."

"Creating music with you makes me unimaginably happy. I imagine all pursuits with you would do the same." He lifted her fingers in his hand. "Have you given much thought to the miracle of our meeting?"

"Every day. Is it real or just some imagined moments on a train?" She shrugged.

"What we have is the most real I've ever felt." He stood and reached for her hand, pulling her to her feet. His arms went around her back, and he held her close as if the two of them were the center of everything important. His face was warm, his eyes full of too many emotions to count. Then he dipped his head, his soft lips finding her ready ones, capturing them, as he pressed his mouth to hers, asking, pleading, pulling all her resistance away. "I love you," he mumbled against her lips.

She smiled. "I love you too."

A loud screeching interrupted them, and a jerking pressure threw them back on their bench. She clutched at his arm as a long, stopping motion pressed her against the seat back. "What's happening?"

"I don't know. Looks like an emergency stop." They peered out the window to a receding terrain.

"We're up high." She swallowed and looked away. "I never notice how high usually."

"Nor I. There's a different feeling about the height when screeching to a halt." He pulled out his pocket watch. "We are on time so far, set to arrive as usual."

A nervous flutter began in her stomach, the slightest hint of worry that she tried to tamp out. "I have our largest concert and event tomorrow, the whole purpose of me attending."

He checked something out the window. She refused to look again. It brought on an ache to her bones and her usual fear of heights.

Erich pointed out the window. "The snow is deep, and it keeps falling."

The train continued its long, halting motion. It was much slower now but still moving, and then they were both thrown back against their seat again. The train stopped.

"What could have happened?" Freya rested a hand on his arm.

"I think we hit snow."

CHAPTER TWENTY-FOUR

SNOWED IN.

A conductor knocked on their door. When Erich slid it open, a man wheeled in a tea cart. "We have hot tea or coffee."

"What has happened?" Freya accepted a cup.

"We hit a snowdrift."

She gasped.

The conductor adjusted the items on his cart, getting a cup ready for Erich. "This happens. It is nothing to be concerned over. If our team cannot dig us out, then another will come. In the meantime, we shall stay warm." The conductor poured hot water into her cup and placed a tea strainer inside.

"Thank you." She placed her hands on each side of the cup. She wasn't cold, not yet. But the warmth in the cup brought her a sense of comfort.

When the conductor left, Erich turned to her. "Except for meeting you, I would say this drift is the most providential thing to ever happen to me."

She laughed. "I quite agree."

He sat back beside her and pulled his blanket up around him. "Now you must tell me three things that make you unimaginably happy."

She settled against him, and they talked for hours. The train did not move, and they didn't either. It seemed every topic was important, and every idea needed to be discussed.

The sky began to darken, and the conductor returned with a food cart. "We have closed the dining car for this evening. It is best to stay here where it will be the warmest." He lifted a table from the wall to hold filled plates in front of them.

"What is the news?" Erich checked his watch again.

The gas lights in their compartment flickered.

The conductor adjusted their food and set out the linens. "It is a rather large snowdrift. The teams are out digging through the snow, but it might take a while. Are you comfortable for the night?" His eyes flicked from one to the other. "And are you willing to let others join you?"

Freya nodded. "If others need a compartment, certainly."

"Do you know if my compartment has extra blankets and the things that this one does?" Erich said.

"I'm certain it would."

They finished their meal. The conductor took their tray, and Freya dozed with her head on Erich's shoulder.

When she awoke, he shifted, and she sat up.

"Tell me what you know about the Maestro," he requested.

She blinked to clear her mind, then sighed. "What is there to tell? I've never seen him. Now that we are delayed, I may never play for him. My chances of being chosen by the Maestro to be his student have now dwindled to nothing." Not to mention that she might have to give up that chance anyway and marry someone of her father's choosing. Was there no way around such a life? Would her father truly not see that a life as a violinist was her only option of happiness? An old, resilient, tiny feather of hope suggested that perhaps, perhaps if she were good enough, if she won enough awards and a professional position, then she would be acceptable to her father just as she was and he could move forward with his business without regards to what she did. The other option sat beside her. Would she leave her father, her dowry, and any responsibility for the railroad to just be with Erich if he would have her?

Erich watched her.

She sighed, then continued. "I've respected him for years. I love his compositions. Every time he writes a new one, my instructor knows to get it because I wish to play everything he writes. It has been my dream for as long as I've known of him to one day have the opportunity to be his pupil and to play with him." Her heart sped up just thinking about him.

"And now?"

"How could you know my thoughts have changed?"

"Have they?" He studied her with unusual intensity.

"I'm not certain they've changed. I would still love to learn from him and to know him." She scoffed. "To *see* him once, honestly. Everyone else has been called back to play for him, some more than once. Except me. But I digress." She toyed with her blanket. "I compare him to you in my mind."

His eyes widened, and he tried to hide a laugh. "To me? And how do I compare to the much-applauded Salzburg Maestro?"

"I considered our time playing together and the things you taught me. Some of it was not easy to hear. But when I was able to apply your suggestions to my playing, it made all the difference. And the things you pointed out were higher-level critiques. I listened to the others' comments about the Maestro's critiques, and I realized that I had already mastered much of what they were working on." She stopped. "I don't mean I've truly *mastered* everything, but I only felt that the suggestions were ones I've worked on before . . ." She felt so comfortable. Words came with ease when talking to Erich, and she certainly didn't want to come across as overly confident or prideful.

"I understand. And I suspect you are correct. You may be open with me." His tone sounded professional. He had returned somewhat to the man who had first listened to her play, who had kept his distance. She watched him, wondering what was on his mind.

"I've asked the conductor to bring my violin. Let's play. If you won't be meeting with the Maestro before your performance, perhaps we can do something now to ensure you are prepared."

She sat up straighter. "I'd like that."

Her violin was out of its case and in her arms in but a few swift movements. She plucked her strings and tuned it by ear.

"Excellent."

She stood in front of him in the center of their compartment. He sat. "Play your audition piece for the Salzburg Orchestra."

"I've already auditioned."

"Please play that first." He added *please*, but he was very much in professor mode, and so she responded as a student and tried to forget that this man had recently kissed her, that she was falling in love with him, and that she might never have him. She played her piece, pleased that she still played it as well as she had prepared for the audition.

He nodded. "And is that how you played for your audition?"

"Yes, exactly like that. I was feeling confident from our last time we played together." She blushed, thinking again on their moments when their instruments felt like one. It had been one of the most romantic experiences of her life.

"I see no reason why you haven't secured a spot in the orchestra."

She widened her eyes. "Do you think so?"

"Yes. Now, please play your solo piece."

"With pleasure. I was disappointed we ran out of time for that on our last train ride." She closed her eyes to gather her thoughts, then played from her heart. It was a difficult piece and would stand out while the entire orchestra played a softer buildup behind her notes. It was high and pleading and strong.

When she finished, he nodded and stood. "Play it again. I will stop you."

She began. After one measure, he held up a hand. "Stop." Then he worked through something very small in that measure. Weeks ago, Freya would have complained about focusing on a detail she considered insignificant, but this time, she knew better. She remembered what the seemingly small changes had done for her playing. She meticulously worked through every suggestion. Once past the first measure, he stopped her again on the eighth. This would be a long session, but she would love every second of it.

By the time they had gone through the piece section by section, he sat back down. And then he smiled. "That was exhilarating."

She laughed. "Was it? I'm exhausted."

"I imagine you are. But I've never . . . You are an exceptional student. I could never have worked a piece like that with anyone else. Now, play it one more time, start to finish, so that I might enjoy your playing. Let's see if the changes have lingered." His manner and tone were relaxed, but she knew she was to play it precisely how they had just worked.

She started on her opening note, and his eyes closed, and his smile grew, and her heart went out to him. She played her notes just as he'd suggested and sent them to him. In gratitude for his time and in love for him, she played her piece for him, until, when she had finished, she was well and truly exhausted, her emotions spent.

And to her great amazement, he dabbed at his eyes. "That was, as I have said, exceptional. Thank you."

She blinked, then curtseyed. "You are the Maestro."

He choked. "Pardon me?"

"I care not if I meet him now. No matter who he is or how renowned, be him English, French, or German, old and grizzled or a young paragon, I have learned from the true Maestro on this train. Thank you."

He didn't speak for many moments, just watched her face, stared into her soul. Then the corner of his mouth tugged up. "Shall we have some fun?"

"Absolutely." She stepped back toward the door to give him room.

He stood beside her, and they played. They picked a common tune to start from, and then each improvised and made harmony and complemented the other's playing over and over again. Until the last light in the sky sank beneath the horizon and the soft flakes still falling were invisible to the eye, their notes lifted to the heavens. When at last they finished, tears of joy streamed down Freya's face.

And then loud applause sounded from the corridor and from the rooms to their sides.

"What?" Freya moved to the door and slid it open.

The corridor was crowded with passengers. All down the row, heads poked out of their doorways. And people stood clapping and cheering for the playing.

Erich joined her in the doorway, and then they both dipped their heads in a sort of bow.

Freya waved. "Thank you. This is all so kind."

When they at last closed the doors, she didn't know what more to say to him. She'd never felt anything so powerful as she did while playing with Erich. They were one in every way. He was the man of her heart, the hope of all her dreams. How would she ever part from him?

In that moment, she made a decision, a bold, brave choice.

She wouldn't.

CHAPTER TWENTY-FIVE

THE NEXT MORNING, ONCE SHE'D washed up, had some breakfast, and cleaned up the bedding in her compartment, Erich returned. His grinning face at her doorway made her laugh again even though she was a bit worried that the train had not started moving yet.

"How did you sleep?" His grin was tired, slightly lazy, comfortable looking, and Freya realized she could become accustomed to just such a look every day of her life from just such a man.

"I've never had a better sleep." She rocked back and forth from toes to heels, a sudden happy energy just at seeing his face making her blissful, more delighted than she'd been in a long time.

His grin turned more sincere, full of purpose. "I admit I enjoy our time together, stuck here with you, although last night when I returned to my compartment, I was a bit lonely."

She felt her mouth drop open and her cheeks burn.

He laughed with his belly and pulled her close, their breath intermingling for a moment. "I wish to be with you always."

Her breath came faster, her lips close to his, so close.

Then he took her hand in his. "Come. Walk with me."

"Yes. I need to stretch my legs. Have they attached the car with the windows on the ceiling?"

"I don't know yet." He swung their hands together. "Let's find out."

They walked the length of the train, not seeing any observation cars, but when they reached the caboose, Erich stepped outside onto the back platform. The freshness of the chill in the air felt exhilarating. The sun had risen in the blue sky. The snow glistened like gems in the reflected light, and the track stretched out behind them.

Her determination from last night filled her with courage. She cleared her throat and turned to Erich. "My father has recently insisted that I leave professional violin behind me and marry a man of his choosing so that this man can run my father's business." She hurried to get all the words out before her voice shook. "I would be a great heiress. I have an extraordinarily large dowry. But I could no sooner live without the violin than I could my own soul. I thought that if I won great accolades, he would change his mind, but he has said that even accolades don't matter to him, not any longer. I can see that a summons from the Prince will not budge his stubborn decision. He commanded me to return home at once, but I traveled here in defiance to that request. And today, I have decided not to return to him at all. If I have to live in poverty, I will do it. If I have to let him down, I will do it. I cannot live without music any more than I could without food." She breathed out. Nor could she live without Erich. She hoped with all her being that he wanted her forever like he'd said.

Erich didn't seem as alarmed as she predicted. He handed her his handkerchief.

She realized her cheeks were wet with tears. "Goodness. Thank you."

"You are a woman of great courage. Do you see those tears?" He indicated his handkerchief.

She nodded.

"Think of the pain and sadness in your life, the loneliness, the years of chasing your dream, the demands of your father."

She dabbed at her eyes again.

"Now, simply let them go. Send that handkerchief out over the wind. You are free. And I will never let you feel those sorrows again."

Her eyes widened. She turned to face the back of the track.

The train started moving in a jerking motion.

Erich immediately moved to stand behind her. With his arms around her, holding her steady, he spoke in her ear. "This is perfect. As the handkerchief moves away behind us, we will move on together. I love you, Freya."

"I love you too!" She wanted to shout the words out over the valley that stretched out behind them, their rise increasing, the incline growing steeper as the train sped up, and she not feeling one ounce of fear. For one moment, she clung to her sorrows and worries, and then she threw his handkerchief into the air and watched it blow away in the wind. The train picked up speed until the white, fluttering memory was out of sight.

Then she turned to him. Freedom surged through her.

He pulled her into his arms and kissed her, this time with a firm resolve that made her cling to him, his mouth promising things his words had not yet spoken. She felt their power flow into her stomach and tingle through her.

She and Erich made their way back to her compartment in a dream. A passing conductor told them all cars were open for entertainment or food. They spent the rest of the day at great leisure. A huge peace had come over Freya, a new surety in her life she had never known. Finally at one with another person, she recognized the loneliness of her life. Her past life. The life she had released over the valley.

And now, she had nothing but hope for her future.

When the train at last pulled into the Salzburg station, it felt completely odd to say goodbye to Erich. She turned to him. "Can we see your father's shop?"

His eyebrows rose.

"And Mozart's home."

"Only the most serious of responsibilities would compel me to deny such a delightful request. Might we visit the day after the concert and ball? Tomorrow?"

"Will I see you?"

"Yes. You can count on seeing me." His eyes said *forever.*

She nodded. "Then this is goodbye until the concert?"

"I will be there."

"Where will you be sitting? I want to find you in the audience."

"You'll see me. I'll make certain of it."

She studied his face, memorizing every line, every expression.

Then he raised her hand to his lips. "Until then." He bowed and left her at the line of hired hacks that would take her back to the boarding house.

But she didn't want to return just yet. She had little reason to. It would be many hours before she needed to dress for the concert, so she told the driver, "Could you take me to the home of Mozart?"

"Certainly, miss. Are you looking for his birthplace, his childhood home?"

"Yes. And I cannot go in. So perhaps you could simply wait while I look?"

He nodded, taking the horse-drawn carriage away from the train station. "If you like, I can give you more of a tour. Are you interested in the musical history of Salzburg?"

"Very much so. Particularly in the violin makers."

"Oh, we have the very best violin maker in the world here. Have you heard of the Schumann violins?"

"Schumann. I have, yes." The S stood for Schumann. Erich Schumann.

"I will show you their shop. And I will tell you their secrets. If you ever come across a Schumann violin with simply the initials, S. W. S., it is an original from the man himself, Herr Wolfgang Schumann. That violin would be worth something indeed."

"Is that so?" The soft sigh that escaped carried a burst of happiness out over the wind. She already knew she had an original violin from Erich's father, but hearing of its worth from this stranger was somehow additionally gratifying. Even more precious was the knowledge that her violin and Erich's were twins of each other.

"And here on the right is Mozart's birthplace, his humble home for twenty-five years of his life. The Haugenauer House, number nine. It's up there on the third floor. Later he moved to Marktplatz Square, but this was where he spent his youth."

She stepped out of the car. "A moment, if you don't mind."

"Take your time."

She paused in front of the edifice, walked the cobblestone path, soaked in the very air, and then entered the carriage once again.

"Is that all you wanted?"

"That's all." She smiled. "I'll be back."

"Shall we drive by the Schumann violin shop now?"

"Yes." The word came out in a breathy whisper. The birthplace of her violin meant more to her than the birthplace of one of the greatest violinists. As they approached the shop, she marveled at the old family crest hanging over the doorway from an upper street sign. The familiar double S weaving together with a W, the very initials she had on the inside of her violin, seemed to call out in welcome. "I'd like to go in. I won't be long."

"Take your time. I'll be waiting right here unless you tell me otherwise."

She slipped out of the carriage, her violin in hand, and stepped into the shop. The place was quiet. A few customers browsed through a row of instruments on the wall. Violins on the top shelf, violas, and even cellos lined one wall.

She deeply breathed in the smell of wood and smiled. The shop smelled like Erich.

"And you are a musician yourself." A young man approached.

"How could you tell?"

"I could point out your instrument, but it's more than that."

Freya glanced down at her case. "I forget I even have this. It's just always there." She laughed.

"But it's the way you smiled just now. You love the smell of the wood."

"And the rosin. And right now, there's a hint of a newly strung bow as well."

"Ah, a true lover of the craft. You're correct, you know. They've just strung some new bows today in the back."

She nodded and then moved to walk the perimeter. "Might I look around?"

"Certainly. Let me know if I can do anything for you."

"Thank you." She walked toward old photographs on the wall.

She recognized Erich immediately in a picture of a young child with his father. So much of Erich smiled back at her in his father's face that she almost reached her finger up to touch the photograph. She grinned. Young Erich held a tiny violin and a bow and stood by his father. The look on his face said he'd much rather be playing the violin than posing for that picture.

She laughed at his adorable face. Then she turned one time in full circle, taking in the shop before she left again out the front door.

When she stepped back inside her hired carriage, the driver turned. "Find what you're looking for?"

"Yes, I have." Then she gave him the address of the boarding house.

"Oh, are you one of the students who will be playing at the concert tonight?"

"I am."

"My wife and I will be there. We never miss it. This year is special, isn't it? We'll be in the back rows, far from the royalty, but in the same room, mind you."

"Yes, this year they've invited all the monarchs in Europe. I am from England, and my own Prince Edward will be there."

"That's something. Well, best of luck to you and your orchestra."

"Thank you."

They pulled in front of her boarding house, and she paid him before hopping out. "Perhaps I'll see you there. If not, thank you for the ride today."

"You're welcome, miss."

CHAPTER TWENTY-SIX

SHE ENTERED THE GREAT HALL where they were to play, her head held high. The students were to make their way to the stage first. The student orchestra would be opening the event with three of their numbers. Their group was one of the first to arrive.

Gertie practically bounced beside her. "Is this really happening?"

"I think so." Freya smiled, secretly thrilled at her scheming. What would Gertie do when she saw Lord Bouchet? And he her? He had said he'd come. He would be there. And her grandmother. And Erich. She smiled. None of this would matter much to her without him.

They took their seats on the stage. Her black gown flowed around her. She held her violin upright on her lap, her bow in the other hand.

Eliza beside her turned, and Freya looked away, but Eliza tapped her shoulder and smiled. She was remarkably pretty with happiness shining from her face instead of her usual frown. "I'm sorry, Freya. I've had a hard time expecting one thing and then always being second to you . . . except once." She looked away and then back. "But what I want to say is congratulations. You deserve this spot. Your playing is beautiful."

"What? Wow, thank you." Freya wasn't sure what to think of this transformation, but she was happy to have the discord between them at an end.

"You're welcome. I wanted you to know. I don't mind being second if it's to you."

Freya switched hands and held her violin and bow with one so that she could rest an arm across Eliza's shoulders. "I appreciate that. I wish you the best today and in all your pursuits as a musician."

"Thank you."

Every student in the orchestra stood as the monarchs from each nation entered. They were shown to their seats in the upper boxes that surrounded the second level above the stage. Freya smiled and caught the eye of Prince Edward when he entered his box. He nodded his head, and she grinned.

"Did you see that?" Eliza whispered. "Did he nod at you?"

"Could have been at all of us."

"That's so exciting!"

The back doors opened, and the rest of their audience poured into the great hall.

The students sat, and soon the auditorium's three levels were filled with the happy chatter of an audience. Freya drank everything in. She experienced no sense of fear, only wild exhilaration to be able to play for so many. For one in particular. Erich. She hadn't yet seen him. But he told her he'd make himself known, so she wasn't concerned yet.

The master of ceremonies for the event stood at the front and welcomed everyone to the concert. As he listed every notable and royal member in the house, Freya's mind wandered. What would her father think if he were to see such an elevated audience? Though a part of her would always wish he would be proud of what she had accomplished, it couldn't matter anymore. That thought made her sit taller in her chair. She wished for a way to support him in his work, but for now, such things were not possible. Perhaps one day they would be.

This was a day to chase her dreams. When it was time, she stood and played a long and true A for her orchestra. They responded, and the brief notes to ensure they were in tune centered her heart. She was ready.

"And now, to open our number, we have a special announcement. The Student Salzburg Orchestra will have the great honor of being conducted by Erich Schumann."

Her heart hammered inside with shock, then pleased surprise. Erich? He would conduct? Thunderous applause sounded, and she almost forgot to stand as he approached. His face was a mask; his professionality had returned, but in his eyes a thousand sparkles beamed at her. He held out his hand, bowed his head to her, and whispered, "Surprise."

She almost snorted but instead kept her smile from wiggling to more than something placid and nodded her head. "Yes."

He winked and made his way to the conductor's stand while she prepared herself to play as they never had before.

When it came time for her solo, their eyes connected, then his closed, and she began. And if it were possible, she was transported back to their compartment on the train. Every note was a tribute to him, every feeling sent out in his direction. The sounds of the orchestra behind her filled her with strength. When she was finished, the one final note lingered until Erich directed her to move on. The audience responded with roaring applause. She sat again, and the piece continued. When Erich's arms dropped, signaling they were finished, the audience jumped to its feet, clapping and cheering again.

Erich bowed, and he indicated to her with a hand. She stood and bowed to greater clapping, and then the whole orchestra stood and bowed.

Freya felt at home. What could be more perfect than this moment?

They played two more pieces to an equally exuberant crowd. And then it was time to announce the awards and those who made the Salzburg Orchestra. The Maestro himself would announce his new pupil and do a demonstration.

Erich left the stage without a further glance in her direction.

She couldn't believe he had conducted. How had such a thing come about?

The master of ceremonies returned to the front. "And now, if you will indulge our students, we have some awards to hand out." He went on to explain all their hard work, how they were chosen from amongst the best in their countries, and how these awards were given to those who would have an opportunity to keep playing at a professional level. He started with an award for every instrument. She would not be receiving anything for violin. The first chair was exempt from individual instrument awards in an effort to recognize others.

Freya was pleased that both Gertie and Daphne had won something. Frank also won an award, and Henry and Tobias received honorable mention. She cheered for her friends.

"And now, the award for most outstanding musician. This award goes to the student who played with the most proficiency, but this student also demonstrated the most significant effort. Many of our students have talent, but the most accomplished among us have learned to couple that talent with work and energy. This student exemplified both, as well as the true heart of a musician. Miss Freya Winter."

She was gratified to hear the most enthusiastic applause came from her fellow students. She swallowed twice to keep herself from crying and accepted her plaque with a brief curtsey and a handshake.

"The Maestro will choose you. I know it." Eliza squeezed her shoulder when she sat down.

Her hope rose. Perhaps.

"And now, one of our most prestigious honors. Every year, the Maestro himself chooses one student as his new pupil. And this year he has chosen again, which he will announce himself. It is my great honor to introduce to you again, our own Salzburg Maestro, Erich Schumann!"

Silence pounded in her ears. She was certain the audience clapped, and her fellow students must have sat forward or clapped themselves. The room surely had other people in it, but to Freya, everything had gone quiet. And Erich's face, full of apology, told her he would not choose her before his mouth announced Gertie as his new pupil. He shook her hand, waved to the crowd, and then said something. None of it registered. Just the silence. Erich. The Maestro. He hadn't chosen her.

He played a simple piece, and Gertie accompanied. Erich's eyes watched Freya most of the time. What was he trying to tell her? Her hearing returned. Freya felt herself clap and smile at Gertie as she slid by to return to her seat.

"And now, it gives me great pleasure to announce the newest members of our Salzburg Orchestra." Erich's voice filled the auditorium. "This year, we had only two openings, and they were given to two students who excelled even the need for the Maestro's instruction. They will learn far more working with the orchestra than they would learn working as my pupils." His eyes found hers again, though still she was too distracted and confused to understand. "Could I have Frank Tolleson and Freya Winter join me?"

She wasn't certain her legs would function, but Eliza nudged her twice, and she stood. Frank was already there, shaking Erich's hand. Erich, the Maestro? Erich, who hadn't chosen her? Erich, who . . . who was Erich? By the time she reached him, her dumbfounded confusion had flamed into a spark of anger.

It must have shown in her eyes. When he reached for her hand, she responded with a certain stiffness. His eyes, full of love and gentle apology, only angered her further. She barely heard his soft whisper. "Forgive me?"

She looked away.

And he laughed.

Her anger flared. Her eyes flashed at him, and she raised her violin and bow in challenge.

He nodded in acceptance and gestured to someone backstage. They brought out his instrument. Erich leaned closer, his back to the audience so they would not be heard. "Frank, I need you to play a simple chord descant to start, and then, if you wish to embellish, you may, but you might notice that our friend Freya here may not leave us much room."

Frank cleared his throat. "Yes, I see that." He looked from Erich to Freya and back. "I didn't know you two were acquainted."

"Neither did I." Freya's eyes must have flashed, and Erich's grin grew.

"And now, our audience awaits." He bowed for Freya to begin.

Instead of their usual country songs, she played one of Erich's own compositions, his most difficult.

His eyebrows lifted in surprise, but he listened for two measures before he joined in a harmony. Freya did not linger for long on his own notes. She trilled and jumped and rewrote even some of the melody. But Erich stayed right with her. Even in her anger, she recognized how very united they were. He seemed to guess her direction before she even knew herself, and his notes matched perfectly. They could have played for much longer to complete the piece, but she noted when he took control of their number. He guided them to a close and then played out their last chords.

She turned and bowed to great applause with a vague sense that Erich and Frank bowed with her, and then she returned to her seat without a single glance again at Erich. She wasn't angry exactly, nor was she betrayed exactly. Whatever it was, the emotion surged inside, and she didn't trust herself to speak yet. Only play. She could use the language of her music only.

Erich continued. "And now I have been asked to play one of my own compositions." He began the piece she had first played for him. She closed her eyes, reliving their moments together. As he moved toward the end, she welcomed the calm peace of the music as he wrote it, but instead of ending how the music was written, he started building in tempo and energy. He was playing his song as she had altered it. She placed a hand at her heart and watched him sway and move, pure concentration on his face as the piece escalated in greater intensity. When it was finally finished, she leapt to her feet, clapping with her instrument and bow under her arm. The audience was on their feet as well. Erich was truly the Maestro. Hadn't she said so herself? His eyes met hers, and he nodded his head. A tribute to her? A message at least. They both knew that music was their language. In playing his own composition with her altered ending, he was humbly admitting . . . something.

The students were dismissed to their reserved seating on stage left down at the front. She and Frank were told to go backstage, where they would meet with the other Salzburg Orchestra members in their green room.

As soon as she entered the room and saw Erich at the front, she knew she'd better figure out her place. He stood on the conductor's platform. He nodded. "Ah, good. Our newest members. Frank, you will sit in that open chair there. And Freya, this is our first chair, Amelia Frankhurst. Please check and tune your violin to hers. It was flat just now."

She trembled. Flat? She'd played before all of those people out of tune? She played and matched her A to Amelia's, then made her way to the open chair. The very last seat.

"Frank and Freya, you are invited to join us for your audition piece number, and in the other pieces as well, but please play the third part. Use the music of your stand partner."

Freya nodded and glanced it over. Very simple, overly simple. But she said nothing. Even though she felt Erich's eyes on her, she said nothing.

"Miss Winter will take the solo in our third piece. Please point out the music to her."

A few gasps followed that announcement, including her silent one in the form of her stomach clenching. But as she turned to the piece, she recognized it as one she'd played with Erich, his own composition again. She knew it well. Did she know it well enough to play a solo? She trembled with the realization that she might not. But she dared to glance up at Erich just then, and the piercing, strong gaze he sent in her direction, the professor side of him she had come to know, gave her strength. He nodded once, and she remembered all his small touches, the emotion, the slight pausing from the other piece, and she nodded in return. She could do this.

Perhaps she might even enjoy it. She would have, were it not Erich. Or perhaps because it was Erich, she could enjoy it more. Her gaze found Frank's, and he smiled. She nodded in return. Perhaps this would be one of the most enjoyable experiences of her life, if not the most memorable.

They called the orchestra to take their seats in the auditorium.

Erich had left the room.

She filed after her partner, grateful she had remembered to grab the music, and prepared herself for her first-ever concert as a professional musician.

CHAPTER TWENTY-SEVEN

HER SOLO HAD GONE BEAUTIFULLY. Their pieces were well received. When the concert ended and the audience filed out, she watched them, all those lovely people who had filled this huge auditorium. And now, smiling, she recognized an audience member. Lord Bouchet waved.

Gertie was standing beside her. "Is that . . . ?" She turned to Freya and then to Lord Bouchet. She lifted her hand to her mouth and swayed on her feet. She gripped Freya's forearm.

"Surprise." Freya grinned. "He's coming to the ball."

Gertie's eyes filled with tears. "But you don't even know him. How did you . . . ? You did this?"

"I did. It turns out I was the woman his mother wanted him to marry. And the two of us did get along very well, but our hearts were elsewhere."

Gertie flung her arms around Freya's neck and nearly knocked her off the stage. Freya laughed, and together they watched Lord Bouchet as he made his way from the room. He turned in the door and placed his hand over his heart, and Gertie gasped. "Does he love me still?"

"He does."

They prepared for the ball together in their room. "I'm going to miss you, Gertie. You've been a true friend."

She stood behind her at the mirror. "And I will miss you. Can we always be friends?"

"Of course." When she turned to hug her friend, she squeezed her extra tight and said, "I'm so happy for you to train with the Maestro."

But Gertie shook her head. "I'm turning down the opportunity. I'm going to tell him that he's crazy if he doesn't train you."

"What?" Freya's mouth dropped. "No, you mustn't do that."

"I know how much this means to you, to your whole life. You cannot give up performing; perhaps your father will listen if he learns this."

Freya shook her head. "I am already in the orchestra, but with or without the orchestra, my father will not change his mind. He commanded me not to attend today. I'm here in defiance of him, and I will continue to play and work as a musician as long as I can even without his approval."

Gertie gasped. "Dare you do such a thing?"

"I dare." She had dared when she had Erich at her side. But this new Erich, this man who had been one person for as long as she'd known him and was now the most celebrated violinist of their day, was he at her side still? She needed to see him again before she knew how much she dared.

They arrived at the ball in their finest dresses. Freya felt more beautiful than she had in a long time, and for the first time, she enjoyed that power, the sense of her own beauty. She made her way out to the edge of the ballroom. She and Gertie told the master of ceremonies their names, and when he announced them over the group, many stopped and turned to them.

Freya smiled.

From across the room, Lord Bouchet began moving in their direction.

"He's coming!" Gertie's voice sounded weak. "I might faint."

"You wouldn't."

"No, I cannot. I don't want to miss a single moment."

Freya grinned when he approached. "Lord Bouchet, how lovely to see you again."

He bowed over her hand.

Freya turned to his mother. "And you as well, Lady Bouchet."

His mother's eyes were pleased, hopeful. "Thank you, my dear."

"Might I introduce the celebrated musician, the Maestro's new pupil, Miss Gertrude Thomas?"

Lord Bouchet bowed over her hand as well. "It is my great pleasure to see you again. Mother, you remember Miss Thomas?"

"I do. A pleasure to see you again." His mother's face seemed accepting.

Freya wondered if her new honors on stage in front of all the royalty had altered Lady Bouchet's impression of Gertie, or perhaps word had reached the dear woman of Freya's own plight, that Freya was lost to her son forever.

The music began, and Lord Bouchet immediately led Gertie onto the floor.

Freya's grandmother approached, and Freya moved to embrace her.

"Oh, you play so magnificently, even better than that Maestro fellow. I was in tears. You must play. We must tell that father of yours."

"Tell me what exactly?" Her father's deep voice startled Freya.

She turned slowly to see her father, Erich at his side. She clutched at her chest.

Her father studied her for many moments, his eyes unreadable, but then he held out his arms. "My Freya."

She stepped into his embrace, tentatively. "Is Mother . . . ?"

"She is well."

Freya's shoulders lowered in relief. "Why are you here?"

"Mr. Schumann invited me, insisted I come, really." His eyes filled with sadness. "I wish your mother could have heard you, Freya." He blinked. "I regret . . ." He cleared his throat. "I regret that I threatened to keep you from something that brings you so much joy. To think . . ." He swallowed. "You have become such a proficient all on your own." He pulled her closer again. "All these people, your award, in a professional orchestra." He shook his head. "You have done all this with me trying to halt your progress. I'm truly sorry."

She hugged him back a little tighter, her emotion almost overpowering her. "Not quite on my own."

She looked from Erich to her father and back.

"This is an excellent young man, this Erich," her father said. "We have come to a good agreement. I heartily approve your choice."

"What?" *Her choice?*

Erich held out his arm. "We shall find out if I am still her choice. I feel some explanations are in order. And I wouldn't blame her if she was still feeling uncertain of me right now."

She nodded to him but took his arm, turning back to her father. "Don't leave. I feel we too have unfinished conversations."

"Yes, for many years to come. You have no fear of missing any."

As soon as she and Erich left her grandmother and her father and Lady Bouchet, she turned to him. "Please start talking and don't stop until all is revealed."

"Shall we dance?"

She looked over her shoulder, the country dance midway through the first couple. "How can we talk of such things while trying to dance and waiting our turn? No. You must hurry and tell all, and then come dance every dance with me after."

He laughed. "Well, that's encouraging. Perhaps I am in better stead with you than I fear?"

"Perhaps."

As soon as they had left the ballroom and found their way to a quiet veranda, he lifted her hand to his mouth. "Yes, I am the Salzburg Maestro. I never revealed myself to you. I never called you back as one of the students. I didn't choose you as my pupil even knowing how much it meant to you. I let you fret and worry about it the whole time without saying a word."

"When you say it that way, my feelings of betrayal grow." She narrowed her eyes.

"As well they should. My dilemma was of course also my greatest joy."

"I don't understand."

"Consider my position. I could not have a relationship with you as a student. I could not choose you as my pupil or even favor you above all others when . . ." He searched her face. "When I love you as I do."

Her hands shook. She began a half nod. "You felt it inappropriate as a teacher to be courting a student."

"And to be awarding my . . . who I hoped would become my . . . but there is more I have to say. I couldn't possibly make you my student." He brought out a single crushed edelweiss from his jacket pocket. "Do you remember the stories of the men who hike to the topmost peak to find edelweiss for their loves?"

"I do."

"When I brought back that bouquet, I had just come from London."

She gasped. "That is when you visited my father." She put a hand to her heart as though placing it there might calm the beating.

"Yes. I knew I wanted you to always be in my life, but I could not approach you, ask you, make any promises until I had spoken with your father. I never felt fully free to pursue you without his permission."

"If I'd known, I could have prepared you. I am embarrassed to think how you were received."

He held up a finger. "You had told me enough. So instead of showing up at his door as a musician, I arrived in my cravat and hessians in the carriage of my family's estate."

She couldn't believe what she was hearing. "Your family's estate?"

"Yes. Through my mother's line, I . . . have an estate in England. A small one. It is run mostly by my steward, but I have always instructed him to invest in the mills in Manchester and have grown a surprising bit of wealth."

"You—you have?"

"Yes. But as you know, I give it little thought." He laughed. "Only you would be able to fathom such a thing."

"I understand completely. That means Father approved of you?"

"He did. We discussed his plans for the railroad and the gas that was found there as a resource. He understands my responsibilities elsewhere and approves of us passing much of the managing to the man who was originally slated to be your husband."

Freya's eyes widened. "Did you meet him?"

"I did." The humor in his eyes exasperated her more than anything. "And?"

"And what? Did I approve of him as your husband?" Erich's left eyebrow rose so high she had to laugh. "Absolutely not. But as the manager of our new company, he will be perfect."

She smiled. "Father approves of you, of this plan." She stepped away and rested her hands on the stone railing, looking out over a beautifully lit garden. "I hardly know what to think." She couldn't remember a recent time when she had moved forward with the knowledge that her father approved.

"I think . . . he has had only your best interests at heart. Misguided though his presumptions were, the man loves you dearly."

Freya turned back to Erich's earnest expression, and her vision blurred. "I feel I need to grasp at that handkerchief we let go in the wind, for some pieces of it belong here for a rejoining to this new life I had imagined for myself."

He pulled her close into his arms. "My dear darling Freya. I have been at great odds with myself these past months and find that only now can I, without restraint, tell you that I love you more than my own life, as much as the music we make together, and want more than anything for you to be my wife." He lowered himself to one knee. "I was prepared to give up what we both hold dear when I talked to your father. I was prepared to be an Englishman gentry only and not a musician if that's what was required to have you as my wife. I invited him to come, to hear us one last time. I offered such to him." He shook his head, as if at the foolishness of his own actions. "But I knew on the journey back to Salzburg that we could never be happy, neither you nor I, without music in our lives. So when your father arrived at my request, he and I had a further conversation right before the ball, and he is in agreement. You and I must both continue our music. We will rely on others to oversee the company. I, of course, will travel now and again to oversee this or that. Your father and your mother will retire to Brighton, and we all shall live happily ever after. If you will have me. Please accept my edelweiss, accept me and all that I offer. Be mine forever?"

Her heart didn't know how to beat any longer, and she was afraid it might leave her chest entirely. She knelt down beside him, placing a hand at the side of his face. "Yes. I am yours forever. I was yours when I thought we would have to defy my family. I am yours now, knowing that we have made everyone happy. I am yours. And I love you with all that I am." She pulled him to his feet.

He wrapped her in his arms against his chest, and the joy that pounded through them both brought more tears. When his lips met hers, it was a kiss full of promise. So much that she dared hope for a life full of music, happiness, and family harmony.

When they paused, she laughed. "About that position as the pupil of the Maestro?"

Erich's face danced with happiness. "Yes?"

"Might there be another opening? I can understand the conflict of interest as a woman you are courting, but as your . . . wife . . ." Her smile grew as she said the words. "Might you be able to add another pupil if one of them was your wife?"

He swung her around. "As long as she continues to teach me as well as learn."

"Agreed."

"Is that a yes then?"

"Yes. Always yes. We could never be apart truly. I am yours."

He held her face in his hands. "I never thought I would be so happy."

She shook her head. "Nor I."

"I love you, my Freya."

"I love you too, my Maestro."

His laughter was lost when their lips touched again. She thought she might fly away on the wind in search of that lone handkerchief she'd sent on a journey. For every wish she'd given up lost to the wind, another was coming true right in her path. His lips slowed, and she responded with all the love she could find inside. Freya clung to him, asking for more, more, so much more, until she could hardly find her breath, and they stopped, his eyes searching her own. Nothing more needed to be said. The music for a waltz started, and the soft rhythm filtered out to them on the veranda. He cradled her in his arms, and they were one in their own moonlit dance, she and Erich, her Erich from the train, her handsome stranger in the hat, the once poor music instructor turned renowned musician, turned English gentleman, but always her love and her own Salzburg Maestro.

ABOUT THE AUTHOR

JEN GEIGLE JOHNSON DISCOVERED HER love for British history while kayaking the Thames as a young teenager. Now an award-winning author—including the Praiseworthy Award for romance and the Foreword Indies Gold in romance—and mother of six, she loves to share bits of history that might otherwise be forgotten. She has become a prolific author with more stories in her heart than can possibly be told.

VISIT SUBSCRIBEPAGE.COM/Y8P6Z9 TO RECEIVE JEN'S newsletter for free books and new-release notifications, and follow her on social media.

JENGEIGLEJOHNSON.COM

FACEBOOK: FACEBOOK.COM/AUTHORJENGEIGLEJOHNSON
INSTAGRAM: INSTAGRAM.COM/AUTHORLYJEN/
PINTEREST: PINTEREST.COM/AUTHORLYJEN/

It Started in
BUDAPEST

SPRING 1900

"COME ALONG, MOLLY," HER MOTHER called. "Your father and Matthew will be waiting."

Molly tucked her hands under her arms and hurried along behind her mother. "'Tis a shame we cannot ride the *Grande Roue*," she said.

Her mother stopped and turned so abruptly that Molly collided with her dark-blue suit. A wire stem from the silk flower spray pinned to her mother's lapel stabbed into Molly's chest.

"I'm just as sorry as you, but time, Molly. Time." Her mother pursed her lips at her.

Molly rubbed the wound. As usual, her mother had completely misunderstood. She'd only meant that to board the passenger box and ride the giant metal wheel into the sky would have been a once-in-a-lifetime experience. Not that she wanted to go back.

"Besides," her mother continued, "is it fair for you, of all people, to keep Matthew waiting for his supper?"

Though her mother never said it outright, her meaning was clear—she blamed Molly for Matthew's illness. He was the son. The one meant to carry on the family name. Her father's factory was called Thomas Cooper Lace. There should be *and Son* attached to it.

Matthew was her twin, but before they were born, Molly had stolen all the strength and left Matthew with none. She'd always had perfect health. He had been sick his whole life. Most of the doctors were surprised he'd managed to live this long.

All Molly wanted was for Matthew to have a whole life. A real life. The kind of life Molly had.

Her mother was not wrong; it was Molly's fault, and she would not keep his dinner waiting.

"No." It was not fair.

Her mother nodded once and began walking again at a pace even a race-horse would have had trouble matching. Molly trotted along behind her, letting her mother clear a path through the crowds of people at the Great Paris Exposition.

Tomorrow, Molly would board the Orient Express with her mother, father, and Matthew. In sixty-seven hours, they would arrive in Bulgaria, on the coast of the Black Sea.

Except that Molly would not.

She had plans of a different sort that not even Matthew knew about. Secret plans she had told to no one. Plans that would heal her twin brother once and for all. In fact, it would make him live forever.

Her mother swerved to the right. Before Molly could make the adjustment, she collided with the broad front of a black suit coat.

"Oh, I'm so sorry," she said, dipping her head. It was then that a cold wetness seeped through her thin shirtwaist. The man had been carrying something that now drizzled down the front of her clothes. It smelled like a lemon grove in summer. Or at least what she imagined one would smell like. She'd never seen a lemon grove herself. She'd never left England before now, and lemons certainly didn't grow in the fields around Nottingham.

"I beg your pardon, miss," the man said. "It's my fault." He had no trace of a French accent, but it wasn't quite an English accent either.

Molly glanced after her mother, but she had been devoured by the crowd. The man held out a white handkerchief. He had dark hair and very round, dark eyes. There was a young lady beside him, about Molly's same age, carrying a gleaming white parasol and dressed in soft summer white and a straw hat fluffed so high with white feathers that it looked like a pillar of light reaching for the clouds. Even her boots were spotless white.

Molly shuddered and took a step back. "You're very kind, but I never touch anything white."

The man's eyes flashed over to his angelic companion in flowing white. "I beg your pardon?"

"I can't," Molly explained as she removed a pink handkerchief from her handbag. "Not white."

His eyes came back to her, taking in her soft-blue shirtwaist. Not the most stylish of colors, but Molly did what she had to do. Dark-blue skirt. Leafy green handbag with yellow and soft-pink flowers stitched on it. Even her stockings were dark blue, not that he could see them. She wasn't a harlot.

She dabbed at the spilled ice on her shirt. "Smells nice though. What is it? Or should I say, what *was* it?"

"Iced lemonade." The man laughed. His companion said something to him in French that sounded very much like a chastisement.

Molly had studied French, of course, as did all properly educated young women. Upon arriving in France, however, she'd discovered that French in a primer book and French in France were not the same thing.

Molly opened her mouth to speak, but at that moment, a young woman appeared wearing the largest peach-colored hat Molly had ever seen. It was all feathers and brims. Between that and the pillar-of-light hat on the lace woman, Molly was forced to conclude that her own hats were clearly undersized.

"Right, then," Molly said, setting hat troubles aside for the moment. "I'd best catch up to my mother, else she'll end up blaming me for all that's wrong in the world. Enjoy the exposition. I hope you have time to ride the grand wheel. And don't forget to visit the Eiffel Tower. They've painted it yellow just for the fair." She gave both the man and his snowy-white companion a dip of her head, then pushed off through the crowd, already regretting the loss of her mother, who was extremely proficient at cutting a trail. Molly tucked her hands into her folded arms and plowed ahead, praying that nothing white would find her.

She'd gone about ten paces when a man stepped in front of her.

"Excuse me," he said. It was the same man who had shared his iced lemonade with her shirt. "Allow me to pay for your soiled clothing, at the very least." He held out some folded banknotes.

"But, sir, it was I who barreled into you. I should be offering to pay for your lost lemonade. Perhaps we can call it even."

"I insist." He pushed the banknotes closer.

"It will wash out."

"Please."

The notes were francs. By tomorrow night, she would not even be in France. But the distance between herself and her mother was beginning to worry her. Not because she didn't know the way back to her hotel but because her mother would never let it go that she had caused them yet more delay.

The edges of the notes were white, so Molly opened her bag and held it out. They might prove useful if she ran into any unexpected trouble carrying out her secret plans.

He stared at her for a moment, then pushed the money into her bag. "Now I can leave Paris with a clean conscience."

"That's one thing that's clean, at least. Thank you."

He laughed, and his dark eyes lit up. She stared at him for a moment. "Uh. My mother is not a patient woman." Molly motioned toward the exit. "I really should be going." And before he could delay her further, she tucked her hands in once more and hurried off.

One time when Molly was young, her mother had tried to cure her by dressing her in a solid white frock. In less than twenty minutes, Molly had shredded it. Her mother had swatted her bottom with a wooden spoon until Molly couldn't sit for a week. All the good it did her was that now she also feared wooden spoons.

Molly wedged her way through the exit and strode along for nearly half a block before she found her mother coming back for her.

"My goodness. How can you be so slow? And what on earth have you done to your clothes?"

"Someone spilled lemonade on me." The sugar had dried stiffly in the spring sun, puckering the fabric where it had soaked. "I'll wash it when we get to the hotel."

"For heaven's sake. How can one person attract all the misfortune of the entire family?"

"Well, I'm here now, so let's go." She had just turned nineteen, far too old to be chastened in the streets of Paris.

Her mother set off again at her deerhound pace. Molly looped her hand through her mother's arm so they would not be separated again, and they reached their hotel just as the electric streetlights were coming on along the Champs Élysées.

She followed her mother into the elevator, and the operator closed the metal grate doors and whisked them up to the third floor. In their room, her father was standing, staring out the window. Probably wondering what was taking them so long to return from the exposition.

Matthew lay on the bed, reading *Treasure Island*. It was his favorite. He seemed more pale than usual, but that may have been because of hunger.

"You're back," he said. "At last, we can eat."

"Change quickly. We have a table waiting downstairs." Her mother sat on the other bed and put her feet up. They had been walking all day, and Molly's toes were cramped inside her boots.

"What happened?" Matthew asked.

"Some man had the nerve to dump his lemonade across your sister's chest," her mother said.

Matthew turned to Molly with wide eyes.

"Mother. It wasn't like that at all." She took a change of clothes behind the dressing screen. "Matthew, really, it wasn't like that at all. Mother was walking so fast, and I was trying to keep up, but she swerved, and I crashed into a man drinking iced lemonade. He was very kind and extremely apologetic and a perfect gentleman."

"Was he handsome?" Matthew asked.

Molly paused as she pulled a clean shirtwaist over her head. She hadn't given it much thought at the time, but yes. He was handsome. Quite handsome. "It doesn't matter," she called over the dressing screen. "He was already with a lady."

"Was *she* handsome?"

Molly stepped out and turned her back so Matthew could do the buttons. "She was dressed all in white. Head to toe, like some sort of lace mummy."

Matthew sat up and swung his feet over the edge of the bed, then started on her first button.

Mother brushed his hands away. "You're far too old to be helping each other get dressed." She set to work on the buttons. "If only I had a tuppence for every time I've told you that, we'd be living in Buckingham Palace."

"We spent nine months naked together in your womb, Mother. I hardly think there's anything we haven't seen."

Matthew snorted behind her.

Her mother swatted her on her shoulder. "Molly Cooper, you watch your mouth." She finished the last button. "Thomas, do something about your child."

Her father took his bowler from the coat stand and tugged it onto his head. "It's a bit late in the game, isn't it, to make much difference now?"

Her mother rushed to the mirror and straightened her hat. Matthew rose from the bed and smoothed the front of his coat as he crossed the room toward the door. Lines of pain crisscrossed his face.

Soon, Matthew. Soon.